"I'm worried,"
Scott said with a frown.

"I know," Jacqui replied.

"The city's gone crazy, and it's less than four weeks until Halloween. My crew will take over on the three days before Devil's Night. But a pyro just isn't the same thing. I don't know *how* to anticipate a real nut case, how to prepare for him, how to stop him."

"Scott." Jacqui's voice held a warning tone.

"Erase *nut case*. Substitute *troubled gentleman*. I'm trying to adjust to your lingo, petunia, but where I come from, a jerk's a jerk. Some people are just born bad, although I know you don't believe that." He frowned, reached over and brushed some powdered sugar from her cheek. Their eyes met. Lightning again.

Dear Reader:

No doubt you have already realized that there's a big—and exciting—change going on in Intimate Moments this month. We now have a new cover design, one that allows more room for art and has a truly contemporary look, making it more reflective of the line's personality.

And we could hardly have chosen a better month to introduce our new look. Jennifer Greene makes her second appearance in the line with *Devil's Night*, an exciting and suspenseful tale that still has plenty of room for romance. Old favorites are here, too. Barbara Faith's *Capricorn Moon* and Jeanne Stephens's *At Risk* show off these two authors at the top of their talent. Finally, we bring you a newcomer we expect to be around for a long time. Once you read Kaitlyn Gorton's *Cloud Castles*, you'll know why we feel so confident.

In coming months, look for favorites like Marilyn Pappano, Nora Roberts, Kathleen Korbel and Paula Detmer Riggs, as well as all the other authors who have made Silhouette Intimate Moments such an exciting—and romantic—line.

Leslie J. Wainger
Senior Editor

Devil's Night

JENNIFER GREENE

Silhouette Intimate Moments
Published by Silhouette Books New York
America's Publisher of Contemporary Romance

SILHOUETTE BOOKS
300 East 42nd St., New York, N.Y. 10017

ISBN: 0-373-07305-4

First Silhouette Books printing October 1989

Printed in the U.S.A.

JEANNE STEPHENS

loves to travel, but she's always glad to get home to Oklahoma. This incurable romantic and mother of three loves reading ("I'll read anything!" she says), needlework, photography, long walks—during which she works out her latest books—and, of course, her own romantic hero: her husband.

Prologue

Sulfur was the devil's smell. He loved it.

Until he struck the match, the basement had been in total darkness. No more. The small flame illuminated the pool of charred wooden matchsticks at his feet. The blaze hissed and then steadied into a perfect yellow teardrop.

Sweat broke out on his brow when the flame started to walk down the matchstick. Waiting for the pain was always the worst. The top of the match blackened and curled. Down went the flame, lower, lower, until the bit of fire licked at the pads of his two fingers.

He never moved, although he was always amazed at how one tiny match could cause such a scream of a burn. The pads of his fingers were already blistered, not just from this match but from all the others.

In seconds the match sputtered out, but his fingertips still felt on fire. Nothing hurt like a burn. Nothing. He had a vague recollection of his father coming at him with a poker when he was ten years old. That had hurt, too.

His father had been an intense, powerful, virile man. When he set fires, he no longer hated his father, because he understood. He had precisely what his father had had. The power. The intensity. The virility.

The match, though, was out, and the darkness started to smother and close in on him. He lurched to his feet and switched on the light. The glare of the single light bulb upset him. His stomach suddenly thudded with anxiety. The only thing out of place in the entire basement was the puddle of dead matches on the floor; yet for a brief moment he couldn't remember coming down here, and if he'd struck all those matches or if it had been someone else.

Shaking his head to clear it, he found a whisk broom and meticulously swept up his mess, then deposited it in the blue trash container by the washing machine. He replaced the lid precisely, as if that could make everything normal again.

It didn't work. Nothing had been normal lately. The short blackouts of time kept reoccurring. So did the devil moods—the rage, the fascination, the anxiety. Like boxes in the attic, he'd forgotten those emotions for years. Now they were starting to take over his life.

It was her fault. Jacqui's.

Even thinking of her, he felt the power, the intensity, the virility denied him in life. With fire, of course, he had it all. Fire was the only possible way he could pay them all back.

He hadn't decided yet whether he was going to start with Jacqui—or end with her. It was an important decision, and he was trying to make it carefully. There was no room for mistakes. No one in a million years would believe him capable of real power; he intended to prove them all wrong.

When he set the city on fire, it would stay lit.

For Jacqui, though, he wanted something special. He couldn't stop thinking about it. Some would say, what the hell; if she's going to die, it's all the same. But that wasn't true. He wanted to give her the anticipation, the fascination, the waiting.

He wanted her to know he was coming.

Chapter 1

He whispered things to her. Wicked, delicious, sexy things. His hands were hot. They melted her skin and she climaxed yet again, this time with an unbelievable explosion of colors and textures and sound.

Mostly sound.

In the darkness, Jacqui's eyes blinked wide. Sexual abstinence was playing increasing havoc with her dream life. There was no explosion, just as there was no man lying next to her. If she didn't know better, she'd think she was hearing the caterwaul of a smoke alarm in the distance.

For all of three seconds she lay still. It wasn't possible. One fire, maybe. Two stretched the imagination, and three fires in three months moved right into the realm of unjust, unfair and just plain unreasonable.

The unjust, unfair and unreasonable smoke alarm continued to scream.

I don't believe this. Her eyes squinted at the bedside clock and registered the ungodly time of 3:02 a.m. as she hit the carpet, naked and barefoot. En route through the darkened hall, she scooped up the fire extinguisher—a new one—from the linen closet. A slight whiff of smoke greeted her in the kitchen. She flicked on the light, blinked hard at its brightness and felt her heart squeeze tighter than a fist when she saw smoke eddying at the bottom of her basement door. *Come on, God. Is this fair?*

The minute she opened the basement door, her ears suffered the full abrasive pitch of the smoke alarm—a panic-inducing sound if ever there was one. Pelting down three steps, she saw charcoal smoke billowing around the middle of her basement floor. Not a little smoke, but lung-choking, thick, ugly clouds of it. It took a lot to make Jacqui totally lose her sense of humor.

She lost it.

Vaulting back up the steps, she slammed the basement door and reached for the kitchen phone. On the second ring, 911 responded. The calm cool voice asked the same questions Jacqui had been asked before—name, address, directions, nature of the fire if known, how extensive—and delivered the same list of instructions. Stay away from the fire. Shut down power, if possible. Close doors and windows. Get out of the house.

When she hung up, she spotted her raincoat folded over the kitchen chair. She pulled it on and pushed her slim white hand through her shoulder-length tangle of blond hair. *Stay away from the fire. Get out of the house.*

Such good advice. For several seconds, she obeyed it, because for several seconds, it was easy to convince herself that the fire was a figment of her imagination. Everything around her was normal. Outside, this twentieth night of September was as black as pitch and the grass dew-drenched. From the window, the lake looked like an obsidian blanket, peaceful and quiet.

Nothing looked wrong—outside or in. Her purse and briefcase were still stashed on her white wrought-iron kitchen table. The pile of mail lay untouched on the counter. Her kitchen was all white except for the plants—ivies and philodendron and dieffenbachia and fig. In the daytime, her kitchen had so much light that the plants grew in spilling, disorganized, cheerful profusion. She'd gone to bed knowing they needed watering. They still needed it.

Nothing could possibly be wrong—except that smoke was still seeping under her basement door. And the clock's minute hand had only moved four dots since she checked the last time.

You're not qualified to deal with a fire, and you know it, Jacqui Hughes. Fires are their business, not yours. Your business is being a psychologist, which means you are an expert at teaching people not to overreact to emotional situations.

The mental lecture shouldn't have been necessary. Jacqui never overreacted. Hadn't she stayed calm on the Fourth of July when a spark had ignited her porch carpet in the middle of the night? Hadn't she stayed collected on the night in mid-August when the box of rags in her garage had decided to spontaneously combust? And both times, the firemen had been as consoling as her insurance man. No one had been hurt. Damages had been minimal. There was no suspicious "cause" or fault. She'd been urged to take the attitude that occasionally, regrettably, nuisance fires simply happened.

That attitude was undoubtedly sensible, justifiable and rational, but at the moment it struck her as the pits.

Other Detroit suburbs had lakes, but few as secluded and cloistered as Silver. The mortgage payments on the house would have cowed the less optimistic, but Jacqui had taken one look at the place and fallen in love. This was *home*.

She checked the clock again. Barely another minute had passed. Waiting, though, just wasn't going to cut the mustard. Snatching the unwieldly extinguisher again, she headed for the basement stairs.

Halfway down, she had to stop in confusion. For all the thick clouds of smoke, she saw no flame, nothing specific to aim at. The heaviest smoke clustered around the water drain in the middle of the floor, which didn't make sense. How could a water drain catch fire? At age twenty-seven, she hadn't accumulated the years of treasures and savables that her parents had. Her basement had a washer and a dryer and a clothesline, some suitcases under the stairs, an old steamer trunk. Maybe it was the trunk? Only she couldn't see through the smoke to *find* the trunk, and the alarm kept screeching like a grating scream of pain.

There was a level where Jacqui always felt alone. But not like this. Not totally alone, not heart-pounding, pulse-thudding, stomach-dropping alone.

Come on, Hughes. Would Arnold Schwartzenegger's sister be dithering in a situation like this?

Determinedly she climbed down four more steps. Her sweat-slick hands groped for the nozzle handle of the extinguisher. Plucking the pin of the fire propellant, she aimed the nozzle as if it were a machine gun and let it rip.

The blast of propellant gas gushed out in a thick white foam and blended with the smoke. Neither was breathable. The extinguisher was so awkward and heavy that her hands trembled and her arms ached. She just kept blasting it. It supposedly only took minutes to empty the whole extinguisher; it seemed to take years.

As though someone had flicked on a light switch, the nightmare was suddenly over. Jacqui, arms huddled around the waist of her trench coat, coughed like mad. She retreated to the top stair of her basement steps to survey the wreckage...only to discover that all the sound and fury hadn't added up to tiddledywinks.

Certainly there was smoke, but it was dissipating fast. One small basement window was broken, but both her washing machine and dryer looked unharmed. A white silk blouse still hung on the line, untouched, as did a delicate blue camisole. The antique steamer trunk she'd bought at a rummage sale had taken the brunt of the fire. It looked shriveled and charred—irreparably—but all in all it was still just a trunk, a place to store some out-dated textbooks she should probably have thrown out years ago.

She was still numbly staring when she heard the clumped boot steps of two firemen coming up behind her. Turning her head, she saw they were both in turnout coats and helmets. "Don't yell at me," she said wryly. "But the fire's definitely out, and I'm terribly sorry to have called you in the middle of the night for nothing. I know it doesn't look like it now, but there was an unbelievable amount of smoke just a few minutes ago. I had no idea what I was dealing with—"

"No problem. *Always* call, honey. That's what we're there for." The tall, thin one had the wherewithal to disconnect her smoke alarm—she could have kissed him.

The other fireman was a chunky, burly man she recognized from the Fourth of July. He touched her arm and urged her back into her kitchen. "You've really had your run of bad luck lately, haven't you? We'll finish checking it out and get that trunk out of the house. Shouldn't take us more than a few minutes. You take it easy, okay?''

She didn't want to take it easy. She followed them downstairs and then held doors while they carried the trunk from the basement to the back lawn. Although the trunk was no longer smoldering, they insisted that it was a standard safety precaution to remove it from her house. She followed the firemen outside. ''Fine,'' she said distractedly. ''More to the point, could you tell what caused the fire?''

The big burly one kept sneaking smiles at her, probably because she looked like a darn fool, clutching herself in the trench coat and dancing on one bare foot and then the other on the cold wet lawn. Her next fire, maybe she'd have time to dress in a business suit. Better yet, there wouldn't be a next fire.

''There's the broken glass of a pop bottle on the floor in your basement,'' the older man told her. ''Our guess is that a kid threw a pipe bomb through your window—''

''*Bomb?*''

''Take it easy. Not 'bomb' like in terrorists,'' he said soothingly. ''A homemade pipe bomb, like the kind kids have been making since the beginning of time. A rag for a fuse, gunpowder probably out of a bullet. You got a neighbor with teenagers?''

''I don't know. I only moved here about six months ago. There are houses all around the lake, but I'm kind of secluded on the ravine here. I also work so many hours that I just haven't had the chance to meet many neighbors.'' She rubbed two fingers at her temples hard enough to make dents, her mind less on neighbors than on her older brother. Jack had made a pipe bomb fire-cracker when he was fourteen.

Jack had a Huck Finn grin, a love of building things and an idea he could make a firecracker that could make a big "boom." When their dad had discovered the project, he'd nearly grounded Jack for the rest of his life, but her brother had never intended more than innocent mischief. For that, Jacqui had called out a fire truck? "Look, I'm really sorry to have bothered you. Three o'clock in the morning, and I admit it was awfully easy to panic..."

She was still tendering apologies when a dark car pulled in her driveway behind the fire truck. Her yard light illuminated the Detroit Fire Department's insignia on the car door, which struck her as strange—Detroit and its suburbs were the same as other countries but the detail hardly concerned her.

Her feet were numb. Cold air liberally drafted up the hem and cuffs and down the throat of her raincoat. She was exhausted and increasingly embarrassed at having caused so much trouble for nothing, and she desperately wanted a mug of tea. As it happened, extricating herself from the scene was hardly a problem.

The man who climbed out of the car had his face completely shadowed by a fireman's helmet, but her two firemen obviously recognized him. They strode toward the stranger with welcoming yelps of "Llewellyn!"

Jacqui thought dryly that either God or the devil had arrived, because she was abandoned as fast as a skunk site. Under the flashing red light of the fire truck, the three men indulged in a lot of fast conversation with enough deferential overtones for her to gather the new arrival was hot cheese.

If they wanted to chat all night on her back lawn, it was all right by her. All she wanted was tea. Once inside the kitchen, she filled a pot with water, flicked on the burner and then, regrettably, had to throw open a window. The waft of freezing air made her shiver all over again, but it was better than the smoke smell. Anything was better than the smoke smell.

For bare seconds she caught her blurred reflection in the windowpane. Her light blond hair couldn't have looked more disheveled if she'd just climbed out of a man's bed. Her face was pale and her eyes looked huge. *Dammit, are you going to cry on me, Hughes? It's over. It was nothing. Since when do you fall apart over nothing?*

It took her an extraordinary amount of time to line up tea bags and mugs and spoons. Her fingers all seemed to have metamorphosed into thumbs. She felt an invidious shakiness from the inside out, as if someone had thrown her into the snow. Foolishness. There was nothing to be upset about now. No danger existed and the fire was out. Her home had never been threatened; it was just a kid's prank.

The kettle started whistling at the same time that she heard a rap on her door. "Miss Hughes? I should have introduced myself outside. I'm Scott Llewellyn."

"It's Jacqui, not Miss Hughes, and come on in. I was expecting you—or one of you. I'll make you some coffee. I know there's some form you have to fill out." She swung the copper kettle away from the burner and stopped abruptly.

"No coffee for me, thanks. But I would like a quick look around after we finish the fire investigation report."

"No problem. Have a seat." If her tone was cheerful, her mood was utterly distracted. She had hardly expected the fireman to walk in wearing tux and spats, but the other men had greeted Mr. Llewellyn with a lot of kow-towing deference. As far as she could tell, he looked fresh from a street fight.

He wasn't built tall, just tough. His jeans were tight, he wore his gray sweatshirt inside out, and his chin had a disreputable night beard. A shock of unruly, undisciplined jet-black hair framed his angular face, and his eyes were that same snapping black.

Looking at him was like being plugged into a source of earthy, physical, blatant sexual energy. The chin was pugnacious, the nose decisive, and he reeked vitality even at this ungodly hour of the morning. His gaze took in the room faster than a camera flash, noticing everything from her cranberry leather briefcase to the forgotten pearl earrings she'd dropped on the counter earlier.

Then he focused on her, a swift sweep from her bare feet to the open V of her trench coat to the exhaustion in her pale green eyes. His study wasn't long, just thorough.

"Were you hurt?" he asked immediately.

"No, not at all." Quickly she turned around and reached for the jar of instant coffee. Her nerves were suddenly jangling, her heart pumping an uneasy beat. *What do you expect, Hughes? It's the middle of the night, and you just had a fire.* Determined to appear relaxed, she calmly and competently made tea and coffee.

Lots of coffee. When she pivoted around with the steaming mug, she discovered that someone had already lined up several steaming mugs in front of Mr. Llewellyn. "By some remote chance," she asked dismally, "did you just get finished telling me that you didn't want any coffee?''

"That's okay. I changed my mind, and heck, when I'm in the mood I can easily drink three at a time." Humor laced his tenor, but so did compassion.

"I'm not usually so scatterbrained," she defended herself as she sank into the closest kitchen chair. "Actually, I'm never scatterbrained. I've just recently developed a real aversion to fire alarms in the middle of the night."

"So I understand. In fact, if I were you, I'd be skipping the tea and dipping into the cooking sherry. Don't hesitate because I'm here."

She didn't want cooking sherry, but she wouldn't have minded a tranquilizer. She guessed he intended to sound reassuring, but his battered tenor was nothing you'd ever hear in a church choir. That voice rubbed across a woman's nerves like sandpaper. "Are you sure you want to bother with this report tonight? The other firemen probably told you that the fire was nothing more than a kid's homemade firecracker—"

"So they said." So far those devil-black eyes had yet to stop prowling her face. He scratched his whiskered chin as if to announce what an innocuous, harmless man he was. Mr. Llewellyn would be innocuous on the same day it rained cats. "You've had your run of fires recently, haven't you?"

"If you're about to go into your fireman's reassuring monologue, don't bother. I've heard it all before," she said dryly. "Some kid's prank is not worth a federal case, right? And the other fires were even smaller. You people are going to start thinking I call 911 the minute someone strikes a match."

"Sometimes a kid's prank is worth a federal case, but we'll get to that later." Abruptly he frowned, uncoiled from the chair and closed her open window. The temperature in the room threatened frost. Belatedly she realized that she was still shivering—and that he'd noticed.

"I'll go through the question part of this as quick as I can." He unhooked a beeper from his belt and dropped it on her table, then settled back, a scuffed boot cocked on a chair rung and his blank form propped negligently on his knee. His first questions probed for the obvious statistics: her full name, address, her profession, marital status. "Age?"

"Twenty-seven." She figured he had five years on her, maybe six. She was good at reading people—it was what had led her into psychology—but she couldn't read him. His cocky, easy posture didn't match up to the deeply grooved stress lines on his brow. His grin was irreverent, but his eyes held no hint of laughter.

The other times, the firemen had rushed through their required reports to get them over with as quickly as possible. Mr. Llewellyn was nothing if not thorough. He was also imaginative, because he asked questions she knew perfectly well weren't on his form.

"What kind of clients do you take on?"

"I already went through all this the other times with the other firemen—"

"I know you did. But just once more?"

That coaxing, battered tenor again. She sighed. "I have a private practice with two other psychologists. Primarily I work with troubled teenagers, mostly referred through the court system. And before you even ask the next questions—*yes*, some of my kids have been in trouble for arson, and *no*, none of them had anything to do with this fire. Or the other fires. They're my kids. I know them.''

"I'm sure you do. Which ones did you say had records for arson?''

"I didn't say.''

"That's okay. We can cover that now. What were their names?'' With his pen poised over the form, he glanced at her with encouragement and expectation in his smile. When her only response was a dead stare, his smile gradually upgraded to the kind of dominantly male grin that snuck up on a woman. First his bottom lip crooked up, then there was a gradual display of even white teeth, then a dance glinted in his eyes like an invitation to mayhem.

She acknowledged the effect of that grin, but at her worst—and she was certainly at her exhausted worst—she still had a nominally functioning brain. "There are laws affecting confidentiality in my business, Mr. Llewellyn. I couldn't give you my patients' names even if I wanted to.''

"No?" He took a stab at looking innocent and failed. "I guess I knew that. It just temporarily slipped my mind—and make the name Scott. You call me mister and I'll be looking around the room for my father. Anyway, we'll get back to your 'kids' another time. Let's move on to neighbors...." She gave him the same answer she'd given the firemen. "You live alone?"

"Yes. But I've got a part-time handyman, Joe Mc-Graff, who's around a lot." She sincerely doubted that *anything* slipped his mind, temporarily or otherwise.

"Known this McGraff for long?"

"Long enough to know that he's a sweet old man with a crippled leg. He fixes more than I can afford, he works harder than he should, he pretends to work less hours so I won't have to worry about paying him—"

"Mark off one saint," Scott murmured. "How about family?"

"The usual two parents. Also an older brother, Jack. The crew lives in Lansing. I can't imagine why you're asking this—"

"No special family problems? No Aunt Matilda with a grudge? No Uncle John jealous over the family silver?"

She cupped her chin in her palm, starting to feel amused. "If you're that desperate for family skeletons, the best I can offer is my Great-Aunt Marie. She drinks. Are you going to write that down? I haven't seen her in thirteen years—she lives in Los Angeles. She's going on eighty-four—"

"Okay, okay." Scott's eyes never raised from the paper. "Recently kick a man out?"

She blinked. "No."

"Got a man friend pressing to move in?"

"No."

"Any estranged ex-husbands hanging around? Anybody you recently sent away with your basic dammit-she-said-no type of grievance?"

"I should live such an exciting life," she said dryly. "What is all this? None of the other firemen asked me these kinds of questions."

"Would you believe they leave me behind because they're nice and I'm nosy?" When she didn't buy that, he dropped all pretense at flippancy. Like Jekyll and Hyde, the boyish grin disappeared along with the sassy dance in his eyes. The serious Scott had a box of a jaw, the crow's feet of a man who'd faced his share of sun and sorrow, and the keen, sharp vitalness of a man familiar with authority. Jacqui suddenly knew exactly why the other firemen had treated him with such respect.

"I'm not looking to pry out of some prurient interest," he said quietly. "I am, however, looking for some answers. You're an unusually beautiful woman, which you know. What you may not know is that revenge and jealousy are two of the most common motives in fire-related crimes—at least in those caused by adults. If you've got a man causing you a problem in your personal life, I'd appreciate your honesty. I'm not just talking about a guy you turned down or kicked out. Maybe there's somebody who feels competitive at work, jealousy in the family, a neighbor with a grudge?"

"Honestly, there's no one." She took a breath. "Don't you think you're going off in left field here, talking about 'fire-related crimes'? A kid threw a firecracker through my basement window tonight. That isn't funny, and believe me, I'm not laughing. I was scared out of my mind, but I also work with children. Even the most innocent of kids' pranks have been known to get out of hand before."

"If it was a kid's prank," he agreed.

He was beginning to upset her. "It had to be."

"Why?"

"For the obvious reason." Agitated, she lurched up from the chair and reached over the table for one of his cooling mugs of coffee, ignoring her poured tea altogether. "I'm just me. I work twelve hours a day, I come home beat, I have a reasonable circle of close friends— mostly people I work with. My worst vice is overdrawing my checking account twice a year—I forget to add it up. I also get punch-drunk at a plant sale. I'd love to develop bigger vices, but there's no time. The closest I've ever come to an enemy is on *Miami Vice*. Are you getting the picture?"

"Yes. Miss Hughes—"

"For heaven's sake, would you cut out that 'Miss Hughes' business? You'd think I was 103," she said crossly.

He swiped a hand across his whiskered chin. "You're tired, I know. You have to be."

"That's like saying there's snow in December. Of course I'm tired. It's four o'clock in the morning."

"And you've had two other fires before this," he said quietly.

"Small fires, yes. But they didn't have anything to do with this one. Didn't you talk to the other firemen? On the Fourth of July, the carpet on my back porch caught fire in the middle of the night." She lifted her shoulders. "They didn't know what caused it. Fireworks? Ash blown in the wind from someone's beach fire? And in August, some rags caught fire in my garage. That was probably my fault. Stupid, keeping piles of rags around, but it just never occurred to me . . ."

She stopped talking when she realized he wasn't listening. Instead, he was studying her again. Some men found the arrangement of blond hair, fine bones and pale green eyes attractive. Scott seemed to find her face a source of worry, frustration and stress. The furrow between his brows deepened.

"What's wrong?" she asked.

"Nothing. You sound very sure your fires were coincidental."

"Do you have some reason to think otherwise? The other firemen—"

"What I think is that you've had about all you can take for tonight." Again, his gaze prowled her face. Both his boots hit the floor with an abrupt clunk. "I know how late it is, but if it's okay by you, I'm going to do a quick safety check through your house." He crossed the linoleum to her living room doorway, glanced at the white carpet and immediately hunkered down to unlatch his boots. "You don't have to come with me if you don't want to. I won't be more than a few minutes."

"What kind of safety check?"

"Electric cords, switches, that kind of thing." He made them sound as boring as dust.

"Now? Wouldn't it wait until tomorrow?"

Evidently it wouldn't. He was already striding through her living room in stocking feet. Pushing a hand through her hair, she trailed him as far as the doorway.

Her living room was a long rectangle of lemon and white with splashes of green from plants. The white marble fireplace had been a disaster when she'd moved in. Reglazed now, it was an elegant beauty. The china hutch and Queen Anne chairs had been inherited from her grandmother. Jacqui had reupholstered them herself in lemon velvet and made the most impractical choice of white carpet because she knew the room would rarely be used.

He took one look around and immediately slowed his aggressive pace, which made her smile. It was like watching a hockey player delicately tiptoe through a department store lingerie section. Scott wasn't much of a tiptoer, but he tracked every lamp cord, then checked the locks on the long narrow windows and the latches on the front doors. "A two-year-old could get past that bolt," he accused her.

"Good grief. What does that have to do with fire safety?"

He hunched by her fireplace, fooling with the damper and vent switches. "Got a flashlight?"

She brought a flashlight and crouched next to him, looking up where he did—heaven knew why. A chimney looked like . . . a chimney. Black and sooty and dark. "I always figured Santa Claus got the raw end of the deal," she murmured.

His chuckle was throaty and hoarse.

"What are we checking for?" she asked him.

"Just looking for loose bricks." He knew that wasn't the total truth. Certainly his palms were running inside the chimney's rough surface, but his sense of sight was otherwise occupied.

Jacqui noticed he was looking fiercely, protectively, at her. Adam had had a disastrous problem with forbidden fruit. From the distance of spare inches, Scott's eyes traveled her disheveled hair, bare mouth and long white throat as though he'd just discovered temptation. A temptation he didn't want. A temptation that annoyed him. And a temptation that lured a softness into the man's eyes she would never have anticipated.

She felt an unexpected burst of sweet, lush heat in her bloodstream, darkly sexual and stunningly strong. For the first time since she woke up, she forgot about fire. For the first time in years, she felt something wild and feminine shift inside of her, like moorings ripped loose in a dark wind that had come from nowhere.

Her fingertips chilled as if she'd just touched danger, when he hadn't touched her at all. A clock ticked somewhere. Their eyes met—his as bold as brass, with just a trace of deprecating humor—and then he lurched to his feet. "Believe me, I won't take up much more of your time. I'll finish the rest as quickly as I can."

He covered the rest of the house at the speed of a track sprinter, never coming near her in the process. The ranch house was laid out in an L; once past the kitchen and living rooms, he strode for the bedroom wing.

There were three rooms in the back. Her study was done in corals and browns and wicker. It was the place she did her reading and relaxing, where French doors led to a patio that overlooked the lake. He didn't notice patios any more than he noticed the ivory lace slip on the floor in the bathroom or the rumpled sheets and spilled pearls and shoes in her ice-pink bedroom. He was only interested in switches, electric cords and the locations of her fire alarms, which he told her. Several times.

When he reached the last door at the end of the hall, he tested the knob. "You keep this room locked?"

"Yes. But it's just a storage room. There's nothing to look at." The fib slipped from her tongue before she could bite it back. She rarely lied and never well. It was just that her studio was something fragile and private that she didn't want exposed. The fire had already exposed vulnerable emotions, a feeling of violation. Now a stranger she didn't know from Adam seemed to be exposing other equally disturbing emotions. She'd had enough, that was all. Was there a law that said a woman had to be rational at four o'clock in the morning? "Honestly, you don't need to go in there."

He raised one dark eyebrow, and she could feel color flush her cheeks. He knew as well as she knew that one room was as likely to have the same number of switches and electric cords as any other. She thought he was going to comment—was afraid he was going to comment—when the look in his eyes unexpectedly gentled and he took his hand away from the knob. "We don't have to do anything else tonight. I can see you're dead on your feet. I'll get out of your hair so you can get some rest."

"The report's done, then? You don't have any other questions?" She followed him back into the kitchen, where he stuffed his feet into the scruffy boots.

His words were like buttered bullets, fast and to the point. "I haven't even started, but we've done all we're going to do for tonight. Would you do me a favor and not touch anything in your basement or the trunk outside until I've had a chance to get back here? Are you going to be around tomorrow?"

She shook her head. "I have to be at work."

"Do you have a way I could get back in your basement tomorrow morning?"

"My handyman should be here."

"He'll do. And in the meantime, how long is it going to take you to go through your client files and come up with some kids that have been in trouble for arson?" He carted coffee cups to the sink and rinsed them out as if he owned her kitchen.

"Didn't we recently play this record? My kids' names are confidential."

"We'll talk about that." He spotted a scratch pad by her phone and started scribbling. "As soon as you go through those client files, I want you to call me. Here are two numbers where you can reach me, but if you haven't called back by tomorrow night, I'll be getting back to you."

How could anybody be such a steamroller at this hour? "Look, I haven't slept all night, and I have a full schedule of work tomorrow. You're making this sound awfully urgent, don't you think?"

"Yup."

"Anybody ever tell you that you could use a course in reassurance techniques?" She asked dryly. He responded with a ghost of a grin, picked up his report and headed for the door. "Wait a minute, I don't understand. Believe me, you're welcome to investigate from here to forever as far as I'm concerned—I really don't need another fire as long as I live. But don't you think you're making too much of this? You can't possibly devote this kind of time to every kid's homemade firecracker—''

"Normally, no." He started to say something, glanced at her and checked it. "No more worrying tonight, all right? The point is that you're not going to have any more fires, Jacqui. None. Zip. Zero. And we'll talk about how we're going to make sure about that when you call me tomorrow. If you're at work, that's just as well. I'd like a look at your office, anyway. Think you'll have time to go through those files by noon?"

"Noon? You have to be kidding. There's no possible way I'll have that kind of free time, and I told you my kids weren't involved."

By the time he'd let himself out the door, she'd given up talking. Mr. Llewellyn was deaf to anything he didn't want to hear.

Long after he pulled out of the driveway, she lingered at the window with her arms wrapped around her waist and her bare feet freezing on the cold floor. The house was suddenly silent—not the peaceful quiet she always relished at the end of a day, but an uneasy, wary silence.

She'd never been afraid of living alone, but at the moment she felt like a child in the dark, expecting a monster to step out of the closet. She rubbed her cold arms fretfully. Until Scott had walked in her door, she'd thought she was handling the fire incidents sensibly and rationally. Certainly she'd been scared by the fires. Everyone was afraid of fire.

He was the one who'd made them into something more. She had the shaky, disturbing sensation of an earthquake coming. Her extremely safe, secure world was suddenly tippy, and for a moment she was starkly aware that the man had upset her more than the smoke in her basement.

And cows fly. Hughes, you're so tired you can't see straight. He's just a man. Now forget about him and fires and pack it in.

Exhausted, she headed for the bedroom. Within minutes she was asleep.

Chapter 2

Scott hadn't faced a problem of such epic proportions in years. Some merciless fiend had vandalized his desk. Reports and files were all mixed together. He foraged deeper and in due time uncovered a two-day-old cup of coffee, three old issues of *Firehouse* magazine, a tie tack—it wasn't his—four pencils, two pens and a year's supply of paper clips.

All he wanted was the police printout he'd bribed from Brickman. The price he'd paid to get at that! If he had to sit through another lunch listening to the entire saga of Brickman's divorce again...

When a long pair of black legs passed by his open door, he offered a somewhat downhearted wolf whistle. The heels backed up. Weighing a solid 185, Luz had all the looks of a hard-traveled road. "One of these days I'm going to haul you up on sexual harassment charges, Llewellyn," she said severely.

"Please? I beg you. I can't think of a better way to get Connolly to fire me." Scott never looked up from the desk. He'd known Luz from his fire fighting days. She was the best dispatcher in the business, which was why he'd taken her with him when Connolly had bullied him into this godforsaken job.

"Nobody's going to fire you if you continue to impress the pants off the city commissioner. I don't know what you told him behind closed doors this afternoon, but he sure left here thinking you were sacred."

"You can always fool some of the people some of the time—and don't remind me of that meeting. I'm already depressed."

"Paperwork got you down? Poor baby," Luz drawled. "Promoted to a classy office. No more burns, no more life-threatening situations, no more terrible hours, nothing to do but read all day and handle an itsy-bitsy problem like Devil's Night." She shook her head. "What on earth are you looking so hard for?"

"A yellow computer printout. I repeat, yellow. With all this manila and white, wouldn't you think it would be relatively easy to find a few yellow sheets of—"

"Yes." She crossed to his desk, neatly withdrew the stapled yellow sheets and handed them to him. "It's a genetic flaw. There isn't a male alive who didn't come out of the womb asking, 'Where?'"

"I'll ignore that insult, because I owe you my life."

"I'd rather have cash, and in the meantime are you aware what time it is? Pack it in, Llewellyn. I won't suggest you should head for home and a good woman—you wouldn't know what to do with a good woman—but you might glance at a clock. It's past seven." She swung toward the doorway and then hesitated. "I hate to break precedent and say something civil after all this time, but if you're not aware of it—'' she shrugged ''—we're all glad you're sitting in that chair. There are even a few of us who think you're doing a passably good job.''

"Hell, you'll make me blush."

"Not likely." She grinned and then left.

Once Scott heard her heels click down the corridor and the whoosh of a door closing, he knew he was alone in the office complex. Before concentrating on the police printout, he pushed back his chair, stood and rolled up the venetian blinds.

Nine stories below, a traffic light turned red, a taxi honked, and the aboveground "people mover" mini-train zoomed by with a blur of people's faces in its windows. Blues and purples backdropped the skyscrapers as the sun set. Neon lights already flashed their rainbow light show. He couldn't see the Ambassador Bridge from here, but he had a peek of the Detroit River, a view of the spiraling Renaissance Center and a look at the cars choked on Jefferson.

Chicago had the better nightlife. San Francisco the class, Houston the architecture, Vegas the fun, New York—hell, New York had everything. But those weren't his cities.

Detroit was his city, his home, his baby.

Scott rubbed the bridge of his nose. His baby was in trouble. The summer had been hot. Detroit's economy was dependent on cars, and cars weren't selling this fall. Unemployment was high, crime was up, and to walk the streets at night you'd better carry a bigger knife. Dope, crime, gangs, slums—every giant city had the same urban problems.

Devil's Night, however, was strictly and uniquely a Detroit phenomenon. When Scott was a kid, he'd rung doorbells and TPed his neighbor's bushes on the night before Hálloween. Times had changed. Since 1983, arsonists had used the excuse of Devil's Night to burn up the town.

More than five hundred fires had been reported in 1983, more than eight hundred the following year. Scott knew the statistics by heart, just as he knew that the task force, curfew and public education had limited the problem in more recent years. Limited. Not stopped it. Nothing had stopped the problem. Everybody and his mother had theories, but no one really knew why it happened. Why fire? Why Detroit? Why the night before Halloween?

The date was stuck in Scott's mind. October 30 was only thirty-nine days away. The troubled mood brewing in the city reminded him of the Detroit riots in the sixties, and Devil's Night was an ideal excuse for every wacked-out crazy to explode. The mayor had an ambitious goal: to cut the devastation by thirty-five percent in the seventy-two hours preceding Halloween.

That goal was fine, but city hall had chosen a man to lead this year's task force who was nothing more than a life-educated Welshman, a man who'd fought literally hundreds of fires, but who knew absolutely nothing about a desk job and never wanted to.

How did Connolly talk me into this? he wondered for the hundredth time.

The phone rang. He turned away from the window to grab it. "This is your nightly call to remind you to have dinner," said the silky soprano at the other end.

The tense, brooding scowl faded from his forehead as he sank into the desk chair and swung his legs to the top of the desk. "I had my dinner," he lied. "More important, did my favorite girl have a good day?"

"Of course. And how many times do I have to tell you? You can lie to a mother, lover, or wife, Scott, but don't try fibbing to a sister. You haven't had dinner. You haven't even thought about it."

"Did you call just to give me grief?" He twisted the phone cord around his hand, eyes closed, letting the pressures and weariness seep out of him as he pictured Phoebe. She'd have three half-open books around her, the TV on, the radio on, her computer on and an open box of chocolates half-hidden under her pillow. "Did you do your exercises?"

"Let's put it this way. I could compete in the Olympics for arm wrestling."

"Cheap talk." He heard her chuckle, but he caught the nuance in his sister's voice. He always knew when Phoebe was in pain. His sister was all sunshine and sass. When they were kids she used to drive him nuts tagging after him. The car accident had happened when he was twelve years old. He'd never forgotten it . . . and never decided who he blamed more for it—God or himself. "Good day or bad day?" he questioned her.

"No codeine."

He knew that was how she measured her days. "Behaving yourself?"

"I seduced seven men, climbed a thirty-seven story building in a single bound and sprinted laps. Shut up, bro. I don't want to talk about my day. I called to talk about yours. Did you call her?"

"Who?"

"Lord, you're annoying." He heard her pop the chocolate—undoubtedly the kind with the liquid cherry center. They were her vice. If he could have been a man at twelve years old, Phoebe might have had the chance to develop far more dreadful, dangerous vices, which was another thing he never forgave or forgot. "Surely you remember calling me this morning? I'm talking about the classy blonde who knocked you for six last night. The one with the three fires. The one who had you rambling on like a bumbling teenager—"

"I beg your pardon?"

"You should. Regularly," Phoebe agreed. "Did you see her today?"

"No. I went out to her house to check the fire site after I called you, though."

"Nothing?"

He squeezed his eyes closed, as though he could squeeze out frustration. "Nothing. Dammit, not a clue."

"And if you're still downtown, you're obviously running too late to see her tonight. So you set something up with her for tomorrow?"

"Yes, nosy."

"At her home or her office?"

"Her office—and how long is this third degree going to last?" Scott murmured dryly.

"Her office... That's unfortunate," his sister reflected. "I was going to suggest that you take her wine."

"Wine? What does wine have to do with anything?"

"Lord, you're dense. I guess if you're going to her office, you'd better skip the wine, Scott, but brush your hair, check for BO, and throw some cold water on your face so you won't look like you've been working twenty-hour days. Where would you be without me to advise you?"

"Happier," Scott murmured. "And I swear you're deaf. Like I already told you, the lady has trouble, and that's the only reason I'm involved. On any other level, we're talking a woman who probably grew up in Grosse Pointe, graduated cum laude from St. Mary's College, has white carpet in her living room—repeat, white—and probably buys her play clothes at Saks.''

''Hey, I'm sitting here bedridden and in pain and pitiful. The least you could do is give me a classy sister-in-law. The last broad you brought around popped gum—''

''Susie was trying to quit smoking,'' Scott defended her.

''Get real. She was a convenient lay. The body was impressive, I'll grant you that, but upstairs we're talking hollow. She hit on you because you were a hero, a fire fighter, all that silly stuff. And you stuck around because you didn't know how to avoid hurting her feelings.''

''Where do you get this language? Pity Dad didn't wash your mouth out with soap when you were a kid.''

''It's a tremendous advantage being an invalid,'' Phoebe agreed. ''You can say whatever you please and everybody feels too guilty to argue with you. You gonna call tomorrow night and tell me how it goes?''

''I'm going to come by tomorrow night and treat you to a marshmallow chocolate sundae. Keep your money handy. We'll play poker.''

''You sure you can handle another loss?''

Scott was smiling when he ended the call, but for the next three hours he never raised his head from the file on the desk. He only quit then because he had to. The pages were blurring and his eyes were scratchy.

By eleven o'clock his city had long turned dark, not unlike his mood. He leaned back in the chair and dragged both hands through his hair. Long before his sister's call, Jacqui had been on his mind. She'd affected his concentration all day.

He could still see her making him all those cups of coffee. He could still see her crouched next to him by the fireplace, with her trench coat gaping half-open, the look in her eyes part promise, part wariness. He could still see her defending the door to her back room, eyes suddenly blazing stubbornness, so damned tired she was weaving. God knew what she was hiding from him. He'd been far too busy feeling slammed in the gut to care.

He was a beer-drinking, blue-collar Welshman who'd grown up on the wrong side of the tracks. One look at Jacqui and he'd known she was out of his league. The fragile profile, the porcelain skin, hair the color of iced champagne. She even moved with grace and breeding. Her body was slender and soft, long waisted, long legged. Dangerous. Touch her and she'd probably bruise.

She undoubtedly liked Dubonnet. He drank draft. She undoubtedly read the *Wall Street Journal*. He read the sports section of the *Detroit Free Press*. He'd bet she was an opera fan. Some date had once dragged him to a ballet; he'd fallen asleep.

Scott had an unfailing respect for the boundaries of class. He knew enough to stay on his own side of the fence with a woman like Jacqui. That wasn't a problem.

The problem was that tomorrow he had to convince the elegant blond lady with the soft, perceptive, lethally emotive green-brown eyes that she had trouble. Maybe big trouble.

She wasn't going to believe it. In his experience, do-gooders like psychologists generally saw life as an extension of charm school. She was not going to want to see any link between her three little fires and Devil's Night, and Scott wasn't absolutely positive there was one. Hell, if he had proof, he would have surrounded her with police protection as fast as breathed.

He had no proof. No facts. And no time, not with Devil's Night looming up on the city like a big, black, threatening thunderstorm. He would have worked twenty-four hours a day now if his body didn't occasionally cave in. Connolly may have conned him into this promotion, but Scott's need to protect his city was its own motivation. He had no time to focus on one woman's lone problems.

Only he was irritatingly afraid that he had no time not to. A man couldn't fight his city's worst fires for fourteen years without developing a gut instinct for the problem. He *knew* fires. He knew the streets. He knew the kind of nuts who came out of the woodwork on Devil's Night, and he knew that one determined firebug could upset a whole applecart of copycat crimes. With equipment and men and resources divided all through the city on Devil's Night, a *real* pyromaniac was almost unstoppable.

A real pyro also knew that.

What he was afraid of—what kept nagging at his mind, gnawing at his nerves—was that Jacqui was a link to the most dangerous kind of fire setter there was.

Scott squinted bleary-eyed through the window and pictured himself telling her that. Actually, what he pictured was her laughing herself silly—and then offering him therapy at cut-rate prices. So much fuss for three little fires?

Only that wasn't, as he damn well knew, the whole story.

At precisely 11:03 the next morning, a white porcelain cup shattered against Jacqui's far office wall.

After a moment's silence, Jacqui leaned forward. The boy sitting across from her was sweating hard through a thin black T-shirt. His lean face was like stone, and he had ice for eyes. The pulse bucked at the bottom of his throat as his shoulder muscles clenched and unclenched. When she took his hands, though—and it was a major breakthrough that Stan let her touch him—she could feel him shaking. "If you think that solved something, you're welcome to have another cup to throw."

"No."

"I have a whole shelf of them. Feel free."

"I said no. Lemme alone!" He jerked his hands free.

"Because it doesn't help," she said softly. "All that anger, Witkowski, but we've got to find something to do with it that does help. Throwing cups doesn't work. Setting fires doesn't work. Violence doesn't work. When are you going to get that through your head?"

He threw back his head and glared at the wall. "I suppose you're going to tell my old man that I wrecked your stupid cup."

She drew his attention back to what mattered. "Do you want out of that house, Stan? I told you I'd go to the judge—"

"No. I don't want out. I just want my old man to—"

"To what?"

The boy glowered as if he'd like to strangle her. "I want him to be different. That's what I want."

She shook her head. "We can't change him. But we can change you—how you deal with your father, how you feel about yourself, how to work through that anger. In time."

He twisted out of the chair. "Yeah? Well, maybe I'm sick of hearing about 'in time.'" He grabbed his denim jacket, making a point of flashing her the swastika pin on the pocket because he knew she loathed it. "You don't keep very good track of your appointments, do you? My hour's been over for ten minutes."

"But you weren't ready to leave ten minutes ago," she said patiently.

"You have to be kidding. I wouldn't come here at all if I didn't have to. And maybe I'm sick of people telling me what to do. Maybe I won't be back next Thursday." The challenge in his eyes was as dark as a dare.

She didn't pick it up. "Maybe you won't, but you can count on me being here."

"I suppose you'd tell that parole dude if I didn't show."

"Are you going to make it my decision if you get locked up again, or yours?"

"Hell. Here we go with the 'meaningful question' routine," he said scornfully. "Don't you ever let up? Do us both a favor and go get yourself laid."

He hunched in the doorway for several seconds—waiting, hopeful, dying for her to respond to the vulgarity. When she said nothing more than, "See you next week, Stan," he scowled and slammed the door—par for Stan—and par for Jacqui that she felt as whipped as a dog when he left.

The boy was sixteen and had been more in than out of juvenile hall for the past three years. Arson was his favorite game, although he wasn't fussy. Any kind of destructive violence would do. His father called him uncontrollable, the judge called him incorrigible, and it was tough to help a boy who drew a knife on every social worker and psychologist assigned to him. He'd tried a switchblade on Jacqui during their first session.

Professionally, she couldn't fault the progress of the therapy. Unresolved anger was at the core of most troubled people. Couple anger with despair and you had something as combustible as TNT. Soon, Stan either had to find a way to vent his anger—or explode. Technically, she knew that any rage transferred to her was a hopeful sign.

All that healthy transference, though, made their therapy sessions as relaxing as an air raid.

When the door opened, she'd kicked off her shoes and was kneading the knot at the small of her back. Sandy's newest version of a hairstyle had tips of green. "Ah... you have a rather antsy man waiting for you in the coffee room. He's only told me three times that he isn't a patient. I think he has a slight prejudice against psychologists—"

"I'll bet he does." Jacqui straightened with a sudden smile. She hadn't forgotten Scott. It was rather impossible to forget a man who called six times in less than forty-eight hours. "Thanks, Sandy. I'll take care of him."

She slipped back into her heels and made a token sweep of her hair before heading for the door. The coffee room was at the end of a long corridor. The walk took her past Jonathan's and Timm's offices—both were in with clients behind closed doors—then two testing rooms, Sandy's reception center and the slightly larger "study" used for group therapy. The place was as familiar and comfortable as her second home. It had to be. Sometimes her days ran as long as twelve hours.

This particular Thursday was scheduled to the hilt, and her step was impatient as she crossed the corner into the coffee room. Abruptly, though, she found herself hesitating.

Outside, the leaves were just starting to turn crisp oranges, soft ambers. Sunlight poured in through the wall of windows, brilliant and bright. It was an innocuously lovely fall day—if one ignored the jarring slam of energy that Mr. Llewellyn represented.

He wasn't dressed in a ragged sweatshirt and tight jeans this morning, but a gray suit—a civilized, formal gray, but the businesslike effect was lost on its wearer. The coat was open and Scott's hands were stuffed in his pockets, revealing the beeper on his belt. His tie hung unevenly. He'd destroyed his hair by dragging a hand through it. He also turned on a dime when he heard the first step of her heel on the linoleum.

She thought she'd imagined the other night: the slug of masculine power, the vitalness, the raw male sexuality that made up most of a woman's more foolish fantasies.

But she hadn't imagined anything. When his eyes locked on hers, she felt the buck and bolt of sensual awareness. The scrape of nerves disturbed her. She was never nervous around men. Sexual feelings were as familiar to her as blue chips to a stockbroker. In a certain sense, they were her job. You couldn't work with teenagers without tuning in to their sexual feelings. Hormones didn't scare her, and aggressive males were her bread and butter. There was no conceivable explanation for her pulse to thump around this man.

Her pulse *was* thumping, though, as annoyingly as a drumroll. Irritated with herself beyond measure, she strode toward him with her hand extended. "Scott." He wasn't expecting the handshake. She wasn't expecting to feel the lightning warmth when his hand swallowed hers. Formality just wasn't going to work here. "Well, you've won," she said wryly. "Heaven knows, I tried to talk you out of this visit six times."

She caught his slow grin but noticed more how fast he severed the hand contact. "Certain things are better discussed in person than on the phone."

"Sure. Births and deaths and IRS audits," she agreed. "You're going to have a hard time convincing me that my fires rate up there at a crisis level. What couldn't you tell me on the phone?"

"I'll explain, but you seem to have people running in and out of this place like it was a bus station. You regularly hire children to man your reception desk?"

"Sandy's in her first year of college. She gets credit for working here, and since most of our patients are young, we like someone of that age at the front desk." He undoubtedly wanted that information like a hole in the head, but the chatter gave her a moment to slow her pulse rate. She'd been with him all of sixty seconds, and already she had the annoying sensation that he'd taken in everything about her.

Her work clothes were basics: camel skirt, silk paisley blouse, pearl button earrings. Jacqui could tell he'd absorbed that sort of thing before his first blink. By the second blink, he'd latched on to the faint mauve shadows under her eyes, her rubbed-off lipstick and the habit she had of twisting her cameo ring when she was nervous. Scott, she thought dryly, faultlessly zoomed in on a person's weaknesses, a perception she highly valued in a fellow therapist and found thoroughly unnerving in a relative stranger. Especially a male stranger.

"You have a place to talk that's a little more private than this?" he asked her.

"My office," she agreed, and motioned him through the far door.

From behind her, he said, "The kid that just left—the one with the scar on his neck and the swastika—was he one of yours?"

"Yes."

"In trouble for arson?"

So it was going to be like that, was it? Once in her office, she closed the door. "Anybody tell you that you're disgracefully nosy? I don't know how long you were at my house yesterday morning, but it was long enough to upset my caretaker, my insurance man and a neighbor I didn't even know I had."

He made the kind of grimace that a kid makes when he's caught with his hands in the cookie jar. "I may have asked a few questions."

"A few? Let's put it this way. You seem to have a small habit of upsetting people in your wake. Including me. You've had me worrying that there's an underground terrorist plot behind my fire. All those phone calls! If you were trying to scare me, you did a good job of it," she scolded.

"Jacqui?"

She'd be damned if he didn't have the sexiest, darkest eyes she'd ever seen. "What?"

"I *was* trying to scare you," he said softly. A load of bricks could have dropped on her plum carpet. She'd never have heard them. His eyes were narrowed on hers, assessing, judging, and then he sighed, a gusty vent of impatience. "Only that's not so easy to do with you, is it? Have you even given one serious thought to your fires?"

"Of course I have." At his deadpan stare, she couldn't help a smile. "All right, *no*. I'm not saying that last fire didn't shake me up to beat the band, but it's not like the house burned down or I lost my last shirt. I've had two full days of patients. I worked late last night with a young girl, and this morning I had a patient at six. The very last thing I have time for—"

"Is yourself?" His quick perception was unsettling, and before she could respond, he withdrew two black-and-white photographs from his shirt pocket—just snapshots, each of men. "The first guy's a man named West, the other is Roberts, but don't worry about the names. Just tell me if you know or might have seen either one of them."

"All right," she said curiously. When he didn't immediately explain, she dropped her eyes to the photographs.

The photo of West looked like a driver's license picture. Sick. Blank eyed. From the expression on the gentleman's face, he'd just tasted eel. As a psychologist, Jacqui's interest was piqued, but she certainly didn't know the man. Roberts's photograph was more difficult. Walk into an office building, and there were a dozen men like Roberts—conservative hairstyle, middle-age lines, vapid smile and an oxford button-down. The eyes, though, were dark and deeply hooded. Troubled.

"Do you know either one of them?" Scott asked her.

"No." She lifted her head. "Is there some reason why I should?"

"Could you have seen either one of them sometime?" he persisted.

"Not West. I'd remember him. In fact, I almost always remember a face, but Roberts..." Her thumb traced the edge of the photo. "I don't know. He has a way of looking familiar. You know. Like someone you've talked to while waiting in a bank teller line or in a grocery store." When she glanced up again, Scott had shrugged off his suit jacket and tossed it on a chair. He was rolling up his white shirt cuffs as though he'd been civilized and proper about as long as a man could stand.

"Keep looking at the one of Roberts. He's got a scar on his neck, hard to see in a black-and-white picture, but it's there."

She saw the scar, a jagged blotch of skin climbing out of the man's shirt collar. In real life, the scar would probably have been red rather than white, and the mark wasn't neat like stitches, but wrinkled like an old burn wound. The physical mar was tiny but distinctive. It should have helped, but it didn't. "He looks vaguely familiar, but that's all I can say. Does it matter?" She added humorously, "What are these, your classic mug shots?"

She expected him to grin. He didn't. "They're just old pictures, but you could make my day if you could be positive you'd never laid eyes on Roberts. Keep studying that one, okay?"

She tried, but neither photograph captured her interest as much as the man roaming her office. Scott had obviously built up some preconceptions of what a psychologist's work space should look like. Judging from his frown, what he saw confused him.

The carpet was plum, the chairs powder blue. She had no desk, and her confidential files were locked in a pecan credenza. Open shelves held games—playing cards, memory games, Clue, Sorry, puzzles—ready to be played on a long low table as big as a door, surrounded by powder blue beanbags for seats. In one spot the carpet was raised to a small dais that was beneath a photographer's spotlight. He stared at the dais for a long time.

"It's a place where the kids can act—or act out," she told him. "Some teenagers shy away from a spotlight, but some really do well with it."

He turned his frown on her. "You're supposed to be studying those photos."

"I did. I've never seen the one man before in my life. The Roberts man—probably, possibly, maybe. I just don't know."

"Okay." But it wasn't okay; she could hear the frustration in his voice. Belatedly she noticed the balled muscles in his shoulders, the lines of stress and exhaustion around his eyes. She worked with too many people not to recognize a man who drove himself too hard. Why he worked so hard wasn't her business, but it was second nature for her to care. Instinctively she moved toward the credenza to pour him a cup of tea, but he shook his head when he noticed what she was doing.

"Are you sure?" she insisted. Her plea fell on deaf ears. He was still busy exploring and motioned toward her shelves.

"What are the games for?"

"The younger the child, the less they want to sit and talk—they want to *do*. In a game, I can usually set up a situation—their winning, their losing, frustration, success, how they handle themselves interacting, how they approach a problem, their attention span."

"I keep looking, but I can't find the couch."

She smiled. "Sorry, no couch."

"You don't do hokey stuff like hypnotize people, do you?"

That time she chuckled out loud. "In most cases, hypnotism isn't any different than a kind of meditation. It isn't 'hokey.' It's a very practical way to teach someone how to relax, how to handle stress and anxiety."

"Where I come from, 'practical' is putting your feet up and popping the lid on a beer if you've had a tough day."

"Sounds great to me," she murmured.

His mouth twisted and she caught a flash of dark eyes. "What kind of comment was that? I expected you to say something judgmental and psychologisty."

"We're going to have to do something about this little prejudice of yours," she said wryly, and perched on the arm of a chair. "Is it just psychologists, or do you have the same feeling for social workers, sociologists—"

"Maybe we'd better move off this subject. The kid that just left do this?" She'd forgotten the broken cup. Before she could reach the pieces, though, he hunkered down and swept them up. "Did he throw it at you? And I don't know why I asked that. You're not going to answer." Still, he pushed. "The kids you work with all as rough as the one I just saw leaving?"

"Troubled kids do troubled things," she said quietly.

"Which means you're not going to answer that question, either." He puttered around with the cup shards until he found her wastebasket. "By some extremely remote chance, did you bother to glance through your files like I asked you?"

"Yes, mostly because I figured you were going to nag me with another six phone calls if I didn't. You want the statistics? I'm currently working with three kids who've had a little trouble with arson, and there are about another seven or eight I've worked with in the past—"

"I don't suppose you'd be willing to show me those files?"

"You suppose right. And I don't know about you, Scott, but I learned about taking turns before I was six years old. You've been asking all the questions. When do I get to ask some? Like who are you? What do you do? Why is someone from the Detroit Fire Department even involved in a Silver Lake fire? Why did you bring in these two photographs? What the tarnation are you making all this fuss about?" She glanced at her watch. "And you'd better start talking fast, because I only have an hour before I have a patient coming in."

"An hour? Then when were you going to have lunch?"

"What does lunch have to do with anything?"

"You skipped lunch to be able to see me?"

"It was the only free time I had," she admitted.

"Same here." With all his roaming and pacing, Scott had yet to come within three feet of her. For the first time since he walked in, he was suddenly still, standing near the far window, with the mist of sunlight behind him. His square jaw was in relief, an unruly shock of hair on his brow, and she could see the tension clenched in his shoulders.

Until that moment she'd assumed his tension was because of his work, his life, some private burden he was carrying, anything—but certainly not her. The way he suddenly looked at her, though, was unguarded and intimate. His eyes had a man's interest and a man's fire, intense and damned unsettling.

Abruptly, he relaxed. A languid grin started to steal up on his face. "I guess," he said slowly, "you're just too high-class a lady to go for pastrami—"

"Corned beef."

"Horseradish or mustard?"

Now there was a test. "Horseradish," she said firmly.

He dug in his pocket for his car keys. "I'll drive."

She shook her head. "You have to be kidding. I'll drive. You're going to be too busy talking."

Chapter 3

The entire city of Detroit had collected in the doorway of Cavalerri's Deli by 12:01. They were short on time, so Scott grabbed Jacqui's wrist and shouldered his way through the crowd until he caught Leon's eye.

Within sixty seconds, they had a booth with a window. Outside of three minutes, heaping sandwiches were placed in front of them. Leon hovered, offering voluble greetings in Italian until their drinks were served.

When he was gone, Jacqui muttered humorously, "I think that's called pull with the owner. And when did you ever learn to speak Italian?"

"I don't. Never understand a word he says."

She raised a brow. "But you obviously know him."

Scott nodded. "Nine years ago Leon had a fire, and his kid was trapped." He watched her pick up the three-inch-thick sandwich and wondered how on earth she was going to make it fit in her mouth. She managed, delicately, which he should have expected.

"The fire was here, at the restaurant?"

"At his house. Rollover had already occurred and we found ourselves in a flashover situation—that's when everything in the room has heated to the point of ignition temperature. You've only got minutes to get out by then, so whoever's in charge of the fire calls off any search or rescue missions. It's all over. It's just too late."

She might not have understood the terms, but she caught the gist. "His child was caught in that? What did you do?"

"I went in and got the kid. Hell, she was just a baby, couldn't have been three years old." Scott didn't have the least idea what he was saying. There was no chance he could eat and talk at the same time under this hazardous level of stress. *Watch your language, Llewellyn. Use your napkin. Don't let the lettuce hang out of your mouth. Chew with your mouth closed.*

This wasn't a date, of course, but he specifically didn't want to spill horseradish on his shirt while he was with Jacqui. He'd be darned if he knew how to force the subject back to fire—correction, to *her* fire. She'd pelted him with questions about his fire fighting history during the drive here. As fast as he answered one query, she had another. A gentleman with manners didn't interrupt a lady, which left shouting a change of subject out of the question.

Two tall men in aviator jackets gave her the eye when they passed. So far, Scott hadn't seen a man pass who hadn't given her the eye. He hadn't picked the place because of Leon but to douse her curiosity about him. The place was him—blue-collar, rough at the edges, no frills or pretense. The restaurant decor was a study in cheap Formica and linoleum and hanging fake greenery. Except where she was.

Sunlight streamed in where she was. It landed on her delicate nose and the tiny cameo ring she wore on her little finger. It spun a sheen in the pale gold swirls of her upswept hairstyle and caught in her smile. She smiled a lot. She also listened as though a man's every word was worth gold, and those damned eyes of hers... In sunlight, her eyes were as green as wet spring leaves and shimmered with empathy and intelligence and perception.

Scott had always related well with women, but not women like Jacqui. The boundaries that separated them were as clear as a fence. She had class, elegance, breeding. It showed in her scent, her smile, the way she walked, the way she saw life. She considered herself quite a realist. He knew better. He thought of the fire in her basement and felt nauseous. He thought of a pyro like Roberts anywhere near her and tasted acid on his tongue.

"How did you deal with it?" she asked, her last chip halfway to her mouth.

"Deal with what?"

"The fear. How did you make yourself walk into all those fires?"

Nobody asked him crazy questions like that. He didn't know what to say. "It wasn't like that. Fighting fires is what I knew, what I wanted, what I did. You have a fire, you don't have time to sit around and analyze whether you're afraid of not."

"I would."

"Yeah, well. You're a psychologist. You're supposed to analyze things."

She ignored that comment and folded her arms on the table, lunch forgotten. Her voice turned soft, intensely soft, as if she were alone in a room with a man who mattered to her. "Scott, you're quick to dismiss the courage involved and just as quick to label fire fighting as your average career. Nothing's that simple. Every story you told me—those were hard choices you took, not easy ones. There has to be a reason."

Restlessness and impatience surged through him. Her fragile alto could woo secrets from a man that he didn't even know he was guarding. He hadn't been tempted in years to tell anyone the whole story of the fire that had paralyzed his sister. The fire that he'd walked away from, or the passing of fourteen years of testing himself to make sure he never walked away from another one. Abruptly he changed the subject. "Jacqui, we came here to talk about your fires, not the generic variety."

Her pale eyes glinted with humor. "That may be what you came for, but I came here to listen. You promised to do all the talking, remember?"

"Yeah, but not about me. If you're done, let's get out of here. You're running out of time, and so am I." When he lifted up to reach for the billfold in his back pocket, he saw Jacqui reach for her purse at the same time. Their eyes met briefly.

"You're the one who came out of your way because of my fires, so lunch should be on me," she insisted.

"That sounds reasonable, only my dad didn't raise any reasonable sons. When you're with me, I pay. And in this place, paying at all is tricky." Leon was capable of quarreling if Scott pulled out his billfold at the cash register, so he tucked a twenty under the salt shaker. "Let's go."

He may have been distracted during the drive to the restaurant, but that wasn't true now. He stayed silent on the drive back to her office, simply because safety took precedence over conversation. Jacqui drove with one hand on the steering wheel and the other fussing with either the radio, her lipstick, the safety belt or the heat.

Her fuel gauge was on Empty. She said she was going to remember to fill it up, but she sounded vague. Fuel gauges obviously rarely troubled her, and she not only drove the downtown streets at corner-careering speeds but ran every yellow light.

He'd never met a woman who needed worrying about more.

"Well…" In the parking lot to her office, Jacqui shut off the engine and plucked the key. "Do you want to come back inside, where we can talk?"

"Here will do." Her office had diverted his attention toward the woman instead of her problem. If her egg-shell-colored compact car lacked legroom, he figured it would be less distracting. He leaned back against the door and tried to ignore the vague French scent that lingered around her. "You know about Devil's Night in Detroit?"

She was in the process of tucking her keys in her purse. She glanced up at him. "Of course."

Her answer didn't surprise him. A city that annually ignited was a little difficult to keep out of the media. But when he told her he was leading the task force, he got a sudden smile out of her, a satisfied smile, as though she'd locked a puzzle piece in place. He didn't want her smile, and he didn't understand it.

"The job of the task force is to set up the curfew, commandeer every spare piece of fire fighting equipment we can beg, borrow or steal, organize command posts around the city—that kind of thing. We don't investigate fires. There are fire departments and police to do that kind of thing, and they do it well."

"If you're trying to whet my curiosity, you're doing a good job of it. I give. If you don't normally investigate fires, why on earth were you involved with mine?" He heard the rustle of her silk skirt's lining when she slipped off a shoe and tucked a leg under her.

"I'm *trying* to tell you. For the past six months, I've been keeping records of any unexplained fires throughout the city—no matter how little, no matter how seemingly unrelated. See, Devil's Night isn't made up of one arsonist, one firebug. It's made up of a bunch of sickos who come out of the closet for the occasion. And then a bunch of maniacs who copycat the sickos."

"Don't say 'sickos,' Scott," she admonished gently.

"Pardon?"

"People aren't sickos or maniacs. They're troubled."

God save him from psychologists. He had a small inclination to shake her and a larger inclination to find out if she kissed . . . elegantly. If she was as crushable when a man held her as she looked. If she tasted as damn good as he was afraid she'd taste.

Abruptly he patted his shirt pocket for a peppermint and popped one. "I don't care what language you use. The point of keeping those records was to identify known, active firebugs *before* Devil's Night and to get them off the streets. There's a level where we can control the pranksters. There's no level where we can control a total crazy. If I have a torch out there, I want to know it, and I want him behind bars before Devil's Night."

"Hmm." Wheels were turning in her head. He saw a quick frown, the glow of intense concentration in her eyes, and then she looked at him again. "Could I help?"

"Pardon?"

"Could you use a psychologist as part of your task force?"

Scott rubbed the bridge of his nose. "We're getting off the track—again—of your fires. Now would you just listen, please?"

"I'm listening." But she smiled, amused at his impatience.

"The other night you had a pipe bomb thrown through your basement window. You weren't the only one. Earlier in the evening, there were reported fires in Birmingham, Livonia and Royal Oak—all homemade pipe bombs of the same kind."

"The same night?"

"The same night. And on the Fourth of July, you had a 'mysterious' spark catch fire on your porch. That same night, there were four other calls for the same kinds of fires."

"But don't you normally have a lot of calls on the Fourth of July? I mean, everyone loves a sparkler, and the weather was hot and dry."

"True. But you also had a fire in August. A box of rags in your garage decided to 'spontaneously combust'—not unusual in a closed-up space after a buildup of phenomenally hot summer days. Only it wasn't hot on the fourteenth of August. We'd just had three days of rain. It's pretty tough for anything to spontaneously combust in that kind of damp and humidity, yet we had the same type of unexplained garage fires called in that night from Allen Park, Plymouth, Northville, Southfield."

He ticked the similarities off his fingers. "Every fire took place in the middle of the night. No one was hurt, and none caused more than nuisance damages. In fact, they were all such minor fires that they'd normally rate no more than a report stuck in the back of a file cabinet."

"You obviously think only one person set all those fires," she said quietly.

"I *know* only one person set those fires, but I can't prove it." Frustration put the snap in his tone. "I've already talked to the cops and the affected fire departments. The consensus of opinion is that the incidents may be stretching coincidence, but without some kind of proof or evidence or a lead, there isn't much they can do. Are you hearing me?"

"I'm hearing that you're terribly upset," she said gently. "Only I'm still not sure exactly why. Somebody's set some prank fires, Scott, but that has nothing to do with your Devil's Night."

"It's got everything to do with Devil's Night if I have a loose pyro out there who's decided to get real active this close to October. I *don't* like the pattern. He doesn't leave any clues. He doesn't leave any reasons. He started the fires all over the suburbs. He was smart enough to make them all real nice and small so nobody would see the link." He shook his head. "I've seen too many fires, too many arsonists, too many pyros. I don't care what I can prove—I know guys like this. They set the first fire and get away with it, and then it's like a fever. They set more fires after that, bigger fires. It's like they're flaunting how smart they are, showing off their power—"

"Or trying to tell someone how troubled they are," Jacqui murmured thoughtfully.

He rolled his eyes toward the ceiling. She *would* see it that way. "Honey, I am trying to tell you that someone's hitting on you. The only thing in common with all those fires is you. You're the link. The only link. Which means that it has to be someone you know or have worked with or who knows you."

"So the two photographs of the men you brought me . . . ?"

Finally she was listening. "Both were sent up the river for playing with matches in the past. Both did their time and are out on parole. Both have skipped parole and are missing."

"You think they're in Detroit?"

"Their home base is Detroit. If you want to talk logically, a scuzz who skips parole should want to take a fast hike and get lost miles from his home base. Except fire setters are a different breed of cat. Torches flaunt what they do. They like to stand around and watch, and Roberts particularly has a habit of—" He stopped.

"Of what?"

But Scott had no intention of telling her that Roberts had a problem with women. Pretty women. Preferably young, pretty, professional women who lived alone. When it came down to it, both West and Roberts had some patterns with women and fire that were enough to make his throat close.

He said nothing, but Jacqui must have picked up something from his face. "I'm sure I didn't know West, Scott, and I'm almost as positive that I didn't recognize Roberts."

Her tone was warm and soothing, as if her only concern was reassuring a man who was nearly going out of his mind with worry. "Am I getting through at all? I'm trying to tell you that you have trouble. Maybe it isn't West, maybe it isn't Roberts. Maybe it's one of a hundred other people with a police record, and maybe it's one of several million people who have no record at all. I don't even know if it's a man or a woman or a kid, but I'm telling you there is someone out there who isn't dealing from a full deck."

"Please calm down. I believe you. I agree with you." He took a long harsh breath. "Was I shouting?"

"Yes."

"I didn't mean to shout at you."

"People shout at me all the time," she said mildly. "You're mad and upset and frustrated and worried. It seems to me a very logical time to shout. It's just rough on the eardrums in this small a car. Anyway, you've told me this whole thing, now what can I do to help you?"

He was still disturbed at having raised his voice around her, but more jubilantly relevant was that he'd finally gotten through. "For openers, I want you to give me your patients' names, the ones who've had trouble with arson, and let me look through those records."

She frowned. "I thought we had all this settled? You know I can't do that."

He fought for patience, which had never been one of his strong points. "I'm telling you that this guy *knows* you. All those fires, but you're the only link. You're the only one who's had every fire every time. The only way we're going to find him is through you. If you're that sure your private life is surrounded by paragons and saints, that only leaves your patients. I want those files."

"I can't." The two words were spoken simply and calmly.

He tried cajoling. "Come on, Jacqui. You gonna make me go all the way to a judge? All that hassle and nuisance for a search warrant. You'll feel mad and I'll feel mad. We'll waste all that time, and in the long run I'm going to get what I need, anyway."

Her smile was as unexpected as a tickle. Before he could stop her, before he had any idea what she was going to do, she leaned over the console. A whisper of French fragrance assaulted him first. It was suddenly so quiet he could hear the sound of sliding silk when she raised her palm to his cheek. The texture of that palm was warm, dry and pampered smooth. And then she feathered her lips over his. Not for long. All he caught was the taste of woman, the tease of sensuality, the lure of something sweet and forbidden and dangerously tempting.

She leaned back before he could exhale. Assuming he could exhale. He had no immediate memory of knowing how to breathe. The kiss had lasted less than a second. For him, it had the impact of a coiling tornado.

Her soft, liquid eyes rested on his face—for a moment he had the crazy feeling she was as shaken as he was—and she had no business looking at him that way, as though she knew him, or wanted to. As though she cared, when she couldn't. There was something else, though, the briefest dark spark of fear in her eyes, and then that, too, was gone.

"In my opinion, you are one good man, Mr. Scott Llewellyn," she murmured. "Full of horseradish, but good." She gathered up her purse and scarf. "I wish you'd given me this whole story the other night. You have an entire city to worry about, you foolish man. You can't spend this kind of time worrying about one lone woman." She pushed at her car door. "I'd like to continue the discussion, but I have to go. My one o'clock just drove in, four cars down."

She climbed out of the car, swung her purse strap to her shoulder and then leaned back down. There was a tease in her eyes, a twinkle. "A warrant," she chided him. "Who do you think you're fooling? I told you half my kids were referred through the courts, so I happen to be just an itsy-bit familiar with the justice system. You have zip to justify a warrant, Mr. Llewellyn, nor is one necessary. Naturally, now that I know what's going on, I'll go back and restudy both my kids and my files."

She straightened and closed the door. He surged out of his side of the car and said over the top, "I want to know what you come up with. And I'm not done with your house. I want to talk to you about locks, alarms, a security system."

"Fine, but not today."

"And I want you to think harder about the people you work with, the people you know. You still have that picture of Roberts. I want you to keep it, keep looking at it—"

"Fine. And Scott . . . ?"

For just those bare seconds a crisp breeze caught the champagne luster of her hair. Her skirt flipped high on her thigh, and the sun flowed on, in, all around her. "Thanks for worrying about me," she said softly.

He made it to his car. He even latched the safety belt and pushed in the key, but then he just sat there.

He told himself that it was professional frustration that had his heart still pounding, his hands still slick, the pulse still thundering in his temples. Jacqui may have listened, but she hadn't really *listened*. She didn't have enough sense to be scared. Her mind-set was too locked in to helping people.

Scott hadn't been that nice when he was in diapers. The guy linked to Jacqui had already set fifteen fires in a sequence of three months. The character showed a real enthusiasm for fire. The next sequential month was October, and Jacqui had no conception of what a real fire lover of a maniac could do on Devil's Night. Scott did. Scott didn't want to help the bastard. He wanted to waste him. Before Devil's Night, and before he came anywhere closer than five hundred miles of that naive green-eyed blonde again.

You are only professionally concerned, Llewellyn. Naturally, justifiably and professionally concerned.

He flipped the key to turn on the engine, thinking, *Yeah, right.*

"Do you see that wall over there, Jaime? I desperately—desperately, desperately, desperately—need a picture on that wall. What I really need is a picture of your room. Do you think you could draw one for me?"

The towhead with the solemn blue eyes never budged from the doorway. "Where are you going to be if I do a picture?"

"Right next to you. Handing you crayons. So you can tell me all about your room at the same time."

"I don't draw good."

"Me either," Jacqui said cheerfully, and offered her hand. "But if we help each other, maybe we can come up with something special."

Ten minutes later Jacqui had her skirt hiked to her thighs and forty-eight pounds of concentrating towhead on her lap. An enticing box of new crayons perched on the table, all sixty-four colors, but the little girl relentlessly chose blacks and browns and drew in huge, stark, slashes.

Every time Scott tried to sneak into her mind, Jacqui pushed him away. A long time ago she had learned the art of emptying her mind of any distractions. The sky could fall and the building flood. For the next forty-five minutes, nothing existed for her but a grave-eyed little girl named Jaime.

An hour later, Jaime was gone and so was Jaime's mother. As Jacqui scooped up the artwork, Jonathan parked himself in her doorway. An empty pipe was clamped between his teeth. This was his newest effort to

quit smoking. "You got her talking. That's better than
the rest of us were doing."

"She talked," Jacqui agreed, her head still down.
Crayons were no easier to evenly stuff in the box today
than they were when she was seven. But crayons were not
on her mind. Neither was her co-worker or her sore feet
or her four o'clock patient due two hours from now.
Llewellyn and that kiss had lodged in her head with a te-
nacity that had her thoroughly annoyed.

"You know what you want to do with Jaime?" Jonathan asked.

"I know what I'd like to do. Love her so much she
couldn't stand it and shoot her mother."

Jonathan's lips twitched. His mouth was surrounded
by a straggly growth of dark beard, an annual growing
event, starting every fall and ending on a barber's floor
in May. "I hope that isn't your best professional opinion, love."

"I wasn't talking professional opinions. I was talking
temptation." A poor choice of words. A pink crayon
snapped in her hands. She tossed it into the trash and
carted the rest of the debris to her shelves.

There was absolutely nothing wrong with kissing him.

She was physical in her approach to people. Always
had been. She touched her patients. She hugged her
friends. Physical affection came as naturally to her as
breathing, and that man distinctly needed a kiss.

It was her business to know when a man was troubled.
Scott was in a high-pressure job, and some men thrived
on pressure. She guessed he was one of them. The fire
fighting stories he'd told her at lunch, though, were about
a man who invited risk, fed on danger, drove himself toward life-threatening situations.

He had an old-fashioned protective streak that touched her, a sneaky sense of humor that made her laugh, and a chip on his shoulder about his blue-collar background that was utterly foolish. His blunt and blatant sexuality could perk up a nun's hormones, but it was the dare-life drive that worried her.

She refused to regret one brief, caring kiss. Her response was the problem, not the kiss. Her pulse was still unsettled, her nerves heightened, her mood hung up on erotic. To have that kind of reaction to such a slight, inconsequential physical contact was—in the vernacular—plumb crazy. She wondered vaguely if she could possibly be coming down with the flu.

"What did he have to say?"

She turned from her shelves to find that Jonathan, obviously between patients, had flopped onto a beanbag. "What did who have to say?"

"Your fireman." His pale blue eyes slid over her face. "Something has you all distracted. I assume it's him."

She heard the edge in his voice and thought, *Please, not today.* The puzzles on her game shelf were in shambles. Her fingers flew as she put them back together, at the same time giving her co-worker Scott's whole rundown about her fires, the other similar fires and Devil's Night. "It's impossible for me to believe that it's any of my kids. Still, maybe either you or Timm might want to sit in on one of my sessions with Stan."

"You've told me about Stan before," Jonathan said.

"I know." Once she finished cleaning up, she dropped into a pale blue chair and tucked a leg under her. "I don't have—and have never had—a patient like him. I know he's angry. I know he's at the stage where he's transferred a lot of that anger to me. But to believe he could act out that anger to the extent of setting fires at my house . . ." She shook her head. "If I've misunderstood him that badly, he needs a better qualified therapist than I am."

"I don't know a better qualified therapist, love. But if you want Timm's or my backup opinion, you know you have it."

"I want it," she admitted frankly. "And I suppose if you and Timm think it's wise, I could bring up some case histories at the Monday staff meeting. I certainly don't want you two affected by something I seem to be inadvertently involved in—"

"Like you said, we'll hit the whole subject Monday," Jonathan interrupted firmly. "In the meantime, what about you?"

"Me?"

"You're not shook up about these fires? As in scared out of your tree?"

She cupped her chin in her palm, regarding him warily. Jonathan's one leg was cocked over the other's knee. The sole of his Reebok vibrated a mile a minute, a sure sign his frenetic mind was working overtime. Jonathan was Mr. Laid-back for his patients. Fortunately or unfortunately, she knew him better than that. "I keep telling myself I should be scared, too," she agreed, "but it's like watching a movie. It's simply not possible for me to associate me or anything in my life with—" she hesitated "—fear. Danger. Malice. To take it all seriously just seems melodramatic."

"Devil's Night is real." Again, Jonathan's eyes focused intensely on her face.

"Yes. And that, I'm fascinated by. The psychology of a fire setter. The motivation of a pyromaniac. I've had my share of patients in trouble for arson, but none like Stan. He sets fires for the power of it, Jonathan. Because he doesn't see that he has power over his life in any other way. We're talking an incredible despair. And it keeps occurring to me that you magnify that type of despair a hundred times . . . and there you have your Devil's Night.''

"You're intrigued," Jonathan murmured.

"Yes."

"By the whole problem of fires and fire -setters . . . or by the fireman? I saw him when you drove in from lunch. You were interested in him.''

Again she heard that tone in his voice. Still, she tried to divert trouble by sounding casual and easy. "Sure, he interested me. For the obvious reason. I just had a few run-ins with fire—enough to know I could live without any reoccurrences as long as I live. He'd voluntarily walked into fires for fourteen years, and not just the little ones, but the big ones, the tough ones, the dangerous ones. I can't fathom that kind of courage.''

"Undoubtedly that's why you were attracted to him," Jonathan suggested smoothly. "The whole caveman scene. Courage. Danger. Physical prowess. How long have I known you now—four years? It's been more or less a point of curiosity to see when, how and what kind of man would finally get to you. Somehow I always thought it would take more than a pair of biceps.''

"Jonathan," she said breezily, "I'll be darned if I know why we go through this every six months, and I don't much care. Why don't you consider a nice cold swim in the Detroit River?''

He never moved from the beanbag, just tried the boyish grin that had nearly worked its charm on Jacqui four years ago. "Aren't you touchy? I was just joking. Since when can't you take a little teasing between friends?''

" 'Friends' is the operative word.''

He stopped trying to smile. His blue eyes bore into her like a cat stalking a mouse, ever patient, waiting. "There was a time we were almost more."

"'Almost' an affair is worth the same as 'almost' in horseshoes and elections. Now could we drop this subject?"

He uncoiled from the beanbag in one long lazy stretch. "For now. Yes."

That was all he said before leaving, but air whooshed from her lungs in a relieved sigh when he was gone. She rarely let Jonathan upset her. She valued working with him. His ability to zone in on the jugular of a patient's problem was uncanny. He was a brilliant therapist, and more than once they'd made an unusually successful man-woman therapist team.

About every six months, though, a disturbingly possessive streak popped out of Jonathan as sure as a jack-in-the-box. She'd turned him down some four years ago. He never let her forget that, and Jonathan knew exactly how to get under her skin. He knew he was capable of making her feel wary, threatened, uneasy.

She knew better than to react to him, but the whole darned day seemed to be one bit of a trauma after another.

By seven that night she was dead beat, starved and would have sold her soul for a long hot soak in a jasmine-oiled bath. As she drove into her yard, the sun was setting on the lake in a mirror of mauves and silvers and midnight blue. Her house, which should have been peacefully dark, had windows blazing more lights than a department store having a sale.

She reached for her briefcase and climbed out of the car. Her gaze was still bemusedly fixed on her lit-up windows when she glimpsed the scruffy old man sneaking around the corner of the garage. His hobble was stealthy and his watery blue eyes had a blank stare. Gray fringed his temples and emphasized his harsh, weathered features, and his mouth never budged from a flat, emotionless line.

Faking a scowl, she slammed the car door and said severely, "All right, what is this, McGraff?"

"What's what?" The old man's tone was as belligerent as hers.

"You were supposed to be gone long before three o'clock, and you know it."

He applied his fixed stare to the fender of her car. "Didn't want you coming home to a dark, empty house, not after all that's happened. And like I told you before, I got nothing better to do than wait around, so it's no big deal."

"Arthritis pretty bad tonight?" she asked gently.

He immediately stopped rubbing his right leg. "Had better days. Had worse ones, too." He moved past her as though he was passing a bee, giving her a wide, evasive berth. "Got your basement cleaned up. Piled up the wood and stacked it so you could have a fire. Finished up half the storm windows. Do the rest tomorrow."

"Thank you, you stubborn, bullheaded old—" She quit name-calling. It never did any good. "I do not want you waiting for me, McGraff. You know I keep odd hours."

"Yeah, yeah. Go git your dinner and quit bugging me."

"I love you, McGraff."

He just kept walking down the driveway, but for an instant she thought his profile twisted in an unwilling smile. One of these days she was determined to get a full-blooded laugh out of him, maybe even get him to tell her something about himself.

More immediately, she had some pinched toes, tight muscles and the nag of a weary headache to take care of. Once inside the house, she sifted through the freezer for a frozen dinner, thumbed through the mail and poured herself a glass of Madeira.

The original owners of the house had had the courtesy to install a pink marble bathtub. An hour later she was in it with the same glass of Madeira on the ledge beside her. She used her toe to turn on the hot water faucet. The water slushed down, burning, delightfully hot, and mixed with the oil she'd added to create a steam of sweet jasmine that should have soothed the most frazzled nerves.

It would probably have worked for her, too, if she didn't have three open textbooks perched precariously on the bathtub rim. When she reached for the wine, a little water dribbled on a page. She paid no attention.

The psychology tomes had several case histories on pyromaniacs, but those she was already familiar with. There was ample material on the nature of traumas that might drive a person to set fires, but absolutely nothing on courage.

In time she gave up, closed the texts and dropped them out of the water's way. Still holding the glass of Madeira, she sank up to her neck and sipped, letting the rich, robust flavor linger on her tongue.

Courage fascinated her. The fear of fire was as instinctive in most people as the fear of snakes. People risked pain and danger in various ways and for various reasons, but most had a natural, primitive fear of being burned.

What Jacqui couldn't understand, she could rarely let go of. And she couldn't understand a certain brand of courage—the courage it took someone to risk the awesome fear of being burned to set a fire. The courage of a man like Scott, who had chosen to risk the awesome fear of being burned in order to put out fires.

She frowned, irritably aware that every time Scott sneaked into her mind, her response was a lunge of emotion. Inexplicably he drew her, like the whisper of an erotic rush, the promise of something special that could be. And he repelled her. Like a wash of cold-water sanity.

It was her own flaw, of course. A lack of courage. When push came to shove, she could enter a smoke-filled basement alone. She didn't panic if a patient like Stan drew a switchblade on her. She had no fear of storms or the dark or living alone.

A brand of fear, though, had always colored her personal relationships. She never minded the climb to the cliff, but as a fair number of men had discovered, she never jumped off. Jonathan, in one of his nastier moods, had called her the last of the vestal virgins.

He was wrong. She'd had relationships, successful ones up to a point. With her patients, with her family and friends, she gave two hundred percent of herself. All her life, friends had counted on her. Both her parents were overachievers. She was the one who'd held the family together through the rough times, even as a kid. Her patients had needed her. To her knowledge, Jacqui had never let anyone down—except herself.

Whatever man she'd been involved with had always believed the relationship was thriving until she started withdrawing. A therapist should certainly be able to analyze her own behavior, but the physician heal-thyself theory didn't seem to work. She accepted other people's needs. When her own kicked in, she simply grasped at some vaguely subconscious anxiety. Fear took over, that was all, something like the catcher in the rye. She wasn't so afraid of jumping off the cliff, but that there'd be no one at the bottom to catch her.

Is that your considered professional analysis, Hughes?

She leaned forward, and turned the knob on the drain. In a slush and sluice of water, she stood up and reached for a towel. In her professional analysis, she was boiled to a wrinkle.

She still hadn't finished her one glass of wine.

And she still hadn't managed to get one Scott Llewellyn off her mind.

Chapter 4

Saturday night Jacqui wakened from a dead sleep to the sound of a branch slapping against the window. Her bedroom was dark and the house still. Sleepily she fluffed her pillow. Her eyes were already half-closed again when she noticed the light seeping under the bottom of her bedroom door.

There couldn't be a light. She never left lights on before going to bed. Ever.

Well, obviously you forgot this time. Sleep was imminently more desirable than thinking about her electric bill, but old habits died hard. Groggily she forced herself out of bed, grabbed a bathrobe and belted it. By the time she reached the door, her fingertips were unaccountably icy and her pulse was racing. Scolding herself for acting paranoid, she impatiently turned the knob.

Light immediately blazed in her eyes. The hall light, the study lamps, the bathroom overhead, even the kitchen and basement—every light in the house was on.

Fear didn't shudder through her, though, until she traveled the hall and found her always locked studio door ajar.

Before going to bed, she'd spent an hour with her clay, working on a bust of one of her patients. The bust was terrible—one of her worst—and heaven knew she was a laughable failure as a sculptor. She pursued the hobby because it helped her in her work and because she loved it. For the same reasons had never exposed her vice to anyone. It was her business, no one else's.

Someone, though, had made it their business this night. The working lamp she'd left off was now on and deliberately twisted toward the clay model of Stan Witkowski. Under the light's harsh glare, the boy's face looked so surrealistic and sinister that nausea rose in her throat.

Jamming off the light, she relocked the door and stood there shaking like a goose. Fear, like a sniper, hit her all at once. She could hear, smell and taste it.

She forced control by taking several deep breaths and then started moving. One glance in her den showed that everything was where it should be. Magazines were where she'd left them; her briefcase was still open, with the same splash of papers strewed over the desk. No one had touched the living room. Even a scoopable pair of garnet earrings still lay in a crystal dish, where she'd dropped them. Her kitchen still had a dirty glass on the counter, the same apple sitting by the sink, the dish towel tossed near the stove.

There'd been no vandalism. She kept looking, hard, but there was no sign of a thief or prowler. Nothing was wrong anywhere.

Except for the lights.

And the silence.

There wasn't a sound in the entire house except for her shattered breathing. Everywhere she looked there were blaze-bright lights glinting down at her. Every light winked menace. Every lamp glowed a threat, and the clawing feeling of violation kept coming.

She wouldn't have minded a nice, clean thief, someone who wanted her microwave or TV. Her microwave and TV were untouched. Nothing was damaged. He hadn't even stirred the dust. *All* he'd done was go through every room in her house and turn on the lights. As pranks went, this one was harmlessly laughable.

Only she wasn't laughing. Her skin was crawling as though she'd been locked in a closet with spiders, particularly when she realized he'd been in her bedroom. What other conclusion could she reach? She'd locked the studio before going to bed. The door only had one key. That key was kept in the top drawer of her bedroom dresser. In order for him to get the key, he not only had to know where it was, but he must have entered her bedroom while she was sleeping.

She slept buck naked, always had. There wasn't a pajama or nightgown made that didn't make her feel tied down, and anyway, who cared? *Maybe he looked at you, Jacqui. Maybe he was close enough to touch. Maybe he was close enough to . . .*

In five fast strides she reached the kitchen telephone, punched in nine, then one, then hesitated. Hanging it back up, she raked both hands through her hair. *What are you going to tell them, Jacqui? That your lights are on? They'll probably send you to one of the psychologists in your own office.*

Blindly, mindlessly, she started sifting through the clutch of papers on the counter, wading past bills and mail and notes to herself until she finally came up with a telephone number written on a scratch pad.

Her breath was still coming in patches. She told herself not to dial until she'd calmed down, but that was like waiting for Godot. Her mind sent out sensible instructions about thinking rationally and gaining control. Her body just wasn't getting the messages. Her hands trembled so hard that she had to dial twice to make the connection, and then all the phone did was ring. And ring. And ring.

You're overreacting, kiddo.

You bet your sweet petunias I'm overreacting. Dammit, Scott, answer your phone.

On the eleventh ring, someone picked up the receiver. There was a dull thud, a muffled four-letter word and then a groggily growled, "Let's hope like hell you have a damned good reason for calling at—" a brief hesitation "—2:49 in the morning."

Her eyes squeezed shut, and she suddenly had the hardest time swallowing. Scott was obviously mad. She didn't blame him. It was an unprincipled hour to call. Already her fear was ebbing away from simply hearing another human voice—*his* voice. Fresh from sleep, Scott had a voice that made a woman think of sin, sex and beds. Those distracting illusions were a good jolt of common sense. He undoubtedly had someone with him. He was single; it was Saturday night. She whispered a desperately low, "I'm sorry I woke you, Scott. Go back to sleep—"

"Jacqui?"

How could he possibly have recognized her from one choked whisper? Her tongue tripped out an unwilling, "Yes."

"Where are you and what happened?"

He certainly woke up with a snap. His bark-rough tenor should have soothed her. Instead, she felt the idiotic sting of tears in her eyes.

She made a gesture with her hand that he obviously couldn't see—a gesture of helplessness and anger and confusion. Emotion suddenly poured out of her faster than water from a spilled bucket. Nothing could stop her. She couldn't help it. "Nothing happened. That's what's so... silly. I mean, there's no crime, no fire, no nothing. I started to call the police and hung up. What on earth were they supposed to do, come here and turn off my lights for me? Good grief, they'd laugh at me. *I'm* laughing at me. I don't even know why I'm calling you. I never panic, Scott, but for a few minutes there I was just so scared and I—"

At first he couldn't make any sense from what she was saying. She didn't have to make sense for him to react. Snapping on a bedside light, he grabbed for his shirt. "Shh, Jacqui, tell me slower."

The longer she talked, the faster he moved. Emotion seemed to transfer direct through the phone wire. As she calmed down, he revved up. Stomach stinging acid, he carried the phone as far as it would go so he could reach his jeans. Cradling the receiver to his ear, he tugged them on—and without underwear, that made the zipper tricky. "You checked your doors? They're all locked?"

"Yes, they're all locked. That's half of what's so unbelievable. He locked up after himself. Talk about your considerate prowlers...."

Her laugh was shaky, low. Scott felt his jaw muscles tighten. "Sweetheart, do you have a gun?"

"A gun? Of course I don't have a gun."

His mouth twisted in a wry grimace as he tugged on his socks. He should have known better than to ask the question. Jacqui Hughes wouldn't own a gun. Not in this life. A beautiful young woman living on a relatively secluded property alone . . . but no. It would never occur to her to have a weapon of any kind. He reached for his shoes. "Are you absolutely positive he's gone?"

"Yes."

"How are you positive?"

"Because I am. He isn't here. I know he isn't still here. You know how you can sense someone in a house when you're completely alone?"

He usually respected anyone's instincts. More than once he'd trusted his life to his own gut instincts. Jacqui's intuition, however, totally failed to reassure him. "Where are you?"

"You know where I am. I already told you. Home."

"What *room*?"

"The kitchen. Good grief, who cares?"

In his head, he could see one petrified woman with misty jade eyes turning quickly—too damned quickly— back into a psychologist. He said firmly, "Because I want you to stay there, by the phone. Don't go near the basement, don't go near the closets, and definitely stay inside. After I hang up, dial nine and one and let it hang. You hear a mouse squeak, you dial the last one."

"Scott, that's silly. He's gone. Like I said, there's nothing to call the police for. I can certainly turn out my own lights—"

"Don't touch the lights, honey, and the only reason you're not calling your Silver Lake cops is because I am. If nothing else, maybe they can catch some fingerprints. Now, your cops should be knocking on your door within a fast fifteen minutes, but it'll take me longer. I'm a good forty-minute drive away from you."

"You don't have to come." She let out a long, low breath, so long and low she might have been compressing it for hours. "You're right about the police. Fingerprints never crossed my mind, probably because I was so busy being a hysterical wimp. The wimp has now recovered enough to feel darned embarrassed to have bothered you at this hour," she said humorously. "When I grabbed the phone, all I could think of was that you were the one person who knew about my fires. I knew you would believe me."

"I believe you. But you're wrong."

"Wrong?"

"I do have to be there." As fast as he punched the disconnect button, he dialed the Silver Lake police. In principle, he had no jurisdiction over the suburban fire or police departments—Devil's Night was a city problem. He could demand cooperation if he had to, though, and besides that, he had a voice that carried dominantly well over Ma Bell.

The whole time he was barking at the Silver Lake boys, he stared at the walnut-paneled walls of his apartment bedroom. The room was austere: gray carpet, white sheets, no pictures or doodads anywhere. He didn't live here. He lived at his job.

For years, he'd also lived for fires—the chance to walk into one, a bad one, to feel the heat and smell the scorch of danger and know he could conquer it. He didn't have a do-gooder bone in his body. He simply had a sister named Phoebe. A dozen times, a hundred times, a thousand times he'd proved his courage by other men's standards. Not by his own. Dominating all those years was a search for the one fire that was an honest test of a man's bravery. He'd never found it, and once Connolly had talked him into the promotion, the chance to test himself was gone.

Hanging up the phone, he found a jacket and his car keys and pelted down the back steps toward his car. Bunched clouds hung low in the sky. A chill wind fretfully hurled leaves and debris. He could smell rain coming.

And for the first time since he was twelve years old, he could smell fear, almost as if he was about to face that one fire, that one test that mattered. What if that bastard was still there, lurking in the basement, waiting in some closet? If the devil put one little finger on her...

He didn't stop to think how, when or where Jacqui had started to matter this much. He just jumped into his car, put the pedal to the floor and ran the first red light.

An hour later, rain was pitching and tossing against Jacqui's kitchen window. She heard the slam of brakes outside. She'd been entertaining two of her local policemen.

The one, John Henry, liked his coffee black. The short, jowly man with the marine haircut was Hank. He not only liked coffee but sugar cookies to go with it. They had arrived shortly after her call to Scott, looking stiff and official. Once the rain had obliterated any chance of a prolonged outside investigation, they came inside with their fingerprint kit, and she started the coffee. Their stiff, proper postures had disappeared with conversation. She'd deliberately cracked the first joke to put them at ease.

The whole night had taken on a surreal cast for Jacqui. The woman who'd stood petrified under the silent blaze of lights had disappeared.

Panic never solved a problem. Control and rational thinking solved problems. And when push came to shove, there was no one but yourself to depend on. She'd been taught that, believed it, and the ingrained lesson had never been more valued than tonight. The police hadn't been there ten minutes before she discovered they weren't going to do anything. There was simply nothing they could do.

Once she understood that, she let a nice, fat layer of numbness settle over her. The numbness worked beautifully until she heard the slam of brakes in her driveway. Both policemen lurched up from their chairs even before Scott reached the door.

He blew in with a gust of wind and pelting rain. Maybe his jacket hung open and his chin hadn't seen a razor for hours, but she noted with no surprise that John Henry stood at rigid attention and Hank lost his low-key humor the moment Scott started leveling questions.

He barely glanced at her. He was too busy mercilessly grilling her local police. She looked at him, though. She'd nearly convinced herself that any sense of danger was a figment of her imagination until he walked in.

He had dangerous, dark eyes, she thought whimsically. They were as dark and mobile as a gray-black thundercloud. He stood with his legs slightly spread, his hands loosely on his hips and his hair matted with rain. It was a dare-anything posture, and the look of him dented her soft shell of numbness as nothing else could have.

She was coming to understand that her conflicting feelings for Scott all came from the same source. For what he believed, for what he wanted, he'd dare anything at all and to hell with anyone's civilized rules. She wasn't sure whether that thought was tremendously comforting . . . or badly disturbing.

In time, he ushered the policemen out, closed the door and latched it. The silence only lasted seconds. If he'd barely glanced at her before, his gaze ripped from the top of her disheveled head to her bare feet now.

Her eyes were the color of cognac, he thought fleetingly. With the skill of a chameleon, she'd changed moods since their phone call. Then, she'd been scared witless Now, an easy, welcoming smile courted her lips. Normal color tinted her cheeks, and she was wearing a long blue robe that looked French-boudoir elegant and crushably feminine.

He valued strength in a woman, but Jacqui knew a dimension of the quality he was unfamiliar with. The strong women he knew were tough, streetwise, survivor smart. Jacqui hadn't a hard bone in her body. Her strength was all on the inside, and he had a measure of it now in how high she held that chin and how tightly she clutched the lapels of her robe.

He figured she was about a finger snap away from breaking down . . . and wouldn't admit it to Saint Peter, even right at the gates.

"Still a little shook-up?" he asked.

"Not at all. I'm sorry you ended up having to come all this way."

"Forget it. Cops treat you okay?"

"Like I was a Lindbergh in a kidnapping case," she said blithely. "Would you like a drink? I know I have some brandy and wine around."

"Thanks, no. Too late for booze."

"Coffee?"

He smiled but never took his eyes off her face. "Too early for coffee. Have any milk?"

"Milk?" She turned her head before moving toward the refrigerator. "Somehow I didn't figure you for a milk drinker."

He wasn't, but caffeine was going to keep her up, and booze was the last thing to give someone in shock. And she was in shock, whether or not she knew it. "Pour us both a glass? I heard what the guys had to say. Now tell me your version."

"It was like a scene out of the Keystone Cops," she said humorously. She carted the milk to the counter and reached for glasses as she closed the refrigerator door with her hip. "They came out of their cars with guns drawn, took fingerprints all over the place and asked enough questions to fill a thirty-page report—which is fairly humorous, considering they didn't believe me."

He hadn't expected the police to take her seriously, but she'd clearly thought they would. She spilled the milk because her hands were shaking. She swiftly moved in front of the spill so he wouldn't see it.

He tossed off his jacket, since there wasn't a chance in hell he was leaving.

"Not to misunderstand—they treated me like gold, but I gather that was mostly because you made the phone call. Is there anyone in the entire county who doesn't know you, Llewellyn?" When he didn't bite on the question, she continued. "They were not only nice, they were honest with me. Sure, they found some nice clean fingerprints, but those will probably end up mine or McGraff's. They're going to run McGraff's through their computer, but like they said, if I trust my caretaker, that's an obvious dead end. Finding any footprints or shoe tracks outside was another dead end from the minute the rain started. So... there's nothing more they're going to do. There's nothing they can do."

Her eyes flickered briefly at his when she handed him the glass of milk. He wondered if she had any idea how lost she looked or how much the policemen's visit had upset her.

"The real truth, though, Scott, is that they didn't believe I had a prowler," she said wryly. "Why should they? Not a lock was touched, not a window was broken. Nobody had taken anything. I figure they have me pegged as a suburban socialite who got scared of the dark after being the victim of a few prank fires. They even had an answer for my fires. Affluent teenagers with too little parental supervision, etc., etc."

Abruptly Scott lurched to his feet to prowl her cupboards. He found a package of Fig Newtons and a bakery spread of already opened sugar cookies. If milk didn't put her out, a complex carbohydrate might. Something had to.

For the briefest moment, her smile slipped. "Scott, if you don't believe me, no one will. There was someone here. I didn't turn on those lights myself."

"I know, Petunia." He handed her a sugar cookie. Then he nudged her milk closer and sat down. The nickname seemed to both distract and honestly amuse her. He was already aware that from the time of her phone call, he'd fallen into that pit of nicknames and endearments. Once you step in quicksand, it's hard to pull back. Besides, he'd have called her anything to get that look out of her eyes.

"And it wasn't just someone. It was the same man who started my fires." Although she hadn't wanted the milk, she took a sip when she sat down. "I know he didn't start a fire, but the game was exactly the same. He aimed to scare, not hurt. Warn, not damage. And he wanted to threaten, but to do it in such an innocuous way that the police were yawning on their way out the door. When you think about it, he's not only smart but quite a charmer.''

"How about another sip of milk?'' Scott coaxed. Her tone was gay, party light, chitchat conversational—and guilt was tearing at him. He'd talked to her about protection, then failed to follow through. Well, he'd hounded an investigator from the National Board of Fire Underwriters, contacted the state fire marshall, phoned an old security man, nagged the state police about Roberts and West. That was nothing. Talk, not action. He'd been so busy—his own job was a twenty-four-hour-a-day worry—and he'd been sure that she was temporarily safe.

"He needs to be found," she told him.

"Yes."

"That gets a little tricky when even the police think he's nothing more than a naughty little prankster." She smiled. "I guess that leaves the job up to me."

"Wrong, Petunia," Scott said swiftly, firmly. "It's up to me, not you. And I know you're scared, but—"

"Being scared is a waste of energy. Finding him is what has to happen, and when it comes down to it, what can you do? What can anyone do? I'm the one he's singled out, so he's obviously my problem."

"Honey..." But there was no stopping her talking for love or money.

She gulped down a little more of her milk. "There are obvious advantages to my being a psychologist. I know a little about the nature of the beast. I don't believe in 'typical cases,' but many fire setters follow a pattern—disadvantaged background, sometimes less than bright, often a broken home, often sexual promiscuity on the part of both parents. Oddly enough, most pyromaniacs have a physical scar or defect, possibly as a result of the

father's excessive punishment. The father is often a severe punisher if not a downright abuser, while the mother's weak, both morally and emotionally. There comes a
point where our victim runs away, both physically and
emotionally, into a fantasy life—''

"You just keep sipping there...."

"Hmm." She lifted the glass and took another small
gulp. "He frequently sets his first fire in late adoles-
cence. Where he's coming from is despair, and what he
wants is power. Fire is power as he sees it—all the power
he doesn't have in his own life—but unfortunately that
fantasy high doesn't last. It doesn't solve anything, and
so he has to set the next fire. And the next. A true pyromaniac has no fear, Scott. No fear of being burned, no
conscience about hurting anyone. He does it all in a fantasy."

Again, Scott lurched up from his chair. He couldn't
just sit there. The differences between them were chasm-
deep. She wanted to talk about "disadvantaged backgrounds" and "fantasies." Unlike Jacqui, he'd *heard* the
scream of a child trapped in a burning building from a
fire set by a pyro.

He wanted to immediately sling Jacqui over his shoulder and kidnap her to a nice fireproof vault in the Arctic
Circle, where she'd be safe. That being a difficult op-
tion, so he tried to concentrate on milk, in the form of
getting her a second glass. She'd finished the first, but it
hadn't worked. She wasn't calming down but revving up,
and no matter how rational her words, her eyes were still
wild and lost.

Bending in her refrigerator, he noted Brie, Madeira,
avocados and white-wrapped luncheon meat. Last he
looked, his fridge stocked old Milwaukee and a little bologna. His bologna hadn't been butcher wrapped. She

had horseradish, though. It wasn't as if they had nothing in common.

She blinked when he handed her the second glass. "I thought you were the one who wanted milk?"

"I'm drinking, too," he assured her, and lifted his glass.

So did she, but she forgot it too quickly. "I've done enough research to form a psychological profile, but the profile fits a lot of people. I can't just peg someone in the slot. From everything I know, I'm positive my 'friend' is male, but I can't tell you his age. I can't even be sure if he's young or old, and this whole thing started three months ago. Obviously something acted as a catalyst for him at that time, something connected with me, but there's just nothing that I can remember...."

She pushed at her hair. "I can tell you this. He's dangerous. Terribly dangerous. He's long past his first fire, and when you add up the rage, the despair, the lack of conscience... And my particular 'friend' is not dull but extraordinarily bright. He's clever enough to plan small details, outthink all the major dimensions of a problem. He turned on my lights to play with me, Scott. I don't even want to think about what this man is truly capable of."

"Jacqui?"

"Hmm?" She focused blindly on him.

"You're going to bed now, honey."

"Pardon?"

"I said it's bedtime." His voice was gruff. He'd assumed it would help her if he let her talk it out. He'd been wrong.

She wanted to see her pyro as though he were a neat little psychological puzzle. She wanted to play it that way very badly, so badly that she didn't even know she was falling asleep in her chair. Her calm control was as fake as tinsel, and her eyes mirrored fears that she'd relived enough. Once she'd given up holding her robe closed, the neckline had gaped open. Her long white throat was exposed. Her skin had no mars, no flaws. If vulnerability had a color, it would be the exact cream-white shade of her flesh. Scott wondered how the hell long Jacqui had demanded this kind of strength from herself.

It was definitely time to put her to bed, and with that sole goal in mind, his feet hit the floor. "Come on, Petunia. You're beat and I'm beat. I know you'd like to solve this whole thing tonight—preferably entirely by yourself—but it's almost five in the morning. Tomorrow I'm going to hit you with a lot of talk about security systems for this place, and I expect we'll have a good long argument about your job and my job and what you are not going to be involved in. But not now. We both need some sleep."

Immediately she stood up, too, with an appalled look at the kitchen clock. "Lord, I'm sorry. I know it sounds unbelievable, but I honestly didn't realize what time it was. I didn't mean to ramble on and keep you up, and I never once thanked you. For coming, for being here..."

For believing me, was unsaid, but he heard it in her voice. "You can thank me in the morning. Won't be all that hard to do, since I'm staying."

"Here?" She looked startled.

"Not precisely here." He gave a wry look at her kitchen chairs. "I had in mind your den. It's a long drive back to my place, just to turn around and come back here in the morning. You have a problem with that?"

His tone was aggressive, and he backed it up with a don't-mess-with-me scowl. She looked at him for several seconds and then murmured, "No."

She laid too much trust on the line with that single syllable, he thought irritably. Jacqui was going to be a nightmare to protect. He urged her to finish her milk, but that was hopeless. At the rate she sipped, she wouldn't finish the glass before the twenty-first century, so he scooted her and the milk toward her bedroom, zapping out lights as he went.

"Time to put the whole thing out of your mind, and that's going to be easy to do. If so much as an owl hoots, I'll hear him and take care of it. Nobody's going near your door, because I'm going to guard it like my sister's virginity.... Do I hear laughter?"

She chuckled—the first honest chuckle he'd heard from her all night—but it didn't last nearly long enough. "Scott, if you're staying because you think I'm afraid, honestly, it's unnecessary. You've done enough just by being willing to come here at this horrible hour, and I'm fine. Totally fine."

He could see how "totally fine" she was. He suffered through a vague description of where he could find sheets and pillows. If it was up to her, she'd be making up a bed for him. He had to get firm again.

Once he closed the door to her bedroom, he glanced at his watch. Anticipating a solid ten minutes of silence, he found the couch in her den, the low volume on her television's remote control and tuned in to an old Marlon Brando movie. Brando was giving the rush to Eva Marie Saint, but Academy Award performances couldn't hold his attention.

His conscience fed him a steady scolding about not belonging here. Jacqui was certainly being chased by a loose fruitcake, but every loose fruitcake in the city was hardly his concern. This particular creep was an active firebug, and any pyro coming into his own before Devil's Night was potentially Scott's problem, but even that reasoning was hazy. Catching criminals was a cop's job. He wasn't a cop. He had his hands full with the task force and the curfew, logistics, personnel, equipment. Hell, he had more than his hands full.

So. He didn't belong here.

Only he didn't seem to be moving real fast toward the door. The thing was that he could make the cops protect her, but he couldn't make them believe her. And no one was going to protect her too diligently if they didn't believe she was in serious danger.

She's not only *in* danger, Llewellyn, he thought wearily. She *is* danger.

At least she was for him. He couldn't shake the picture of her soft, shock-dazed eyes from his mind, or of her elegant hands, clutched knuckle white on her robe when he'd first walked in. He'd have wrapped his arms around her if Jacqui had been anyone but Jacqui and he'd been anyone but who he was. It was totally inappropriate for him to feel a ripening sense of excitement anywhere near her. The cadence of her voice moved him. Hell, the look of her throat sent a vivid bolt of heat through his bloodstream.

If he was a smart man, he'd move quickly toward the closest exit. He wanted to leave, even saw the wisdom in leaving. If the combined forces of the CIA, FBI and the Green Berets agreed to surround her house until Devil's Night, he might have considered it.

But then again, maybe not. If Scott knew one thing in life, it was fire, and pyros could slip through the cracks as easily as a mouse could steal into a closed cupboard. The idea of trusting someone else to protect Jacqui made him feel as restless as a caged cougar.

He checked the dial on his watch again. Every muscle in his body was tight. He was in a fine mood to slam the nearest wall. Instead, he was stretched out with a pillow behind him when she reappeared in the doorway, still wearing the long blue robe, still barefoot.

He'd guessed she would make it ten minutes. His usually sound gut instincts were way off kilter. She'd made it a full fourteen.

Chapter 5

Scott raised his arm and beckoned impatiently with his fingers. "It's about time the reaction hit you. Come on over here."

Jacqui, at that precise moment, couldn't seem to move. She had no idea what had happened to her when she walked into the dark bedroom. Her skin had turned cold and her lungs had constricted. She'd forced herself to climb into bed and then lay there like a shaking aspen.

The police hadn't believed she had a prowler for a number of reasons, but one outweighed all the others. Human beings couldn't walk through locked doors. But her prowler *had*, just like a ghost or goblin in the night. She knew the image sneaking through her mind was ridiculous, but it clung tenaciously. If the devil could get through locked doors once, he could do it again. Anytime he pleased.

She'd bolted out of bed like a two-year-old having a nightmare. "It isn't reaction that's hitting me. It's foolishness. I know you want to sleep, and I don't want to bother you. If you don't mind, I just want to sit here for a minute.''

"If you want to know what I mind, it's a darn fool woman who thinks she has to be some kind of pillar of strength. Other people can shout, right? Other people can feel scared, but not you. Hell, I saw you serving the cops coffee. Shame on you for not cooking them a seven-course dinner. Sure wouldn't want to give anybody the idea that you're upset. Who the hell taught you to be so hard on yourself, Petunia?''

She would have answered him if he'd given her a chance. At the same time that he was scolding her, he lurched up, dragged her back with him onto the couch and tugged her—awkwardly—onto his lap. As honorably as a priest, he covered her thigh where her robe had parted. As impersonally as a brother, he jammed her cheek to his shoulder and wrapped his arms around her.

She suddenly found herself shuddering, hard—not necessarily because of her prowler. It had always been easy for her to hold, never so easy to be held. It had always been easy for her to express compassion for others' needs, never so easy to accept need in herself. Everyone she knew had always counted on her to have an iron core, yet her heart was suddenly beating, beating, beating... and Scott was still delivering his gruff brand of common sense.

"It had to catch up with you sometime," he said impatiently. "When a son of a sea dog threatens you, you're supposed to be scared, and I don't want to hear any more psychological crap about how troubled he is—"

"But he is—"

"I don't care what *he* is. I care what *you* are. *He's* just fine—probably sitting in his own home with his feet up, sipping a Coke, pleased as punch with his night's work. You can't let the devils win in this life, Petunia, but there's a time to fight back and a time to admit the boogeyman won this round...."

Her hair was a tangled mess that smelled like gardenias, which Scott ignored. The side of one breast crushed against his ribs, affecting his heart as though he'd just started down a steep toboggan run. He ignored that, too, and judiciously kept his eyes away from the open throat of her robe, because she wasn't wearing anything beneath it. Actually, he couldn't *know* that. She *could* be wearing a bra, underpants, whalebone corset and a chastity belt.

He just doubted it. Her flannel robe was long, but not thick—at least not thick enough. The breast crushed against his chest was distinctly unencumbered. The fanny wedged on his thighs made the intimate imprint of a woman's shape. He knew the exact moment when she stopped shuddering and warmth started to flood her skin again, and he had no regrets about holding her. If it had been Phoebe, he'd have had his arms around his sister long before this. Human contact was a basic remedy for fear.

Only she wasn't his sister, and that issue of basic human contact was affecting him. The temperature below his waist had risen ten degrees. His nerves felt coiled up in barbed wire. He couldn't breathe well.

The problem was worse than chemistry, more serious than desire. A man did certain automatic things for a woman in trouble. A man had certain automatic rights to do different things when the woman in trouble was the woman he loved.

You had the right to protect a woman you loved. The right to yell at her when she needed yelling at. The right to make love to her until she couldn't see and couldn't think and the only thing in her head was passion, not fear.

And to keep his mind off that dangerous track, he kept talking. "So you're just going to sit right here and know damn well you're safe and watch Brando on the waterfront. I don't want any arguments, you understand? Jacqui—"

His voice scratched with alarm when she suddenly raised her head. When she'd first walked in, the lack of color in her face had scared him, and her eyes had been haunted. Now her cheeks were a healthy pink and her eyes had a hint of wet, luminous mint.

"I came in here feeling close to hysterical," she murmured.

"I know, that's what I've been—"

"It's very hard to get hysterical when you can't get a word in edgewise."

"I'll shut up. Immediately."

"I'm afraid that's not going to solve your immediate problem."

"My immediate problem?"

"You're about to get kissed, Scott. Try to bear up. I know this makes you nervous."

When she turned in his lap and framed his face with her palms, Scott stiffened as though he'd swallowed a cup of starch. She paid no attention. Her lips brushed his once, a kiss for all his mother-henning. Her lips brushed his a second time because he was a goblin chaser, a man unbeatably qualified to make a woman feel protected and secure.

She had no idea why she kissed him a third time. She was in trouble by then, she knew that. Between a fire and a prowler, this seemed to be her week for trouble, but this was danger of an entirely different kind.

Heat flowed between them like bubbling lava. She'd anticipated the warmth, not the heat. And Scott may have exercised reluctant forbearance for her first two pecks, but when he kissed back . . . he kissed back.

Textures surrounded her like mist. His dark hair shone under the lamplight. The stubborn line of his jaw was rough whiskered, while his mouth was impossibly, unexpectedly soft. She tasted of milk. He tasted of peppermint, and she could feel his heart buck the moment their tongues meshed.

His fingers tunneled into her hair without breaking the kiss. Tongues mated, hot and wet, two tastes becoming one, and the pressure of one kiss suddenly blurred into the next. She felt the tip of his tongue on her throat. She knew her hands were climbing the rough wool of his shirt.

They were alone. She'd never been this alone with a man, not in this way. They shared fear this night. He let her know it. He would put himself between anyone and anything that tried to hurt her. He let her know that, too. His kisses lacked finesse. His touch was more pagan than practiced, more rough than skilled. She knew wild in the wind, not in a man.

Somewhere, an autumn rain had turned into a branch-tossing, wind-hurling gale. Somewhere, a TV screen flashed mute psychedelic patterns of black and white.

She didn't care. She'd walked into the room with a desperate need to be held, a need she could never have spoken aloud. Her need, though, had been so easy to fulfill. His drew her now.

The couch springs creaked when he eased her horizontal. There was no room. Pressed against the couch back, she had to twine her legs with his to keep him from falling. She had to wrap her arms around him to protect him. He hurt. He was lonely—possibly, impossibly, as lonely as she was.

He kissed with a raw, real hunger that called to her. The flat of his palm on her throat made her pulse soar, her skin sear. His hand skidded down, sweeping over her collarbone and shoulder inside her robe.

He tucked in a kiss; she caught the black diamonds in his eyes, and then his palm traveled down her spine. He spread his fingers, cupping her hips and scissoring her closer. Sometimes he touched skin. Sometimes he caressed through the fabric of her robe. He didn't seem to know or care what he touched, as long as it was her.

No one—no one—had ever wanted her like this. Rain hissed against the window. The lamp flickered. A bolt of lightning streaked the night sky at the same time that Scott's bearded jaw rubbed kisses down her throat. Down the swell of her right breast. Down to a nipple hidden modestly by a pale blue flannel robe. It wasn't hidden long.

His tongue was a pagan lash of fire: rough, not soft, arousing, not appeasing. He wanted to ignite, not soothe. Her whole body brazenly arched to meet the lick of his tongue. Her breasts hurt, swelled. He kneaded them in a way that made them hurt more.

Her fingers curled on his arms, making dents as they traveled up his shoulders. Inside the collar of his shirt she found a scar, a smooth line that dipped toward his chest. It was a large scar, a badge of pain. He'd hurt sometime. Badly. And while his palm still cupped her breast, still roughly teased and wooed the soft white flesh into fevered swelling, she drifted light kisses on his mouth. Sipping kisses. Kisses to erase any pain he'd ever had.

She heard him groan, and then he took her mouth as she was terribly afraid he would take her. He was earthy and he was bold and he was rough. His wildness was enough to make her world spin silver. The room was dim and stuffy and shadowy, the couch too narrow. He didn't care. He wouldn't care. What he wanted, he took, and he obviously expected a lover to be equally physical, equally demanding, equally uninhibited. Equally free.

She wasn't earthy, she wasn't uninhibited, and she'd never demanded anything from a lover in her life. Scott invited her to be weak. She was never weak. He invited her to celebrate need, but for her, intimate needs were a source of fear, not celebration.

For those few brief moments, though, she tasted the tang of all those nameless things she'd been afraid of forever. She could lose control with him. She knew it. She could become blindly, intimately, soul-bare honest with him. She knew it, and her heart inhaled the hint, the promise . . . that he could be her catcher in the rye.

She was breathing desperately hard when his hand hooked hers from its traveling path down his hip. "No." He said it harshly and hoarsely, but the message in his eyes—crystal black by the blurred glow of lamplight— told her something else. He'd been as stunned by the magic as she'd been.

He was also in a faster hurry to deny it. Jerking to a sitting position, he pleated her robe edges together at throat and thigh. "I haven't been this close to hot water since I was sixteen. Not this kind of hot water. Anyone ever tell you that you could tempt a saint?"

"No." She waited to feel caution. It didn't come. So fast, too fast, she'd plunged into dark, deep, uncharted waters with him, but the wariness that dominated her nature was momentarily overpowered by wonder.

He was the one upset. Desire had stamped his face with hard lines, but his eyes were sick with guilt, and his tone had an unraveled hoarseness. "Jacqui, I didn't intend that."

"I didn't, either."

"You were scared and shook-up and not yourself. The last thing I meant to do was take advantage of you."

"You didn't."

"Yes, I did." In the process of clawing a hand through his hair, he abruptly made a harsh sound in his throat and leaned toward her again. "You need a robe with a zipper. If you don't have one, I'll buy you one with a zipper. This robe won't stay closed."

"I think that particular horse is already out of the barn, Scott."

"No, it isn't. Nothing happened. Nothing was going to happen. I don't know what I was thinking of—"

"I certainly do," she murmured.

He shot her a look—a repressive, intimidating scowl, spoiled entirely by the dark glint of humor in his eyes. "Would you do yourself a favor and quit looking at me like that?"

"Like what?"

He said gruffly, "Like temptation. Like willingness."

"I was tempted. I was willing," she said softly.

"Because you were shook-up. Enough to want to wrap around something. Anything. I was the closest body around; you know damn well I care about you, and there's nothing wrong with that, as long as you weren't worried I'd get any strange ideas about what was really happening."

It was too late. She was already having strange ideas. Spears of desire were still slicing through her. Like hot, humid weather, there was no relief. He was still close.

Grabbing her grandmother's afghan from the far chair, he crouched over her and tucked it securely around her. The shameless idea wouldn't leave her: she wanted to lay there with him. She wanted to be taken. By him.

He switched off the light, then the television. The room blanked of light and color. "You sleep. I'll be right here. You're safe."

"Scott—"

"Shh."

She heard him drop into a chair. After that the only sound was the rain falling. The darkness of the night closed around her, exhaustion hitting her in waves, but she couldn't let go of what had just happened. "I did not use you because I was afraid."

"Okay. Shh."

"I'm also not in the habit of throwing myself at a man. Any man. Because if that's how it looked to you—"

"That was *never* how it looked to me, Petunia. Now be quiet."

"I'm not asking for anything from you. If you want this whole subject permanently dropped, we'll drop it—"

"Good."

"But not until I tell you that you're special. A wonderfully special man. You care from the inside out, and you're honest and compassionate. Also sexy. Good grief, are you sexy. I like what happened, Llewellyn. It makes me darned nervous, but I liked it. That doesn't have to mean anything, but I'm certainly not going to let you go to sleep with some silly, stupid, idiotic idea that you were taking advantage of me—"

"Dammit." He used the chair arms to vault himself upright and stalked toward her in the dark. When he leaned over her, he was a massive shadow against the silver rain drizzling at the windows. "I swear you could make a scoundrel feel good about himself. The only one special in this room is you." His lips brushed her cheek, then found her mouth. His kiss was short and liquid, a sip of tenderness, a taste of something that lingered as elusively as love.

He pulled back quickly. "Now will you sleep?" he scolded.

She whispered, "Yes," and did.

Mondays were always the pits, but this one had been one long exercise in waiting for the other shoe to fall. Scott was just reaching for his jacket when the tall, nervous man knocked on his open office door.

"Sir? I'm John Borwell, *Daily Press*. Could I have a minute of your time?"

"That depends on how literally you mean that 'minute.'" Scott tugged on his jacket. Borwell was young, regardless of the head of thinning blond hair. The kid had an Adam's apple bigger than a rock and the look of predatory hunger that Scott was beginning to associate with reporters. Borwell's *Daily Press* was one of those suburban rags that generally viewed Detroit as a foreign planet.

"All I'm looking for is a last quote. George Connolly said you were the man to give it to me."

"I take it your article is on Devil's Night? Mind if I see what you have?"

The young man immediately produced his story. Still standing, Scott scanned it, took another look at the reporter and then closed his office door with a frustrated glance at the wall clock. It was going on two in the afternoon. He had a date with Jacqui and a security specialist around three, regrettably on the opposite side of town.

He was going to be late. "You're not going to print this," he told the young man.

"I checked all my facts," Borwell immediately said defensively.

"Facts and context are two different things, and if no one at your paper gave you a fast lesson in that before, you're about to get one from me. Sit down, Mr. Borwell."

The article was enough to make Scott's stomach turn over. The kid was more than a hotshot; the writing was good and every fact accurate.

His quotes were right. The year before, Detroit had had one hundred and forty thousand fire alarms called in, ranking the city eighth in the country, yet the fire department budget ranked lower than seventy-eight other cities. The National Fire Protection Association recommended a certain minimal response to every fire in terms of ladder companies and personnel. Detroit's fire department was notoriously understaffed.

"I figured you'd be with me on this," the young man said nervously. "If anything, I was trying to take a sympathetic slant toward the fire department. I know Detroit isn't the only city suffering from budget cuts, but I don't see how you guys can operate—especially with Devil's Night coming—under conditions this tight financially."

Scott perched on the edge of his desk and sighed. "You want to print that 'sympathetic slant' come November, fine. You publish it now and you're going to hurt people. Innocent people. Badly."

"I don't understand."

Scott knew he didn't. Borwell had unearthed more than old statistics; he'd come up with new ones. Drug- and fire-related crimes had been on the increase since the summer. The city had suffered an explosion of fire alarms in the past three months. If the pattern continued, Detroit would go up in smoke on Devil's Night.

Days before Jacqui had had a hard time understanding why he was so concerned with her lone fire setter. This was, of course, precisely the reason. Her torch didn't function in a vacuum. He had set more than a dozen fires in three months. Each of those fires was a catalyst for another firebug to copycat him. Arson was like chicken pox: catching. Although he had not told Jacqui, copycat fires had been streaking through the city since her fruitcake had started operating.

"They had a saying in the sixties," Scott told the reporter. "If you're not part of the solution, you're part of the cause. If you print an article like this, Borwell, you give a kid with a box of matches ideas. When you give an arsonist attention, you give him reason to believe he has power, and reason to believe we're helpless to stop him. In other words, you're giving a fire setter fuel and inviting him to use it."

"There's nothing in that article but the truth," Borwell insisted.

"Yeah? Well, maybe you'd like to hear another version of the truth." Impatiently Scott pulled out a three-page list from his desk drawer. "Start with this."

Borwell obediently reeled off items from the sheet. "A dozen AR monitor receivers, oxygen resuscitators, three dozen 1-SP half backs, two hundred foam jets, sixty power packs..." He glanced up.

"That's new equipment, most of which any urban fire department would give its eyeteeth for. It'll be on board at least seventy-two hours before Devil's Night. So will a dozen spare engines, ten ladder companies and more personnel than we've ever had going into a Devil's Night."

"A dozen..." Mr. Borwell, scribbling frantically, suddenly looked up. "How did you get that out of city hall?"

By selling his soul, but Scott figured the *Daily Press* didn't need that answer. "The point I'm trying to make is that we're prepared. You tell the pranksters out there that we're waiting for them, it gives them every reason to stay home on Devil's Night. We have never been more prepared, and that's the truth. You ever talked with a fire crew, Mr. Borwell?"

"No."

Scott nodded. "You battle a fire armed with three things. Trust in your own skills, faith in the guys you work with and confidence in your gear. City hall came through with our gear, and we have the best men—our own and on temporary loan—in the Midwest. I know that because I personally know every one of them."

Borwell was still writing. "How many casualties do you expect from your fire crew on Devil's Night?"

"None."

Again, the reporter looked up. "Obviously, there have to be casualties. There always are."

"I worked as a fire fighter for fourteen years and was a chief a good share of that time," Scott told him. "I never lost anyone on my crew, and I have no intention of losing anyone on Devil's Night. You might also keep in mind that hundreds of people are involved in the task force—not just fire fighters, but police, volunteers, city employees. You get that many people together with the same goal, the same dedication, and you bet we'll have an effect."

Borwell was impressed. Scott wished he was.

In principle, he hadn't told the reporter anything but the truth. The troubled mood bubbling through his city was real and dangerous, but his task force was the best. The first arsonist with a lust for loot, the first kid with the goal of devilment, the first gang headed toward an empty warehouse—come Devil's Night, Scott had the equipment and personnel to deal with those kinds of problems.

That was the total truth, but there was another total truth. There was no way—*none*—to anticipate or outguess a true pyro.

The reporter wasn't gone two minutes before Scott pelted down the back stairs toward the parking lot. He'd had a short conversation with the state police that morning. The good news: West had been nailed. The bad news: Roberts had been seen in Detroit as far back as four months ago. Roberts only preyed on single blondes. He liked operating in the middle of the night, and he didn't care to leave clues or incriminating evidence. A sweet single blonde with a smoldering garage in the suburb of Troy, though, had IDed him from mug shots two days ago.

Scott's blood pressure soared every time he thought of Roberts anywhere near his city. The idea that Roberts could be Jacqui's bastard though, and Scott came close to climbing walls.

His car engine zoomed. He slammed it in Reverse. The security specialist's office was on Eight Mile, and he'd have to battle expressways to get there. Rolf Baker was the best in the business; Scott had filled in Baker when he'd made Jacqui's appointment, and she had irritably assured him that she could certainly follow through without his being there.

He bought that the way he'd buy swampland in Arizona.

Yesterday morning, after personally installing two yard lights and smoke alarms in every room, he'd cluttered her kitchen table with catalogs on locks and security systems. Jacqui had gotten a look in her eyes... His mother got that same look every time she picked up a screwdriver.

"Are you at all familiar with this kind of technical equipment?" he'd asked Jacqui.

Her response had been a briskly offended, "Good grief, Scott. You think I live in a closet just because I'm a psychologist? Everyone knows something about electronics these days."

So she knew tiddledywinks.

He passed two semis and zoomed in behind a Corvette, whose driver instantly slowed to a crawl. The red light atop Scott's car was both a blessing and a curse. Other drivers assumed he was a cop, and there was nothing like a cop on the road to screw up traffic for miles. He passed again, feeling the adrenaline pump of agitation and frustration.

Both were becoming familiar emotions around Jacqui. He still hadn't forgiven himself for what had happened Saturday night. The Jacquis of this world weren't for him, and a good man never took advantage of a vulnerable woman, ever—no exceptions.

Only it hadn't been that simple. Jacqui wasn't that simple. She was twenty-seven. She couldn't be unfamiliar with passion; yet she'd responded to the slightest touch as though she were being swept under by something new and reelingly powerful.

Dammit, he'd felt the same way, and he didn't have the excuse of any innocence in his soul. Maybe that was half the problem. Scott lived with guilt and scars; yet she had blindly, generously opened her arms to him. It was as if she knew. She had offered the kind of come-alive sensuality that made a man feel hopelessly powerful, good about himself, whole, accepted for exactly who he was.

And he'd felt as if he'd have happily clawed Mount Everest fingernail by fingernail to have her.

On Route 275, he zipped down the window and received a full belt of smog, pollution and the sting of cold fall air. His mind was supposed to be on protecting the woman's body, not taking it.

He reminded himself of that several times as his foot pressed the accelerator.

Chapter 6

So if anyone entered your home—via window or door—they would trip this set of numbers, which you would be able to see before entering the house yourself."

"Fine," Jacqui said briskly, and glanced at her watch. Scott had either been held up or was unable to make it. Either way, she had a patient at four and no more time for this nonsense.

Rolf Baker had a funeral director's flare for fashion and a voice that could put a colicky baby to sleep. He was very nice, but as of an hour ago, Jacqui considered a dentist's chair preferable to shopping for a security system. Mr. Baker waxed poetic on the massive differences in her possible choices. All she saw were dials and buttons and more dials and buttons. A few locks and a can of mace couldn't be half this complicated.

"You can change the set of numbers as often as you want. You can also give a set of numbers to someone who regularly enters your house, like a maid or a meter man.

This is all you have to do...." Mr. Baker demonstrated, then glanced at her. "Clear?"

"Hmm."

"The whole thing can be tapped to a police line, if you wish, and it's not dependent on functional electricity, which is to say there's a backup system during a power failure. I can show you how that works."

"No need," she assured him swiftly. "Honestly, Mr. Baker, you don't have to tell me any more. I like this system just fine. Let's just go with it."

"I don't want to hurry you into this," he insisted. "We didn't really discuss the window and door locks. If there's anything at all you don't understand—"

"I don't understand anything about surgery, but that doesn't mean I don't trust the surgeon." She smiled. "Scott obviously trusts you, and this is your field, not mine. Let's just wrap this up, okay?"

"Maybe you could hold up there for about two shakes, Petunia." She barely heard the jangled bells at the door before Scott was striding toward them, his hand extended to Mr. Baker. "Rolf, sorry I'm late."

Mr. Baker filled Scott in. They both obviously shared a love for razzle-dazzle technology that she didn't, which gave her a moment to simply look at Scott.

His cheeks were windburned, his manner authoritative and crisp. He wore a white shirt and a tie under his jacket. Creased trousers stretched over his muscular legs, and he smelled like lime and wind and virile, vital energy.

Whatever insane mood had possessed her Saturday night refused to disappear. Whenever she was near him, she felt wistful, fragile, female. A song of yearning sneaked into her soul, and so did a raft of wild, shameless fantasies.

She wasn't used to having wild, shameless fantasies, and she considered herself as fragile as an army tank. Something was happening to her. She wanted to believe it was only an overdose of sexual attraction, because there was nothing dangerous about an attack of hormones.

She was afraid, though, that the lure of Scott was far more lethal. Every time she was near him, he proved he was a man of the old values: courage, honor, loyalty, protectiveness. He'd been exposed to her at her worst and her weakest, yet he'd made her laugh instead of feel uncomfortable. He also had a dangerous voice. He could coax never-told secrets out of a woman with that rusty tenor, and he'd grilled her well yesterday. He now knew about the day she'd walked out on her boss at social services and had gone into private practice. He also knew she'd been sleeping alone for some time.

Scott had already learned far too much about her. She wished the opposite was true. He hadn't touched her since Saturday, and in subtle ways he made sure she knew he wasn't going to. To a point that was fine. Her heart ran on cautious, wary time. If he was gun-shy of psychologists, she was triply gun-shy of venturing anywhere near emotional white-water rapids.

Scott, though, was troubled. She understood his professional interest. Her prowler/fire setter had the potential to affect his Devil's Night. She was certainly scared silly of her unknown enemy, but Scott seemed to have taken on her case in a personal way. He couldn't let the subject go. His fiercely protective attitude went far beyond the call of duty. Sometimes he had a shadowed look in his eyes, like a man battling old ghosts. This was a presumptuous judgment on her part; Jacqui simply didn't know him well enough to justify such a conclusion.

And it's none of your business, she kept telling herself. *He's made it clear he doesn't want anything but a professional relationship, and you know how outstanding you are at intimate ones. We're talking zip and zero. It's just sex. It has to be, and it'll go away faster than a case of flu if you're just careful....*

She had a stash of inhibitions, a lead vest of a conscience and a past history that should have made it enormously easy to be careful around him. Only he kept doing things. Dreadful, horrible things. Like now, when his gaze only swung away from Mr. Baker for a spare second. In that spare second, she felt washed by the tenderness in his eyes.

He was still talking, though, to Mr. Baker. "Maybe she is that sure, but I'd like a private minute with her before she signs on the dotted line. Mind if we use your office?"

"Not at all."

Mr. Baker's office was as exciting as his warehouse—more dials and buttons and boxes and hanging wires. The only streak of color in the whole room was Scott, who closed the door and then sighed, heavily and with great humor. "Jacqui, you were about to give Rolf the fastest sale in his considerably long life. You trying to give the man a heart attack?"

"I didn't see any point in mincing around," she said curiously. He'd herded her in here awfully quick. She had no idea why. "We talked about all this yesterday. You know I agreed with you that it just makes sense to secure the house."

"I know what you agreed to, but I don't know if you understood what you were agreeing to." Restlessly he threw back his shoulders. A devil of a determined gleam turned his eyes pewter gray. "I didn't haul you in here to sell Baker's services. He's the best I know, or we'd be someplace else. I hauled you in here to handle a slightly awkward subject."

"What?"

"Money." When she blinked in surprise, he said firmly, "You heard the overall price, and you also heard how Baker would be willing to do it, a piece at a time. You put the locks on one month, the electronics the next and so on."

"He explained that," she agreed.

"Yeah? Only I don't want you doing it a piece at a time. I want the whole system in place as fast as possible and preferably yesterday. If you can't swing it financially, I will—and dammit, don't give me that hoity-toity look. There's nobody here but you and me, and I'm not interested in pride. Flat out, do you need some help?"

It took her a moment to recover her breath, not just from the generosity of his offer but from his blunt honesty. In her business, she had to skate around people's feelings with intuitive sensitivity. Scott obviously valued tact on a level with beans. Although he probably wouldn't understand it, she felt as if she'd been handed a treat.

"If I wrote a check for that system right now," she admitted, "it would bounce." She pulled awkwardly at her earring. "Actually, if I wrote any check right now, it would bounce. My checking account is sort of in pitiful condition."

His grin was slow and lazy. "Am I getting the feeling that you regularly fail to balance your books, Petunia?"

"Let's just say that the bank and I are on speaking terms. We should be. We talk often enough." He chuckled. She'd wanted him to, but she also gave him a serious answer. "There isn't any problem as long as Mr. Baker will take plastic. Just because I can't add doesn't mean I'm a spender. I have a reasonably healthy savings account."

"I've noticed before that your idea of reasonable and mine can be slightly different on occasion. I don't want you going in hock to your neck. There's no reason to. I have a nest egg boring itself to death gaining interest—"

"Scott," she said gently, "the offer is appreciated, maybe more than you know, but would you try, sometime soon, to believe I'm not a lightweight?"

"Nobody said you were a lightweight—"

"Someone in this room believes that all psychologists are do-gooders and lightweights. I left home at eighteen. Not only schooled myself but have been putting food on my own table for years, imagine that."

"I didn't mean to make you touchy," he said carefully. "I know you put food on your table. I just figure it's different than the food that I put on my table. Petunia, you're an idealist all day, a Proust reader—"

"Scott?"

"What?"

"You've read Proust, too."

"Honey, try and get real. It took me a GED to graduate from high school."

"I really couldn't care what you graduated or didn't graduate from." She motioned to the cameo ring on her finger. "I'll bet my ring—and believe me, it's a well-loved keepsake—that you've read Proust. Or tried to. Which is about what and all anyone can do with Proust."

He cleared his throat, pushed a hand through his hair and glared at her. "You did this to me yesterday. Confused me. We are not talking about Proust—we're talking about a security system. If you can handle the finances, the next issue is getting it installed."

"Rolf offered—"

"Wait for Rolf and we're talking a long week, if not two. That won't do, not in my book."

"So my McGraff can put it in," she offered.

He shook his head. "Not to judge a man on his looks, but your handyman wasn't exactly born in the electronic age. I have in mind me, and I have in mind tonight." He wagged his finger at her when she tried to interrupt. "I've put together a system like this a time or two before, and I've got nothing better to do on a Monday night but watch football and carry around my beeper. Would you doom me to that kind of boredom?"

"I will not take advantage of you like this," she said firmly. "You've already given me an enormous amount of your time."

"This isn't for you—it's for me. I have a heavy work schedule this whole month, and I need my sleep. I'm not going to sleep if I have to worry about someone crawling through your windows. I'll sleep even less if I think you're worried about someone crawling through your windows—"

"All right, all right." She threw up her hands. "But that's absolutely the last thing you're volunteering yourself for where I'm concerned," she said severely.

"I need you to volunteer for something in return."

She raised her brows. "What?"

"Time." He admitted. "As far as I can tell, neither one of us has any. I can't count on free nights, not through this month. And your daytime schedule's hectic. If we don't clip off an early hour, I'm afraid we're going to have a hard time getting together. How do you feel about five o'clock in the mornings?"

"About the same way I feel about flu."

He winced at her repressive tone. "Ever seen Detroit that early in the morning?"

"I've never even seen my kitchen that early in the morning voluntarily."

He was talking so fast that he probably didn't hear her. "While I'm showing you my city, you can be talking to me about bank tellers and grocery clerks and old boyfriends and that swastika-carrying patient of yours. You can tell me all kinds of psychological mumbo jumbo about pyros, and I'll give you the real-life view, and we'll have an excellent time arguing—"

"Could you hold your horses, please?" She was feeling railroaded. "Exactly how many five o'clock in the morning meetings are you talking about here?"

With an impatient shake of his head, he straightened and reached for the doorknob. "Obviously as many as it takes. Until we have your man identified. Until we have him under lock and key. Until you're safe."

He saw her swallow. He also saw the surprise in her eyes, and his voice abruptly slowed to his gentlest drawl. "Like they used to say when I was a delinquent, Jacqui—you need an attitude readjustment. I know you have a heck of a mind and a nice fancy degree, but there are hours at a time when I have this feeling you left your brain on vacation in Tahiti. I have a vested interest in your fire setter—did you forget that? Even if I didn't, you'd have to be totally off your rocker to think I'd leave you to handle this alone."

The darn woman walked right over, and brazen as you please, soft as you please, kissed him—again.

He thought he'd been doing well at keeping it light and low-key but professional. Distinctly professional. She slid her arms around his neck, and professional went all to hell. He wondered vaguely if the federal government licensed a woman's mouth. They could. They should. They'd better.

She'd barely pecked a kiss and he felt raw.

He'd barely responded before she felt mist swimming in her eyes. "I have also, always, handled my own problems alone. I can't handle this one alone, and I know it and I hate it and you're an extraordinarily caring man, Scott. So caring that you scare the life out of me."

One thing for sure. He didn't understand her. "The pyro's the one who's supposed to scare you, Petunia."

"Yes," she said quietly. "I know."

The following Saturday morning, Interstate 375 was as quiet as a cave. Except for two other cars and one lazily tooling semi, Jacqui was alone on the road. City lights glowed silently from empty office buildings. Skyscrapers rose against a mute black sky. As she'd been discovering all week, Detroit was sound asleep at five in the morning.

Yawning, she took Exit 52 and followed Scott's directions toward the Eastern Market. He'd been most specific, particularly about where he wanted her to park, because the area was on the rough side. Scott's definition of rough, however, was obviously influenced by his overprotective attitude toward women. The aging neighborhood around Gratiot had the look of poverty—forlorn storefronts, an occasional deserted building and yawning gaps of broken windows—but not of danger. As far as she could tell, she was the only one alive and awake for miles.

Except for Scott. The Lord knew where this farmer's market was—she fumbled again for his written directions on the dashboard—but he would unquestionably be there and waiting for her, full of life and energy and zoom.

He'd picked today's destination because she'd never heard of the Eastern Market, much less been there. Likewise, he'd brought a picnic of coffee and croissants to a park bench overlooking the Ambassador Bridge on Tuesday morning. Another morning it had been a stroll through Greek town, and another a soar to the top of the Renaissance Center for breakfast, where they watched the sun rise over the Detroit River.

She'd never done any of those things. He mercilessly teased her about the lacks in her education. Scott loved his city with a passion, but it wasn't the city she was coming to know. It was him.

She'd never argued so much with a man in her life. He'd swore at her when he discovered how her prowler had gotten in, acting as though she'd committed a crime because she kept a spare key on a door ledge. That was no longer possible with the security system installed, a system so blastedly complex that she'd tripped it twice this past week while trying to get into her own house. She'd argued with Scott about that, because he'd been so infuriatingly patient about teaching her the number code.

Although the police hadn't found any stranger's fingerprints, they were now patrolling her property after midnight. She was locked in like Fort Knox. And McGraff had gruffly offered to camp in the room over her garage if she was still frightened. Jacqui had turned down his offer. Enough was enough. When a woman was threatened, she took sensible, practical precautions to protect herself. To live in a padded cell, though, was out of the question.

Scott didn't agree. Scott, in fact, liked the padded cell idea, and he was as frustrated as a leashed bear because they were failing to come up with clear-cut suspects.

Jacqui was less frustrated than frayed at the edges—and not by her fire setter, but by Scott. At five in the morning, the whole world was sleepy and dark. She was helplessly coming to associate the time with coming alive. She'd never had a man look at her the way Scott looked at her, never felt the sizzle and crackle the way she did when he touched her, never felt this exhilarating, bewildering agitation around any man.

All that nonsense should have been obliterated in the process of spending so much time with him. It hadn't. She felt like a reckless child exposed to fire for the first time. The flame was warm, bright and enticing. Although Scott hadn't once made a pass, she saw a come-on in his eyes during the times he forgot to be a rough, tough Welshman. That come-on was desire; that come-on was need; and that come-on was magic. The fire lapped closer every time they were together.

Could we panic just a little less about the complete annihilation of your common sense and a little more about being lost?

She had to be lost. Badly lost. She saw nothing remotely related to a farmer's market. Reaching again for Scott's scribbled directions, she turned a corner, yet saw nothing ahead but a dim halo of light. Four blocks down, she turned again. Abruptly, the roar of a semitrailer revving out of a back alley forced her to jam on her brakes and pause before driving on.

With stunning speed she was thrust into the middle of chaos, an enclave of day-bright life in the middle of the silent city. Trucks of all sizes and types crowded every aisle, every street. A car blithely drove on the wrong side of the road. People were screaming everywhere. A small child darted in front of Jacqui's car. Forklifts zoomed down sidewalks, dodging people while never decreasing their speed.

She miraculously found the space where Scott wanted her to park and, not unexpectedly, saw him immediately striding toward her. She told herself it would be different this time. She told herself that she would be more formal, more careful. He could not possibly be as special as she'd built up in her mind, and she was not a woman to be swept away, ever, by emotions.

Like a damn fool, she was swept away the minute he opened her door. His old-world chivalry and courtly manners were fraudulent. His shirt was red and his grin full of the devil. "Like it?" he demanded.

Formality never worked with him. She should have known better than to even think it. Even before she climbed out of the car, she was laughing. "What have you gotten us into this time? 'Just a farmer's market.' Wasn't that what you said?"

"That's all it is, but it kind of takes a big farmer's market to feed a few million people every week. Come on. Whether you can believe it or not, we'll eventually end up at a quiet place for coffee. You'll get more than an eyeful on the way."

He grabbed her hand. It felt less like a lover's handhold than like a manacle around her wrist. The traffic was madhouse wild, but so was the assault to her senses. The smells were unbelievable. Scott guided her around a truck unloading hundreds of sweet melons. A forklift weighted with boxes of tangy apples zipped past them. The sick-sweet smell of freshly butchered beef made her nose crinkle. Past the beef were warehouses stocked to the rafters with pungent cheeses. Then she smelled fish, peaches, and watermelons all mixed together. A single turn and Scott led her through a block full of vendors selling flowers, perfect dew-kissed gladiolas, a sea full of them.

"Is it always like this? It *can't* be always like this!" She had to yell to be heard over the cacophony.

"It's quiet now—you should see it in summer—but the market never really closes up. It can't. I can't believe you haven't been down here before."

It had never occurred to her before to wonder how a metropolitan city was fed. Scott took it for granted. He was at home in the chaos; there was an electric energy and purpose in his stride that made keeping up with him a major challenge.

She didn't try too hard. There was too much to see. She saw a man unroll a wad of crisp bills inches thick—hundreds, not ones. "This way, Jacqui...." She saw another man carrying a lamb on his shoulder with a pistol tucked in his belt; a policeman passed him and never said a word. "Now in here...." A spit-shiny Cadillac actually drove on the sidewalk in front of them. The man climbing out of it could have starred in *The Godfather*. An older boy passed by pulling a wagon on which lay a long, fat, silver-scaled fish that was as big as he was. The fish reeked. It looked to her like a shark. She smelled fresh onions. She smelled gardenias.

"Jacqui." Abruptly she felt Scott's palms frame her face. His eyes met hers square, full of teasing humor. "People will run you down if you walk around here without paying attention."

"I was paying attention. To everything. This is wonderful!"

"You think so?" Even as he talked, he flagged a passing vendor and dug in his pocket for change. Before she could blink, he was tucking a fresh carnation in the top buttonhole of her cream blouse. The flower flopped. He frowned, adjusting it. His knuckles brushed the top swell of her breast. Their eyes met in an intimate clash seen only by two.

"I love the carnation. Thank you." There was a shiver in her voice that she couldn't help. "Scott?"

"Hmm?" He was quick to pull his hands away, not so quick to stop looking at her. A tortoiseshell comb held back her hair, and her blouse was of some pale, shiny material that looked softer than silk. *She* looked softer than silk. Especially her mouth.

"I'm having a wonderful time," she murmured.

"You're hopeless. You have a wonderful time anywhere," he teased. He had tried to choose places where she'd feel distracted from her troubles, where she wouldn't feel "grilled." Stress inhibited honesty. Stress, for him, though, was the increasing dependence he had on starting his day with her laughter and lighthearted smiles. He grabbed her hand and said briskly, "Ever had a *kruchekee* for breakfast?"

"I don't even know what one is."

"Obviously you've been living too posh, Petunia. About time you had a taste of ethnic." He led her toward the open dark doorway of a weathered frame building. They ducked inside.

A chunky bald man with wild black eyebrows greeted Scott on sight. Jacqui was promptly handed a bakery confection peppered with powdered sugar. Purse dangling from her elbow, she took a bite. The pastry was sinfully light, but powdered sugar flew everywhere. Scott still had her other hand and was barreling through the crowd. "Mama, we need two coffees!"

"Is that your ugly face, Llewellyn?"

A tiny round woman appeared behind the counter. She stood on tiptoe, bussed Scott's cheeks, then kissed Jacqui, too. "She's pretty, Scott."

"Yeah, I know."

"I am amazed you have the brains to have such good taste." Jacqui got a wink, then was handed a sloshing full cup of coffee.

Scott's initial goal was reaching the smattering of tables and chairs at the back of the store, but not unexpectedly, he ran across Jacqui's vice. Curiosity. She never left home without it. There had been a time he'd figured she was too classy a lady to enjoy his city—at least the way he did. Jacqui had a way of mercilessly nicking at a man's prejudices. Now, he just as mercilessly stole her coffee and *kruchekee* and collected a sack from Mama Vitale.

Jacqui had seen old-fashioned country groceries before, but never one like this. The shelves were stocked helter-skelter with foods she'd heard of but had never actually tasted: capers and chutney, Irish oatmeal, Windsor teas, Swiss baby food, Burgundy snails, Finnish red caviar. Beyond these shelves were glass bins of spices, dozens of them, not all exotic but each unfamiliar—sour salt and cassia bud, fenugreek and slippery elm and arrowroot.

Jacqui was so absorbed, she didn't realize Scott was trailing her and sneaking things into a sack until she looked back at him. Everything in the bag was something she'd examined. "Don't get any idea you're buying those things for me," Jacqui warned him.

"If I don't buy something, Mama Vitale's feelings will be hurt. And what would I do with—" he glanced "—Twinings of London tea?"

"Drink it. It's like heaven."

"Wouldn't suit me, then."

"What's a Highland oatcake?"

"You've never had one of those, either?" Into the sack it went as soon as she asked the question.

"I'll pay for it," she said severely.

"I told you about my father. He'd slay me alive if he saw a woman lifting her purse while his gentleman son was around. So would my sister. You want some French nougats?" He glanced at her and grinned. "Have we found the lady's weakness or what?" he asked the ceiling.

"Scott, we're going to need a truck to carry us out of here," she wailed.

"Now, now." Eventually he led her back to the quiet alcove of tables. "The coffee should be cool enough to drink, and we have to get serious here. It's already six. What time's your first patient?"

"Seven-thirty."

"You pack in *every* Saturday starting at seven-thirty?"

"I never plan on working Saturdays. It just happens, and you're a fine one to get bossy. You work harder than I do. What's your sister like?"

"Phoebe? You'd love her. She's impossible not to love. She has a mouth on her like a drill sergeant, but she's smart as a whip, careful with people, sensitive. Beautiful, inside and out." He glowered at her over the rim of his cup. "You're distracting me."

"I'd like to meet your Phoebe."

"That can be arranged. What we're going to do about you isn't so easy to arrange." His mood sobered abruptly. He shrugged off his jacket and cocked his foot on a chair rung. "We're not getting anywhere on finding your fire setter."

"I know."

"I'm worried."

"I know," she repeated quietly.

"I told you Roberts is definitely in the city, and the cops came up with a little more bad news. About twelve years ago, he had a delivery truck and a route that took him in the Silver Lake neighborhood. Your neighborhood. Now, I know you looked through the mug shots, but I think you should do it again."

Jacqui shook her head. They'd tried that. In fact, Scott had dragged her to a police station to check out pictures, not just of Roberts but of other convicted arsonists. But mug shots didn't look like real people.

More relevant, everything they'd done and discussed during the past two weeks had given Jacqui a picture of the pressures Scott worked under, the dimensions of commitment and drive that were integral to him. Any arsonist had repercussions for Scott and Devil's Night that went far beyond her own problem. "How many alarms were there last week?"

"Too many. The city's gone crazy, and it's only four weeks until Halloween." He gulped down the rich dark coffee. "It's like watching bullets being fed into a gun and not knowing where the gun's going to be aimed. My crew will take over on the three days surrounding Devil's Night. We know what we're doing and we'll do it, and I don't care how troubled the city is. But a pyro just isn't the same thing. I don't know how to anticipate a real nut case, how to prepare for him, how to stop him."

"Scott," she said with a warning tone to her voice.

"Erase 'nut case.' Substitute 'troubled gentleman.' I'm trying to adjust to your lingo, Petunia, but where I come from a jerk's a jerk. Some people are just plain born bad, although I know you don't believe that." He frowned, reached over and distractedly brushed some powdered sugar from her cheek. Their eyes met. Lightning again.

She knew he was fighting that lightning even harder than she was. His "Petunia" nickname was one way he kept his distance. Teasing her about her Grosse Pointe roots was another. He saw their different backgrounds as a stone wall he had no intention of scaling, and he'd told her in a hundred ways that she couldn't be safer with him.

He never had to know she was falling in love with him. He wouldn't push it. If a relationship was going to be pushed, it would be up to her. Knowing that should have been a source of security. Instead, it was the precise reason she felt as secure as a nonswimmer balancing at the tip of a high dive.

Scott was no angel. He had a temper, an aggravatingly overprotective streak, a head harder than granite and a rascal's grin. He *was* a rascal, but underneath the tough macho layer was a sensitive man. A lonely man. A man who would risk his soul and his life for anything that mattered to him, a man who buried his secrets far too deeply, and a man who *touched* her every time she was with him.

Yes, dammit, she was falling in love with him. And her heart kept beating the insistent message that she was going to throw away something she would regret all her life, if she didn't have the courage to act on what she knew, felt, wanted, needed.

Anxiety thrummed in her pulse. He couldn't, she knew, love a coward. Which meant that very possibly, very probably and most likely, he couldn't love her. *So run, Hughes. Don't you always?*

Her mind was more than happy to change the subject. "I have an idea for you," she mentioned.

"Shoot."

"I would need permission from my patients to do this, which I don't have right now. I also don't know if it would work out around everyone's different time schedules, but pretending there are no complicated problems for a minute... I'd like you to talk to a few of my kids who've been in trouble for arson. Not because of my fires, but because of your Devil's Night. I have in mind your asking their advice."

"I beg your pardon?"

"You heard me. Hasn't anyone on your task force considered that the people who set fires are a tremendous source of knowledge? Preventative knowledge." She set down her half-filled cup and crossed her arms. "I can't stop thinking about this. Do you understand mob psychology?"

"Are you going to be offended, Petunia, if I confess to not understanding any psychology?"

She scolded him with her eyes. "Mob psychology was what Hitler used, most effectively. He brought the youth together in groups. He got them to believe things that no one in the civilized world believes. And he could do that because in a group situation, a mob situation, each person loses his sense of personal identity and becomes part of the whole. You listening?"

"I'm listening." His eyes softened as he looked at her.

"On your Devil's Night, Scott, there may not be a physical group, but there are still emotional group dynamics going on. Everyone who sets a fire thinks he's becoming part of the whole. Everyone who sets a fire has lost his personal sense of self and is trying to find his own troubled identity."

Scott leaned back, staring at her. "Yes," he said quietly. "I've dealt with riots. I know what you're talking about."

"Talking with my kids may not help. But it could. They're the horse's mouth. They're the only ones who really know what draws them to that emotional 'mob' on Devil's Night. I just think—"

"If you can arrange it, I'll talk to your kids. And be glad to. And in the meantime, I have a suggestion for you."

"Shoot."

"You still haven't told your family anything that's happened?"

"No." They'd been over this ground before. "Telling them would accomplish nothing but worrying them. That's out of the question, and it's not like there's anything they could do—"

"They could be there for you. Where I come from, that's what families are for. In fact, where I come from, you'd be hung up by a lynch mob that included distant cousins if you tried to keep something like this under your belt." He kept his tone light, because he knew Jacqui was sensitive about any criticism of family. He understood loyalty. He didn't understand people you couldn't turn to in a time of trouble.

"That's a closed subject, Scott."

"Yeah, I figured it was, so I'm opening another one. I want you to move into my place until Devil's Night is over." He said swiftly, "I don't have two bedrooms, but I have a couch that suits me just fine. Hell, I'm not going to sleep the rest of this month, anyway. I wouldn't bother you, and if you're worried I'd come on to you, Jacqui—"

She laid a hand over his. There was an intensity in his eyes that bordered on fierce, a tautness in his shoulders that went past rigid. His hand under hers was cold, stiff, tense. "One of these days, I need to know what this is about," she said gently.

"I don't understand."

"I know you care, personally and professionally. But you seem to have a need to protect me, Scott, that goes beyond common sense. I have an alarm system that would take a MENSA IQ to break. Police are zipping into my driveway at all hours of the night. And if one of my patients is the problem, I have confidence in my ability to handle him." He tried to interrupt, she wouldn't let him.

"You have no time to breathe through this whole month of October, yet you have spent an extraordinary amount of time on me and my fire setter. Even assuming my fire lover is the most dangerous kind of pyromaniac, you just plain can't concentrate on one person, one problem. There has to be a reason this matters to you so much."

He tried to jerk his hand free. She held on. He gave her a fearsomely intimidating glare. She'd discovered a long time ago that Scott had no patience. Hers was endless.

"Maybe..." He cleared his throat. "Maybe, a long time ago, I failed to protect someone who mattered to me. Maybe I could have done that if I'd been smarter or braver or wiser at the time. And maybe I just can't take any chances that something could happen to you because of anything I failed to do." The instant she released the pressure of his hand, he said gruffly, "We have to go. It's getting late."

"I know it is."

He carried the sack, and they didn't escape the store without another passionate buss from Mrs. Vitale. Outside was the same chaos of duck-dodge-em noise and activity. He didn't take her hand as he had on the way in.

He strode close or he flanked her protectively, but he made a point of not touching her.

When they reached her car, he took her key to unlock it. Once he opened the door, he dropped the grocery bag inside and returned her key. "As far as plans for tomorrow morning . . ." he began.

She slid her arms inside his jacket and kissed him. The other kisses, perhaps, had been impulses. This one was deliberate. She didn't know who Scott believed he had failed, but she knew he was wrong. Someone had to tell him he was wrong.

She kissed him softly, with moist tenderness. By dawn light, his face was all bones and sharp angles. Engines and voices bellowed all around them, and his gaze held a *Damn you, Jacqui* that announced she was misbehaving again.

She knew that was true, but it wasn't entirely her fault. He closed his eyes under the warmth of her mouth. One mobile kiss ignited memories of tastes and textures and temptations begun on a Saturday night that were supposed to be forgotten. She hadn't forgotten them. Her pulse, nerves, skin, heart suddenly remembered everything he'd made her feel . . . only more.

Tongue touched tongue, where no one could see. Her breasts snuggled against his chest, where no one could see. And she felt the fire of longing as his kiss deepened, as his mouth slanted and claimed hers as fiercely and possessively as a man could kiss a woman. Where no one could see.

His body heated and hardened under her arms. She held tighter. He needed holding.

So did she. Gentleness went up in smoke. His hands dived in her hair and clutched, and desire tore between them like a ripped open package at Christmas. Her knees wanted to buckle, but he was there. His eyes seemed an eternal ebony, his mouth an eternal haven. She started trembling, but no less hard than he did, and this one time was different than all the other stolen kisses. He didn't fight her. He simply got lost somewhere between her fragrance and her skin and her touch and her. She understood, because the complementary emotional explosions were happening to her.

Scott finally found the will to break off the kiss, but the strength to break total contact eluded him. Looking at her was like looking at a promise. Her lips had a bruised softness, her eyes a drugged sensuality. A man could damn near lose his mind when Jacqui made promises like that. He smoothed her hair, shook his head. "I'll be darned if I know how this keeps happening," he murmured. He wanted to smile and couldn't. "I chose a career line where I've known for a long time better than to play with fire."

"Scott?" He was still standing close, still blocking out the whole world with the way he looked at her. "It doesn't have to happen again. Not if you don't want it. I've probably kissed on impulse from the day I was born, but that's with affection, caring. I've never—"

His forehead nudged her forehead. "Are you trying to apologize for coming on to me like sexual dynamite, Petunia?"

"Umm...more or less."

"Don't ever even try to apologize for such a silly thing again."

"Yes, sir."

"You don't have to be careful. Not around me. You just have to be honest." He raised his head, touched her bottom lip with the edge of his thumb. "And I'm being as honest as I know how to be when I tell you that I want you like hell, but that's best left be. Anyone can lose perspective when they're threatened. Danger has a way of confusing judgment. I'm not saying you're confused. I'm just saying I don't think you'd look at me twice if we'd met at another time.''

"Llewellyn?"

He sighed. "I sense back talk coming from your tone of voice. It's not like I haven't heard it every day for the past—"

"I've already looked at you twice. Danger or no danger, I know who I'm looking at. I know who I'm kissing, and I am not in the least confused."

"And you're that positive of what you're inviting, right?"

She hesitated.

"That's what I thought." Before she could blink, he handed her into her car and closed the door.

She watched him walk away and felt vaguely like hitting him. He hadn't given her a chance to explain. Scott being Scott, he simply wouldn't. She'd always intuitively guessed that he wasn't looking for an affair, any affair. He was too old and too complex to play for matchsticks.

He wanted to know if a woman was going to be there for him.

The odd thing was that Jacqui, too, had always held up on that turn of the road. She'd never trusted that a man would be there—really be there—when the chips were down. Until Scott. Until the man who, right now, was walking away from her.

She'd let him down.

Chapter 7

Jacqui didn't pull into her driveway until four that afternoon. She grabbed her purse and briefcase, in a fine mood for a dark, growly thunderstorm.

Naturally, there was full sun. Totally unlike early October, the breeze was balmy. The gold side of her maple's leaves glinted in the sun. Another time she would have planned a fire by the lake and scorched a steak for dinner, but the Indian summer temperatures couldn't woo her. When a woman needed a good sulk, a woman needed a good sulk. Saturdays didn't get any worse than this one.

Halfway to the house, she spotted her caretaker stashing a rake at the back of the garage. She sighed loud enough to be heard across the lake. "McGraff, what am I going to do with you? You know you're not supposed to come in on the weekends."

"Yeah? Well, leaves were coming down faster than rain. If I waited until Monday I'd have had a heck of a job."

"You were waiting for me to get home," she accused him.

"I told you I came for the leaves. Look around you. Leaves. That's got nothing to do with you coming home to an empty house." McGraff pushed at his cap so his eyes were blocked from the sun. Hunched over, he started hobbling toward the road.

"Wait a minute, wait a minute. Since you're here, you might as well pick up your check," she called after him. "I made it out last night. It's right on the kitchen table."

He half turned. "Not like I couldn't wait until Monday—"

"I'd appreciate it if you got it now. Then you can also get me in the house without my tripping the alarm," she said wryly. "Besides that, I could make you an iced tea. You have to be thirsty if you've been working out in this sun—"

"Don't need no tea, but I'll get you in." Head down, he moved ahead of her to the back door and silently punched in the sequence of numbers to open the lock. "Remember you look first, make sure nobody's been in the house who wasn't supposed to be. See?"

She saw that he had the back door unlocked five times faster than she could. Giving him a baleful look, she strode in ahead of him. His paycheck was in plain sight; he must have seen it, yet he'd never touched it. As always, the amount troubled her. "I told you when I hired you what I could afford to pay for the work I had. You keep putting in extra hours—"

"Did I ask you for more money?"

"No, but—"

"Then I don't see we got a problem." He stood in the doorway, folding the check. "You deal with some rough kids today?"

The question stunned her. McGraff hadn't volunteered any chitchat from the day she hired him. Dropping ice cubes into a glass, she poured the tea. "That's my job, dealing with rough kids. But only one's got me going in circles."

"Kid been in a lot of trouble?"

"An understatement. Arson, breaking and entering, truancy, fights, vandalism—you name it, the boy's been in it." She only had to think Stan's name to have her head start pounding again, but she smiled for McGraff. When she offered him the glass of tea, though, he shook his head.

"Sounds to me like the boy's more trouble than he's worth."

"How could a child be more trouble than he's worth? You never give up on a kid, McGraff. Are you sure you wouldn't like the tea?"

He said he didn't want the tea, but he still stood there fiddling with his check for several more minutes. She was about to ask if his arthritis was bothering him, when he abruptly turned and left. He closed the door with a little clatter.

Unfortunately, when she was alone in the house she was supposed to do something clever with the lock. Scott had left her printed instructions next to the door—printed, as if he thought he was communicating to a six-year-old child. If there was one thing she couldn't stand, it was a patronizing man.

A patronizing man you let down this morning, Hughes. She read his instructions and poked in the code numbers, feeling as high as a well pit.

Scott, though, wasn't the only source of her moody blues. Carting her iced tea back to the bedroom, she chucked office clothes for old jeans and a man's sweatshirt. Within ten minutes she had her studio unlocked and had started softening a round of clay by rolling and kneading it.

The skylight shot rays of sunshine on her three long shelves of sculptures. Although most of her subjects were patients, she had busts of Jonathan and Timm, one of her brother, another of an old friend from school. She'd even done one of reclusive old McGraff when she'd first hired him. Her focus riveted solely, though, on the bust of Stan Witkowski sitting on the bottom shelf.

She normally met with Stan on Thursdays. This afternoon they'd had an extra session so that Jonathan could sit in with them. She had decided—and her co-workers had agreed—that because of her fires a second perspective was a good idea. She had prepared Stan long before today that Jonathan would be there. Stan had agreed.

Except he'd changed his mind by one this afternoon. "Get him the hell out of here," he'd said the moment he saw Jonathan. At first, Jacqui wasn't distressed. Any patient formed a bond with his or her therapist; a third person was always an intruder to that relationship. Jonathan was excellent with teenage boys, he worked well with hostility, and he had magic with a troubled kid.

But not with Stan. The boy had stayed sullenly, violently mute until Jonathan left the room. Then—for the first time—Stan had poured out almost a solid hour of emotion.

Later, unfortunately, so had Jonathan. "Look, love, there's no question he's formed a dependency and trust with you, but you know that's a two-edged sword in a therapist/client relationship. He's a textbook classic for the kind of disturbed behavior that could tend toward pyromania. You know it, but you just don't want to see it. I think you're too caught up with him. You care too much. You've lost your objectivity."

Had she?

Frustrated, she reached for her woefully inaccurate bust of Stan. Her fingers traced the cold clay cheeks, aware that Jonathan was right on at least one front. She cared too much. That had always been her flaw as a therapist. With Stan, it was worse because he was so troubled, so lost. His mother had deserted the home; his father had a stream of women and either ignored Stan or abused him.

Yes, she cared. A heartful. But to the point of losing all objectivity?

She'd molded his face more than two months ago, and at the time had chosen one of Stan's most common expressions—rage. His cheekbones jutted out, so did his jaw. His choice of hairstyle made him look the seventeen years that he was, but take away the hairstyle and he looked decades older. The bust's blank clay eyes stared at her, but they were totally unlike Stan's. Stan's eyes were hauntingly bitter, keenly intelligent and as ice hard as he thought he had to be to survive.

Jacqui forced herself to center the bust directly under her work light. The night the prowler had left her lights on, the bust had been placed just so. And just so, on a balmy October afternoon, the face of one bitterly lost boy abruptly took on the shadows of sinister menace. A gargoyle of rage.

Because she was a shamelessly dreadful sculptress?

Or because there was an evil in Stan?

Had she allowed her emotions to affect her professional judgment of what Stan was capable of? As Jonathan said, the boy had the textbook symptomatic background of a potential pyro. If it was as simple as that, though, a doctor could diagnose every illness from a medical encyclopedia. Textbooks left out the human factor of judgment. A teenager who suffered the severe stress of a broken home, abuse and sexual confusion was very likely to have problems—but every teenager with that background didn't set fires.

Stan, she knew, could have. He had the brains, his own car and lots of unsupervised time, but those were just facts, and Stan was a human being. If she had totally misjudged the human being, she had to face that. If he had been the one to set her fires, she not only had to deal with it as the victim, but also as the boy's therapist.

Lurching off the draftsman's stool, she started pacing. She was tired and so sick of the word *fire* that she could scream.

Nothing had been the same since the fires. Her whole life seemed tossed in a whirlwind. Months before, she'd believed in herself, her work, her judgment. Now she had doubts about all three. She'd never fought with Jonathan like this. She'd never had a patient who she'd even considered being afraid of. She'd never doubted her ability to handle a problem alone.

And before she'd been content enough with who she was as a woman...although that problem definitely had more to do with meeting a black-haired Welshman than with being plagued by nuisance fires.

She was so absorbed in thought that she jumped at the jangle of the telephone. Grabbing a rag—her hands were coated with clay—she flew for the extension in her den.

"Hi."

It was a measure of how much time they'd spent together that she recognized the sandpapery tenor from the one short syllable. She didn't *want* to recognize it. She didn't *want* to hear it. She felt thoroughly aggravated that her pulse instantly flip-flopped at the sound of his voice. Cradling the receiver to her ear, she started frenetically rubbing the clay from her palms. *No. I'm not sure what I was inviting this morning, Scott. You scare me and I scare me, and I just plain need a little distance.* She responded to his one-word greeting with one of her own. "Don't."

"Don't?"

"If you called to talk about arsonists or fire setters or prowlers—*don't*. I don't care if your Roberts is driving right outside my window with a lit torch. I don't want to know. I am sick and tired of the whole subject. I mean it. Tomorrow I'm prepared to be rational again, but tonight—"

"Tonight, you'd like to be on a plane to Bermuda." She heard Scott clear his throat. "Whether you believe it or not, that was why I called."

In spite of herself, she was starting to smile. "You have tickets for Bermuda?"

"No, but I seem to have reached the same fed-up stage with pressures and stress that you have. I also have a sister who happens to need a little help this evening, and if I remember right, you've been pushing to meet her. Phoebe isn't as deluxe as a trip to Bermuda, but I guarantee she's a diversion." There was a long pause. "Of course, it's Saturday night. Maybe you had something already planned.''

"I did. A wild, wanton date with a vacuum cleaner and a dust mop." She glanced at her clay-streaked jeans and bare feet. "And honestly, that's a date I'd better keep. Any other time I'd love to meet your sister, but not tonight. If you want it in spades, I'm a mess. I look horrible and I'm tired and I'm mean.''

"Mean? You?"

She heard the amusement in his voice; it pricked her the wrong way. "Mean," she repeated sharply. "As in tailgate-in-traffic, bark-at-little-old-ladies, slam-doors mean. Did you think I wasn't as capable of a bad mood as everyone else? Just trust me. I am temporarily not good company for man or beast.''

"Petunia?"

Darn man. His tenor had gentled, softened, blurred. He probably charmed small children in a crowd with that voice, had little old ladies swooning, coaxed beauties into bed. "What?" she snapped.

"I couldn't give a hoot if you're at your best. You're not talking about a date, we're just talking picking up a pizza and going to meet my sister—and getting you out of that house for an hour or two.''

"I can't." Her head ached, her heart ached, and every muscle in her body was cramped up in anxiety. How could she possibly walk away from that?

"Did you ever do a five-hundred-piece puzzle, Sweet Pea? There comes a point where you stare and stare and stare at the pieces. None of them fit. Walk away from them for an hour or two and a dozen pieces suddenly slot in like magic." Scott's voice was just like that. A murmur of magic. "Come on. Let's get you out of there. It won't kill you to put a Closed sign on worry for a few hours, and it might do a lot of good.''

She wavered, drawn less by the chance to escape her own problems than the chance to make sure he did. "No business?''

"No business.''

"No talk of arsonists or fire setters?''

"None. Zip. Zero." He qualified that immediately. "For this one evening.''

"That'll be an awfully long time for you to behave," she said teasingly.

A moment's silence on his part. "Maybe I wasn't exactly promising to behave, Petunia.''

A moment's silence on her part. "No?''

"No." He murmured, "You've certainly turned quiet. I never thought I'd see the day. Assuming you haven't had a fast change of mind, I'll pick you up at six.''

He watched Scott drive in at several minutes before six. Fifteen minutes later both of them were gone.

He had the kerosene; he had the matches. Her security system was nothing. The fancier ones were his favorite. Picking the lock to her studio the other night hadn't even been a challenge, and that was what he had in mind for the evening. Setting a nice small blaze in her studio.

Unfortunately, there was a siren screaming in his skull. His headache was so intense that he had to set down the container of kerosene and lean against the wall of her garage. Lately the screams in his head never let up. He couldn't think when the pain was that intense.

He was almost sure he'd talked himself out of this. To set any fires right now was to risk exposure. To set a kerosene fire was a dead giveaway that the blaze wasn't accidental. And for huge periods of time, he came as close to loving Jacqui as he'd ever come to loving anyone. The reason he was so angry at her eluded him.

He slumped low, kneading his temples. His breath was starting to come in lunging gulps. If he let it go on, the rage would engulf him, just like the lap of a forest fire, all red-hot flames and speed and pain.

The only thing that stopped the rage was fire. He was never confused in front of the lemon-lick of a roaring flame. It wasn't that he wanted to start fires, but it was the only way. And that was her fault. *All* her fault.

She probably didn't even remember the day in early July, her leaning over him, his head splintering into a thousand pieces, her cool palm reaching for his brow. "Did something happen? Can I help?" Her voice had been musical and low and caring, and after that he couldn't stop thinking about all those stupid, stupid kids in her office. She put in long hours for those nerds, but where had she been when it mattered?

The night his father had come at him with a poker, ligaments had been permanently severed in his right thigh, and his back had been scarred. They'd bandaged him at the hospital, but no one had asked questions. No one had done anything. No one cared. There were no Jacquis in his life then.

Now, it was too late for him.

And definitely too late for her.

The dark-haired fire fighter sniffing around her had worried him at first, but not for long. The fireman was more an issue of interest than concern. Llewellyn had known pain by fire. He always recognized someone else who understood pain by fire. He could spot them on the streets; he could smell them—but the fire fighter was no real threat to his plans.

He'd been making explosives for more than three months now. Llewellyn couldn't stop what he had in mind for Devil's Night; no one could. That power was sweet, and he had the "divide and conquer" principle going for him. The man couldn't protect his city and the lady at the same time.

Waiting, though, was the hard part. In fact, the waiting was starting to tear him in two, increase the inferno of headaches, double the blackouts.

Bending down, he turned the lid on the kerosene. Fumes burst toward him, pungent and strong. He could see the fire in his mind, feel the heat slipping toward him as potent and real as the encroaching darkness. Without fire, the whole damn world would be dark.

Jacqui would know all about that soon.

Real soon.

It was less than a month now, he reminded himself. He could wait that long.

At least he had to try.

Jacqui had slipped off her shoes and curled her feet under her. The pizza was in the back seat, just far enough away to taunt her with its tantalizing aroma. Dusk fell early in October, and the hushed, dark streets blurred past. Normally, riding in Scott's car was an exercise in action and excitement—the myriad of communication devices on his console were always beeping or buzzing— but not tonight. He'd turned them off, and the silence was as soothing and restful as contentment.

"I'm still waiting to see signs of this mean streak," Scott murmured.

"I'll show you just as soon as I find the strength to open my eyes." She turned her head. "There is a slim possibility that playing hooky for a few hours was an excellent idea.''

''There is a slim possibility that you've been under a hell of a lot of stress, Petunia. And you work too many hours.''

''Sometime you'd better look in a mirror. When's the last time you took an hour off?''

''That's completely different.''

''Horseradish,'' she murmured lazily.

He chuckled, grinning at her. Her window was open a spare inch. The breeze was just enough to curl silvery strands of hair around her face.

After sharing hours every day together, he thought he knew her. He'd seen her scared and proud. He'd seen her confident, thoughtful, sassy and argumentative.

He'd never seen her in patched jeans, a fuzzy red sweater she'd clearly chosen for softness more than style and battered Nikes. She'd forgotten to put her hair up, and the only jewelry she wore was a capricious pair of earrings that dangled and tangled in her hair whenever she turned her head.

She still looked elegant. He figured she'd look elegant with the flu. Princesses with silvery-blond hair and delicate features and dare-magic eyes couldn't help who they were.

''Tell me some more about Phoebe.''

''I've already told you a hundred stories. Besides, you're going to meet her in minutes.''

''Then tell me about your brother. Dominick, wasn't it? And your three nephews. I want to hear the story again about how they turned the hose on you when you were dressed for a cousin's wedding.''

He told her, to make her laugh again. Her laughter hadn't been so natural when he'd first handed her into the car. Possibly she'd had second thoughts about attending this outing. He had certainly pushed the boundaries of "strictly professional" in their other encounters, but that element had always been there.

Not tonight. "Strictly personal" was the label on tonight, and that goal had made perfect sense to him when he had been sitting in his office that afternoon. The report in front of him had failed to make sense after a third reading. His mind had the sharpness of dandelion fuzz, partly because he'd been working too many twenty-hour days. And partly because that morning at the market, Miss Hughes had sent his hormones mercilessly trampling toward an abyss—one too many times.

Intellectually, he understood that a relationship with Jacqui was unviable, impractical and probably dishonorable. Jacqui ignored the differences in their backgrounds; he didn't. He figured she would see those obvious differences if they could just meet once in a normal situation, away from fires and prowlers and conversations dominated by anxiety. A threat of danger artificially heightened emotions, particularly sexual emotions. Take away the danger and you had calm seas.

Or that's what he'd hoped. It seemed to be working in her case. Jacqui's head was leaned back, her smile easy, the tension slipping away from her.

His seas were as calm as a tidal wave. The jeans made her legs look long and skinny and sexy. It drove him nuts thinking about her in that house alone, and he didn't care how many cops were patrolling the place or how many expensive locks she had.

To the devil with ethics. He wanted her next to him. In fact, the only thing better than her sitting next to him would be her sitting on top of him, wrapped securely in his arms and being kissed with meticulous thoroughness. First with her sweater and then without her sweater. First with her jeans and then without her jeans.

And if he continued thinking along those lines, he was not going to be able to walk into his parents' house without a considerable readjustment of his body parts.

He turned down the old, tree-lined street. The suburb wasn't fancy. Houses clustered close, most of them two-story frames with shutters and matching fenced yards. His father worked on an assembly line, as did most of the neighbors. If Jacqui had any doubts about his blue-collar background, she wouldn't after tonight.

"We're here?" Jacqui hurriedly retied her shoes.

"And about ten minutes early. Can you handle the pizza?" He had a grocery bag filled with a six-pack, a bottle of Madeira for Jacqui and French nougats for his sister. "Did I warn you Phoebe was going to talk your ears off?"

"Only a half dozen times."

He playfully cuffed her around the neck as he steered her toward the back door. No one had used his parents' front door in twenty years. The back porch used to have steep steps; now it had a ramp. Jacqui shot him a questioning glance, but two people were already opening the back door with voluble welcomes.

"My folks," he said, unable to keep the pride from his voice.

She froze for all of two seconds, then flashed him another look, this one appalled. Possibly, he should have mentioned that she would be meeting his parents. The pizza nearly toppled as she balanced it in one hand while making violent efforts to straighten her hair with the other—her hair looked perfectly fine—then his folks, predictably, swallowed her up and herded her in.

He tried to see the house through her eyes. The kitchen had old-fashioned blond cabinets, a thousand doodads hung on the refrigerator door and jackets hung on hooks on one wall. Once he stashed the beer and wine in the fridge, he followed the sound of voices to the living room.

The room was a study in faded chintz and knick-knacks and furniture that never quite matched because it had never been bought at the same time. His mother was a trophy decorator. If any of the kids had won a spelling bee in second grade, the prize was undoubtedly still on one of the shelves, still being dusted, still on view. Dad brought home his bowling trophies; Dominick had track awards and his electrician's license. Phoebe was the only one with the college diploma, that prominently displayed.

Scott's niche on the wall were the so-called beyond-the-call-of-duty medals he'd been given during his firefighting years. He vaguely remembered dumping them all on his mother sometime and now regretted it. Jacqui was being regaled with the whole family history; his dad was stuck holding the pizza. Scott winked at his father, grabbed the box and then took on the saving of Jacqui. Both his parents were dressed to go out—the reason Phoebe needed someone to stay with her for a couple of hours—but his mother was trying to have a change of heart.

"There isn't any reason on earth we can't be late, Griff. We surely have time to offer Jacqui a glass of something."

Scott stepped forward. "Your son is fully capable of offering Jacqui a glass of something, and if you two don't get going, Phoebe's going to be complaining about cold pizza."

"Phoebe's going to have you all evening. I haven't seen you in almost two weeks, and I'm just meeting Jacqui.... She's a psychologist, Griff, did you hear?"

"You'd probably hear a lot more, Molly, if you'd give the poor girl a chance to talk."

Jacqui had walked in on pins and needles, but Scott's parents clearly had a low tolerance for uncomfortable guests. She had the feeling that anyone who walked in their door was treated the same way—noisily, effusively and with overwhelming warmth.

Griff Llewellyn was an older version of his son. She saw lines Scott didn't have and streaks of iron in the thick dark hair, but Griff had the same blazing dark eyes, the same tough compact build, the same slow smile. Jacqui had fallen in love with that smile on sight. Molly was mite-size, animated and gregarious, but her eyes had a woman's shrewdness, a woman's history of trials and laughter. A strong woman recognized a strong woman. Jacqui had no doubts that for her family, Molly Llewellyn would move mountains.

She never had the chance to form further impressions, because Scott guided his parents relentlessly toward the back door.

"They're terrific," she announced as she heard the car pull away.

He looked at her, unsure whether she was saying the expected thing or if she really meant it. Whatever he saw on her face produced a lazy smile on his. "Yeah, they are," he agreed, walking into the kitchen.

"But you'd think after all the times we've talked, you might have mentioned a few things," she said, following him.

"Like?"

"Like that your sister lived with your parents. Like that I was going to be meeting your parents. Like those seven medals on your mother's wall, Llewellyn— You always have beer with pizza?"

He glanced up from the counter. "Always. Phoebe likes it. Why?"

"Then what's the wine for?"

"You."

She shook her head. She'd seen the defensive tilt in his shoulders when he saw her glancing around the house he'd grown up in. "If you're serving beer, I'm having beer."

He frowned. "You don't like beer."

She searched the counter for napkins. "If you don't quit tagging me with Grosse Pointe stereotypes soon, I'm going to box your ears. Contrary to what you seem to think, I never had a country club membership, and the private Catholic girls' school was force-fed. I didn't attend by choice, so you can just quit holding it against me. Furthermore, I love beer," she assured him, and with a quick glance at the label, "especially Old Milwaukee. Now do we have that settled?"

"Except for the part about beer, I've heard that whole lecture before," he murmured dryly.

"I know you have, but I have to keep on trying. One day I might get through to you. Thank heavens I'm an optimist."

"We do come from slightly different social stratas."

"I'll be darned. Does that mean you don't spit in the bowl after brushing your teeth, just like I do?"

He looked appalled. "You don't really do that."

There was no letting him get away with such sass. She collected the three chilled cans, reached up to touch his lips with hers and stood back long enough to watch his pupils dilate. "I have better things to do than argue with a stubborn, bullheaded Welshman. In fact, I could have sworn the reason we were here was to share a pizza with your sister. The mystery of the hour seems to be, where is she?"

"Back room, off the right. I'll bring the pizza in a minute. You sure you want beer, Petunia?"

She ignored him and headed toward the back room, off the right. There had been a lot of things she had been unsure of coming on this outing—Scott, Scott and Scott heading the list. She'd warned herself that she needed space, not more contact with him, in order to identify, face and deal with her feelings for him.

Poppycock. Fear of what she felt was one thing, but knowing what she felt was certainly another. The look of those seven medals on the wall tore at her—how the hell many times had he risked his life?—and the man was positively hopeless on the subject of women and pedestals.

She wasn't falling. She'd fallen. Deep and hard. No man could make her this furious, this worried, this captivated, this crazy to be with him if love wasn't involved.

Coming out with him tonight, though, the one thing she hadn't worried about was meeting his sister. Scott had talked so often and so much about Phoebe that Jacqui already felt as if she knew her. Juggling the three ice-slippery beer cans, she rounded the hall to the right, expecting to find a small, dark-haired woman with a pert smile, reading glasses perched on her nose and eyes full of life.

"Phoebe?" Since there was only one open door in the hall, that was where she peered in. Her heartbeat abruptly slowed, softened, caught. Scott's sister looked exactly as she'd pictured her. Jacqui had even expected the computer, the books, the chocolates.

But not the hospital bed. Scott had never said one thing to indicate that she would find his sister in front of a pile of pillows in a hospital bed.

"You have to be Jacqui. Come on in! I thought you two were never going to get here." Phoebe took one look at Jacqui's face and rolled her eyes toward the ceiling. "He didn't tell you, did he? I've told him a hundred times not to spring this on people. I swear I'm going to shoot that brother of mine one of these days."

"You'll have to wait in line."

Phoebe roared with laughter, and so the evening began.

Chapter 8

Having to depend on people is the only thing that really drives me crazy. At least I'm not financially dependent. I've built up a good business researching data bases, and I can afford to hire my own help during the day. But the help leaves when Mom and Dad come home. That's when the guilt hits. I can cope fine alone—there are just a few things I can't do without help—but they refuse to go out unless someone else is here. Dominick and his wife hover, drive me absolutely bananas. Scott's my mainstay, although I wouldn't be too quick to tell him that—"

"Tell me what?" Scott carted in the pizza.

"What an infuriating brother you are." Phoebe lifted her arms for a massive hug and got it. "You're looking like hell, as usual. Circles under your eyes—"

"Are you going to start? I just got here."

Jacqui, bemused, watched the two bicker and banter with practiced skill. The love between brother and sister was thick, rich and coated with laughter. For a few moments they were too busy scoring points off each other to drag her into the twosome, which more than suited Jacqui. She needed a minute to both mentally and emotionally absorb the story Phoebe had told her.

Scott's sister had only been eight when she'd been pinned under a flipped car. The spinal damage might have been reparable if the car's gas tank hadn't exploded. The fire had permanently severed nerves in both legs. Although she occasionally used a permanently seva wheelchair, the nature of her spinal injuries made an upright position uncomfortable after any period of time. As she put it, "How many people get to laze around in bed all day? So I take advantage."

Jacqui could see the breezy humor was real. As Scott had promised, Phoebe was simply impossible not to love. She had found the strength to accept what had happened to her and had no patience for anyone who didn't. Her whole room was a testimony to a woman's busy life. The *Wall Street Journal* was tucked to the listings page; stock market tomes were scattered all over the bookshelves. A phone and file cabinet were within reach, and all the equipment involved in her research job was mobile.

Phoebe had a strong heart, a strong mind and a will of iron. So did Scott, Jacqui thought pensively, but not where his sister was concerned.

The moment he'd walked into the room, Jacqui had known who he thought he'd failed a long time ago. She saw it in his eyes, and she felt it in her heart, and she didn't have the least idea what to do about it.

For the moment, though, there was nothing to do but join in on the laughter fest. It wasn't as if either one of them gave her a choice.

"You—cut pizza," Phoebe ordered Scott. "Did you bring my nougats?"

"No one said I brought you any nougats, and anyway, you can't have them now. Even you have to admit that pizza and beer don't go with nougats."

"Nougats go with everything, bro." Phoebe winked at Jacqui. "He's nice. Not real smart, but nice. Dominick's better looking, but Scott's sexier. I wouldn't care one way or another, but you'd think I could have inherited some of the better genes in the family. You've obviously survived his prejudice about psychologists. Either that's an enormous credit to you or you have a saint's patience. Which is it?"

"Saint's patience," Jacqui supplied easily.

"Not you, too."

Once the pizza was devoured, they played euchre on a table that pulled over the hospital bed. Conversation never weighed heavier than the price of chocolates. Scott teased Jacqui as mercilessly as his sister, regularly leaning over to check the contents of her beer can. "She's probably finished four sips now," he reported. "I told you she was quite a drinker, Phoebe. Especially beer."

"I'm just telling you, if he does that one more time I'm going to hit him," Jacqui told Phoebe.

"Now I'm trembling," Scott said.

"You're also losing—beautifully," Phoebe crowed. "Shall we up the stakes, Jacqui?"

"I'm down eighteen cents now. Be reasonable," Scott groaned.

Neither woman was reasonable; they upped the penny stakes to a nickel and ganged up to take Scott for nearly a dollar. He complained loudly and long about Las Vegas hussies. The moment he noticed his sister tiring, though, he slowed the pace. The cards disappeared. The table was pushed aside, the overhead turned off and a soft lamp lit by the bedside.

"You two don't have to go," Phoebe insisted.

"No one's going anywhere."

"Well, terrific, because if you're going to stay, I'd like to show Jacqui something—"

Scott said, "No."

"On the middle of the bookshelf there, on top of the paperbacks."

"You're as bad as Mother."

"It's just a skinny little album. Bring it over here by the light."

The family photograph album was just like everyone else's, loaded with shots that were blurred or too dark or had an occasional head cut off. Inevitably the ones of Scott caught Jacqui's attention. One was of him and a girl on a hot summer day splashing in a lake. She looked sweet and young. He looked like someone a father would take a shotgun to. Another was a photo of him and an older man.

"George Connolly," Phoebe identified. "Everyone in the family loves him but me. Scott was going downhill so fast when he was in high school that I was sure he was going to turn into the family's first black sheep, but no. Connolly had to step in and turn him around— Look at the girl in this one. One glance and you'll know why he dated her."

"When you're bored stiff, Petunia, just let me know and I'll get up and save you," Scott offered from the couch in the corner.

"She's not bored," Phoebe announced, and continued. Picture followed picture and story followed story until she hesitated by one particular photograph. "There was nothing wrong with June. Pretty, isn't she?"

"Very," Jacqui agreed. The woman-to-woman message in Phoebe's eyes intrigued her, although Scott's sister rambled on as blithely as ever.

"Smart, ambitious, down-home values, true-blue. I was sure I'd gain a sister-in-law out of that one, but I think his career got to her. That was the time he was collecting medals right and left. Also landing in the hospital with alarming frequency—"

"Hey—"

Phoebe hurriedly interrupted Scott. "And here's our three nephews. They look sweet, but they're total terrors."

"They take after their aunt." Scott stole behind Jacqui, hooked the album with one hand and circled her neck with the other. The contact sent a tickle down her spine.

"Where are you taking her?" Phoebe demanded.

"Over to the couch. Out of harm's way."

"Heck, you weren't even squirming," Phoebe said disparagingly. "Mom's the one who's got the picture of you naked without a diaper in the grass—"

"Do you have any Rolaids? I need relief," Scott pleaded to Jacqui. She chuckled, feeling an easy warmth steal between them when he drew her down next to him. He slouched on the couch, sprawling out his legs, but his arm stayed loosely hooked around her shoulders.

Conversation gradually quieted, then turned desultory. Peace seeped through Jacqui for that last half hour. Being rib-to-rib close with Scott was part of that peace. Sexual vibrations were muted because his sister was in the same room, yet like a soft secret they were there. Scott was tangibly warm and inescapably male. Every time he glanced at her, she felt something liquid curl inside of her.

The whole evening had been special. Her family wasn't like this, much as she loved them. She adored her brother, but couldn't tease and scold with him the way Phoebe did with Scott. She'd never have walked into her parents' house in broken-soled Nikes and patched jeans. She always felt "on" with people she knew, as well as people she loved, but not with Scott.

The older Llewellyns returned before eleven. Molly tried to coax the two to stay but Scott pleaded tiredness and the long drive. Both excuses were true, but neither explained why he pulled her into his arms the very moment they were in the shadows of the yard between the house and car.

There were no peppery-light kisses to warn her of his mood. Just one kiss. One long, thorough, devastatingly sensual kiss that rocked her into starlight. Dark eyes glinted down at her when he was done. Both were aware he'd initiated the embrace. He wasn't apologizing. "You were good to her. And for her."

"I loved her."

"Yeah, so do I. You never finished that beer, Petunia. See if you ever tell me another white lie."

"Give me a break. I can't seem to gulp down wine in any quantity, either, but a twenty-seven-year-old woman doesn't like to admit in public that she still likes milk."

He chuckled, handing her into the car. Within minutes he was turning out of the suburbs and headed for the freeway. She knew he was relaxed. His job and commitments and responsibilities were waiting to claim him—but not yet. Like her, she guessed, Scott had the ability to empty his mind of diversions when he needed to. He'd wanted an evening of laughter for his sister. And he'd made sure, absolutely sure, that Jacqui hadn't thought of fires and torches and dangers all evening.

She had no desire to even indirectly bring up those subjects, but it was her turn to give, and she saw no other way. Her tone was gentle, low. "Phoebe told me about the car accident. There was a fire?"

"Yes."

"She said you were there. You couldn't have been more than eleven or twelve at the time."

"Twelve."

"I suppose you were too young to remember anything about it."

He glanced at her and said quietly, "I remember it. All of it." City lights flashed, dimmed, flashed, dimmed. A Chevy Nova passed him. "My mother was driving. Phoebe and I were in the back seat arguing. We always argued as kids. This was years ago, so no one was wearing seat belts, and the impact was like being thrown at a wall. The truck that hit us completely turned over our car. Mom was thrown, knocked out. Phoebe was under a side. I knew she was crushed because she was crying, screaming...."

A Saab hovered in his blind spot. He dropped speed, forcing the foreign model to pass. "I was thrown, like Mom, but I wasn't hurt, just bruised and scared. There was this smell of gas, and then there were cops and people who'd stopped, people holding me back when I saw the first flames. Only no one was holding me all that hard. If I'd wanted to break free, I could have broken free—"

Jacqui had guessed what was coming, had been waiting for it. "It wasn't your fault," she said softly. She watched him change lanes, efficiently and with total control. His hands never tightened on the wheel, his foot never wavered on the gas pedal, and his tone was as casual as a spring breeze.

"The facts showed that it was no one's fault. The truck driver had a ruptured brake hose he didn't know about. The doctors said Phoebe's spinal damage happened when she was pinned—they couldn't help that. And the gas line explosion—no one could have stopped that, either. The verdict all the way down the line was 'just too late.'"

She repeated, more slowly, "Dammit, Scott. *It wasn't* your fault."

For the briefest moment their eyes met, his filled with anger and as fathomless as a moonless night. "I've been in a hundred fires where it was 'too late.' I have medals hanging on my mother's wall for battling fires when it was supposed to be 'too late.' The nerves in her legs weren't destroyed until the fire."

"You were a twelve-year-old boy, Llewellyn. You said yourself there were police there, authorities, adults—"

"And I've been in fires since, where there've been police, authorities, adults. Their courage is their problem. Mine is mine." He said fiercely, "She'll never make love. Never have children. Never have some bastard turn her life upside down, never have the chance to fall damn silly in love. You should see how she is with my brother's kids. She adores them—"

"Scott," she asked softly, "what exactly did you expect yourself to do?" He never turned his head, but she saw the muscle in his cheek flex.

"Get her out. Go into that fire and get her out."

"No." Her response was swift, immediate, firm. "You know better. I don't know how long you've let it eat you up like this, love, but in your head you know better. Guilt doesn't belong. Even assuming someone could have done something, it couldn't and shouldn't have been you. You were a child. There's nothing to blame yourself for and there never was—"

His tone cut her off like a razor. "You weren't there. You don't know. And I didn't spill the story to hear some lecture on guilt out of a Freudian textbook. If the time comes when I'm looking for a psychologist's professional services, I'll let you know. Otherwise, lay off. You got that? *Lay off.*"

She fell silent. He knew he'd hurt her and spent the rest of the drive trying to frame an apology that never got said. He had never talked about Phoebe and the accident before, and the experience had left him feeling raw and tight.

That was no excuse for lashing out at Jacqui, but he knew there was a level where he needed it said. He wasn't a patient; he didn't want to be analyzed; he wasn't looking for a therapist. People came to Jacqui all the time with their problems. He wasn't and didn't want to be one of them.

At her house, he walked her to the door, hands slung in his pockets, shoulders braced in the wild night wind. Clouds flew by the sliver of a moon. Trees rustled uneasily, then stilled. For a brief moment he felt the hair rise on the back of his neck. He turned his head.

His imagination must be working overtime, he decided. There was no one there. The lights in her yard just seemed to throw more shadows than the moonlight on her woods and black shadowed lake. Still, he checked to make sure her alarm system was fully functional. And once he was positive no one had been in her house, he broke the silence between them. "I was way out of line, and no, you don't have to worry about my coming in. But maybe you could just kick me in the shin so I could quit feeling like dead dirt?"

Hair streamed across her cheeks in the wind when she tilted her face. He expected to see hurt, if not anger, yet her lips were tipped in a calm smile and her gaze was distracted, thoughtful. "There have been a good dozen occasions when I'd have loved to kick you in the shin, but this isn't one of them. Come in, please. There's something I want to show you." When he hesitated, she promised, "It won't take long."

Still wearing his jacket, he followed her through the kitchen and living room and hall. She stopped at her bedroom, ducked inside and came back with a key in her hand. She fit it in the lock to the last room and switched on a light.

"Look, Petunia, you don't have to—" He knew the room meant something special to her, but she insisted, motioning him inside.

"I think we'd better separate the psychologist from me once and for all, Llewellyn. When I'm behind closed doors with a client, I'm a professional. When I'm with you, I'm just me, just a woman, just Jacqui...and I don't think you'll have any more problems believing that after coming in here."

She turned around. "I never let the police in here the night I had the prowler. I didn't think I had to—they had enough fingerprints from everywhere else. Even if they didn't, this is my place, my space, my corner where I block the whole world out. You can see it's a studio."

He saw. The skylight, the white walls, the three shelves of busts, the mounds of clay and the draftsman's stool and long Formica table. Most of all he saw Jacqui. He'd learned a long time ago that she had a fear of showing weakness.

She was showing it now. Her eyes were brazen with vulnerability, her face pale, and she was talking ten for a dozen as though the words had to be pushed out. "From the time I was ten I wanted to sculpt. From the time I was ten and a half, I knew I was no good at it." She tossed off her jacket. "You closely guard your feelings about your sister, Scott. This is what I guard closely. I'm not trying to say that's equal, only that I have a soft spot, too, a subject where I just can't handle people poking too hard."

He leaned against the white wall by the door, hands still tucked in his pockets. She wandered toward her shelves, touching one clay figure and then another. Her chuckle was sudden, soft. "I'm terrible. In fact, you can't get much worse than this." She motioned. "Some are patients, some are friends, but just as many are simply people, someone's face that bothered me in a crowd. I like to think that it helps to 'learn' someone by sculpting them—sometimes it does—but I really only do it because I love it."

She shot him a tentative glance as if expecting him to comment, but he was too afraid of saying the wrong thing to say anything at all. Those eyes of hers were so watchful, so wary.

"I do it because I love it," she repeated, "but as for why I hide it..." She shrugged, her smile dry. "You don't have a coward's mentality, Scott, so it's hard to explain. I was raised to be an achiever, to excel. I came home with *A*s or I didn't come home. Mistakes were frowned on, not because my parents were cruel but because they wanted their kids to be the best. You started something and you finished it, and you did it right or you didn't do it at all."

It was harder and harder for him to keep silent. Too easily she created pictures in his mind—pictures of a little girl who was shot down if she didn't bring home those *A*s, a little girl who was careful not to bring home any mistakes or problems. Jacqui wouldn't want to bother anyone. Hell, Jacqui served coffee to the firemen at her own fire.

She'd also listened to him the whole ride home about his sister. And then he'd shot her down.

She grabbed a rag and started swiping at a streak of clay on her worktable. "If you're picking up what I'm trying to tell you, Ms. Hughes, psychologist, has made a career out of not judging people, partly because I know what it's like to be judged. Even when I take off the name tag, though, even though I know better, I'm still my own toughest jury. I hide things I don't do well. I can't seem to take emotional chances that other people handle naturally. I am capable of being an extraordinary coward...."

He couldn't keep silent. "That's not at all true, Jacqui—"

"Yes, it is. In fact, we're talking a coward of epic proportions this morning." She dropped the rag, wound her arms around her chest and then unwound them and tugged at an earring. "If you'll remember, you asked me if I knew what I was inviting. I believe you were referring to your favorite hocus-pocus psychologist's habit of throwing her arms around you, and I never gave you an answer."

"I never expected one."

"You deserved one. Otherwise, you had every reason to believe I was teasing you or leading you on or using you. For the record, none of that multiple guess is true, but..." She lifted her hands, feeling awkward and awful. "The whole truth is that I have no idea what I'm doing. Not when I'm with you. Not when I'm near you." She tried a humorous smile. "If you were ever curious as to how many men I've kissed, it has to be close to five zillion. But I haven't been involved—physically involved, intimately involved—with a man since the last blue moon."

"That long?" he murmured.

"That long."

"I didn't know there were 'five zillion' men that stupid, Petunia, but I'm damn glad you're selective."

Her eyes fired like emeralds. "Get me off that pedestal, Llewellyn. I've been just as tempted as any other woman. Being prim-proper selective wasn't the issue. Being scared was."

He pushed off the wall. "Sex was like sculpting?"

"Pardon?"

"Something you figured you weren't good at?"

She frowned. "I wasn't talking about sex—"

"One way or another, you seemed to be talking about getting bare with a man." He strode forward and snatched her jacket to drape over her shoulders. "We're going outside."

"Now?"

"You have no idea how badly you need a walk."

"I don't need a walk."

"Then you have no idea how badly I need a walk."

She muttered humorously about madmen as he led her through the den, but Scott heard the relief in her voice. She wasn't seriously opposed to a walk. If he'd suggested digging a ditch, she'd probably have agreed to that, too. She would probably have agreed to anything that was a total change of venue and subject. Spilling emotions was an upsetting and exhausting business, and Jacqui, Scott well knew, had gone further than she had intended.

She badly wanted to let it go.

He didn't.

He had to turn off the alarm system to unlock her French doors, and then he had her outside. The yard light pooled yellow circles on the wet grass. Clouds still clotted around the crescent moon, echoing the clot of thick dark emotions affecting his heartbeat. A wild, branch-tossing wind warned of winter coming, but the wind had more bluster than chill. He knew she wasn't cold, and his own body temperature was soaring.

Once past the yard light, the shadows grew dusty and the trees blurred and rustled. Although he set the ambling pace, he also relentlessly steered her toward the darkest section of trees. Though the lawn had been soaked, there was no grass in the woods. The ground was blanketed calf-high with crisp, crackling leaves. She kicked up a shoeful, laughing.

Her laughter shut off when he deliberately pressed her against the gnarled trunk of an old oak. Her eyes flew up to his, startled, confused. He ducked his head and found her mouth in the darkness. Found, took, and with no mercy and no quarter, seduced.

Pinning her flush against him, he let heat surge from him to her. He was aroused. He wanted her to know it. He was stronger than she was. He really didn't mind if she knew that, either.

His mouth nipped, tasted, rubbed and then sealed over hers. The kiss was hard and thorough, a man's stamp of dominance. She tasted like the only woman who had ever driven him clean out of his mind, which was exactly why he'd dragged her out here.

Second thoughts lapped at him. He mentally pushed them back. His better sense tried to warn him against heading into deeper, darker waters than he could handle, but the only devil driving him was catching her response.

That wasn't difficult. Jacqui kissed without caution, yielding with a fierce wildness that was as giving as she was. At least that was how she was with him. And how she was with him was also a reason he'd dragged her out here.

He buried kisses deep in the hollow of her neck and secreted another cache near the shell of her ear. By the time his mouth sank onto hers again, his control was unraveling—not what he wanted at all. What he wanted was what happened: her fingers curled around his hair-covered wrists and then climbed up his arms and around his neck. His kisses had been rough, aggressive, selfish. If she had any sense, she'd have slapped him. Instead, her head tilted back, inviting the pressure of his mouth again, welcoming it.

He tore his mouth free. He saw her through a mist that was supposed to be clear, wanted her with a heart-slamming intensity that was not supposed to happen. He grappled for the words in his head that had seemed so clear in her studio. Her lashes sleepily swept up, though, distracting him. Moonlight reflected the sheen of yearning and desire in her eyes.

He had to fight to find those words, then to deliver them with care. "When two people make love for the first time," he murmured, "they generally get hung up on nervousness. What if she turns off for a scar? What if he sees I'm sweating? It's a test. Sex the first time is always a test." He eased her down to the bed of leaves. "Do you know what I'm talking about?"

Her eyes suddenly locked on his. "Yes."

"The more you think, the less sexy you feel. Will I please him? Will I please her? The more you worry about being judged, the more honest desire gets lost." He made his jacket into a pillow and his arm into a support for her, drawing her close. As close as a match and its own flame. "So the man forces it and the woman fakes it and the whole thing's nervous and not real at all. Ever had that happen to you?"

"Yes." Her eyes were dazed, confused, defenseless.

"Well, you damned well shouldn't have, Petunia." She blinked wide in shock. He combed his fingers through her hair. Moonlight flickered through the branches, haunting her eyes. To keep his mind off her mouth, he scolded her thoroughly. "If you had time to worry about performances, you picked the wrong turkey. And if you had time to be careful and polite, you were in bed for the wrong reasons, and I don't care how many lovers you've had. We're under an oak tree. Do you feel the acorns under the leaves?"

"No."

"*That's* how it's supposed to be." He kissed her once, then again and again. And that would be the end of it, he told himself. All he wanted was to show her that sex wasn't like earning *A*s, that making love between the two right people with the right feelings had nothing to do with judgment and tests. His so sensitive and perceptive psychologist was all screwed up. He'd wanted to set her straight.

"There's nothing wrong with you. It's not like your sculpting, you goose. You taste like honey—" he showed her "—and the scent of your skin could drive any man crazy—" he showed her that, too "—and how you figured you weren't good at this is beyond me. I—"

"Could I interrupt this lecture?" Jacqui murmured.

"No."

"I just wondered if this was the only reason you brought me out here. To ... um ... scold."

Something was going wrong. He couldn't see her eyes, because she was rubbing her soft cheek against his whiskered one, making every muscle in his body buck. He knew she'd asked him a question, but then she whispered lost, wild kisses on his brow, his nose, his mouth. He forgot the question. Put to the test, he wasn't sure he could come up with his own name.

There was a stick under her back. He found it, threw it. He swept her mouth with his tongue, pulled her arms around his neck and wrapped a leg around her. Every time she moved, leaves crackled like paper beneath her. The leaves clung to her back, sprinkled in her hair, and when he rolled her on top of him, they rained all over him.

For a brief moment, time was suspended when their eyes met. Both were breathing hard, both were covered with leaves, both were warm from the inside out. Jacqui let her full weight blanket Scott so that she could touch his face with shaky, soft fingertips. "Feel any acorns?" she whispered.

"Don't get sassy. You're in trouble."

"I've been in trouble since the day I met you. And I think—I'm becoming very sure—that you're in just as much trouble as I am."

"You still have plenty of time to sock me in the eye. And I'm sure as heck not going to let anything happen to you in these woods." He wanted to say more. Talking was an enormously helpful way to gain control, to keep his mind off her soft eyes and the intimately feminine shape of her and her moonlit mouth.

But then she whispered, "I'm scared. Can you understand? I'm scared of needing anything this much. Of wanting anyone this much. And it's not going to work out, Scott. I'm going to disappoint you, but—"

There was no chance of his talking after that, because he eased his mouth over hers. He intended the kiss to be melting and tender, but Jacqui's fingers tunneled in his hair, deepening the kiss, darkening it.

Need nicked him, as sharp as a spear. Want seared him, hotter than fire. His tongue plunged into her mouth. Hers was waiting for him. And all he knew was that he couldn't stand for her to be afraid or worried—not with him, never with him.

She murmured something low and hoarse when he rolled her onto her back again. He slid his hand under her sweater and flicked the catch of her bra. He could have been more gentle. He wanted to be more gentle, but when he rained a sluice of soft kisses on her mouth and throat, her hands tentatively fumbled at his shirt buttons. Her fingers ripped at those same buttons when he took her mouth with earthy hunger and lusty boldness.

The princess was really in no mood for tame, polite love play. A lick of flame wouldn't please her. She wanted a conflagration, preferably immediate, and she nearly got precisely what she was asking for when her palms skimmed his bare chest, unraveling thatches of hair, teasing his nipples with the scrape of her nail tips. Her teeth nipped the tight orb of his shoulder. The nip delighted him. It seemed to shock her, because for an instant he caught her eyes, liquid and bewildered, and she suddenly tensed.

Not for long. His knuckles pressed her abdomen as his fingers searched for her jeans snap, then the zipper. So many clothes. He pushed up her sweater and glimpsed the crushed fabric of a white bra in the moonlight. Her choice of chaste lingerie was going to amuse him in the morning. Nothing amused him now.

Cold air shivered over her small white breasts. The tender flesh barely filled his hands, and her nipples were tiny, dark, exquisite. He licked both to points, roughly, not softly, because her whole body bowed and tensed beneath his in reaction to that tongue play. His palm slid down her pearl-white abdomen to the open V of her zipper. Even open, her jeans fit tight. So did his hand.

His fingers bridged a thin band of nylon, then soft tufts of velvet down. He cupped her, and she nearly cut off the circulation in his hand when she catapulted toward him in response.

A dozen times he told himself to slow down. A dozen times he told himself to at least carry her to the house, that this was crazy, that he was crazy, that she couldn't really want this, that there were reasons why this was wrong. Every thought that formed dissolved. Jacqui was breathing hard now, as she should be, inhibitions abandoned, as they should be, coming alive as a woman, as he'd only dreamed a woman could come alive, for him, with him.

She wasn't afraid now. A woman's potent sensuality was in her eyes. Scott wasn't sure if he was more entranced or more alarmed. She went after an open-mouthed kiss and got it. She went after a search-and-discovery mission connected with the fit of his jeans and maybe found more than she bargained for. If her gift for torture was newly acquired, Torquemada would have hired her on the spot and to hell with references. She tenderly stroked. She brazenly rubbed. She played...and he desperately wanted her to feel that freedom, but there came a point when he hooked her hands and took control.

The wind screamed and the leaves crackled, and he saw the look on her face when she heard the rasping downhill track of his jeans zipper. Her eyes were on fire, reckless with desire and impatience, and lush—that lushness shook him—lush with love.

Darkness swirled around them when he covered her, wrapped her legs around him and took her. She moaned a "yes," the sound as wild and lost as the wind. He captured that sweet sound with his mouth and set a driving rhythm to match her need, her fear, her pleasure, her passion.

The fire wasn't supposed to take him, but it did. This was for Jacqui. That was how it started and that was how it was supposed to end, yet madness tempted him. She was the madness, with her yielding kisses and the feel of her thighs flexed so tightly around him, and she kept whispering those yeses, each one more willful, more wanton, more wild. Her voice touched something deep and lost in his soul, her touch unraveled secrets guarded for years, and the worst madness of all was that she made him feel loved.

When the first shudders of ecstasy took her, she called his name. Maybe that was the first moment he realized the power she held over his heart. She knew him. She knew his faults and scars, his temper and flaws, yet it was still his name she called like a celebration, his body she claimed with both need and tenderness.

He threw back his head at the moment when a man is as vulnerable as a man can be. Although he believed in no illusions, he could have sworn they rode the wind, ran through fire, captured stars. His fragile, silver-haired princess claimed to know nothing of love. He was the one who knew nothing. She knew it all.

And all he could think, all he could feel, all he could believe . . . was that he'd die if he lost her.

Chapter 9

Something oblong and hard poked into Jacqui's spine. Her jacket hung from a nearby bush. Her sweater was bunched up to her armpits, and as far as she could tell, she had leaves everywhere from her ears to her fingernails.

Odd, but she didn't move. Odder yet, she had the vague, shameless wish to climb onto a rooftop and sing. If it wouldn't have taken so much energy, she might have.

Eyelids at half-mast, she felt wonder still flooding through her like warm spring rain. Branches rustled wildly above her, trees shook their leaves. The moonlight tossed shadows. She'd always loved her woods but hadn't been near them for weeks. She'd been too afraid of a man who set fires in the middle of the night.

It was night now. Her pulse was still skidding from an emotion not unlike fear, and the man wrapped around her, still trying to recover his breathing, unquestionably set fires. Scott's eyes had been a blaze and his kisses had burned, and when his hips had rocked against her, she'd felt the scorch of the hottest fire.

Certainly she had felt desire before, but the blaze, the burn, the scorch just didn't happen to her. She had also previously been to bed with someone she'd deeply cared for, but even deep, honest caring hadn't made a difference. As fast as the lights went out, her mind tuned into a woman's inadequacies and a woman's vulnerability and a woman's past history of climbing emotional cliffs.

These few lovers she'd had a long time had ago had never known she'd wakened in the morning unsatisfied. The best of men were easy to fool. Jacqui knew all the physiology and psychology of sexuality, but the therapist and the woman weren't always in accord. The woman in Jacqui knew well that sometimes it was just plain easier to fake it.

The 170-pound man currently crushing her ribs had never given her the chance to worry about it, she thought fleetingly. Scott not only took a woman to the cliff—he pushed her off.

He'd also been there to catch her when she shattered into a million pieces.

"You still breathing?" Scott murmured.

Her eyes opened to find Scott appraising her with ruthless intensity. His gaze scanned her scrambled-leaf hairdo, tangled clothes and long bare legs on the blanket of leaves. His smile came on slow, like an exultant wave consuming the shore. No mother anywhere in the world would have trusted that grin near her daughter.

"No question what you've been doing, Petunia." His voice was gruff and low—a man's vulnerable gruff, a man's tenderest low. He dropped a soft, reverent kiss on her lips. "I've seen you beautiful in pearls, but I have to tell you that you're even more beautiful draped in early leaf. We're talking sinfully breathtaking—and no, don't you dare go shy on me.''

"I'm not shy," she denied, yet had never felt more shy in her life. She had a good look at Scott when he leaned back. His black hair was disastrously disheveled...because of her hands. His shoulders were brazenly bare. In the darkness, she couldn't see the scars hidden under the short tangled fur on his chest, but she'd felt them, explored them. Intimately. And even in the dim light, she could see a dark mark in the hollow of his shoulder. It wasn't a scar, but a love bite.

Since no other half-naked women were running around the woods, she must have put it there. Inhibitions separated men from the beasts. She was a woman who valued control, and too few minutes ago, her control had taken a vacation. She closed her eyes again.

"This is no time for a nap," he scolded. "We'll both catch our death of cold that way. Upsy-daisy."

Other lovers may not have moved her, but they'd certainly been more romantic. She was propped up and then left standing naked from the waist down while he fooled with *his* jeans. Most embarrassingly, he then fooled with hers. "Lean on me," he advised. He fed one leg, then the other, into the jeans.

He zipped, kissed, snapped, kissed, jacketed, kissed and then hauled an arm around her neck. One was given the impression he expected her to walk to the house. Her knees felt like jelly and her ankles felt no stronger than wet noodles.

"We'd both better hit the shower. I think we have a matched set of leaves in our respective belly buttons."

"Scott..." It was like him to be common-sense natural and easy. But not *this* common-sense natural, and not this easy.

He'd just turned her world upside down. She didn't pretend to have the ability to read his mind, but she had certainly been the one lying under him a few minutes before. He'd been caught up in the same tailspin.

Whether or not he knew it, he had made love to her like a man who was desperate to hold and be held, a man searching for something lost in his soul, a man who needed in a way that had shaken him.

He had made it impossible for her not to respond. He was an impossible man not to love. And now he was characteristically moving a little too lightly and a little too fast. It was as if he was going to make very sure she didn't have time to dwell on regrets.

"That's not what happens to me," she said clearly, and added, "ever."

She knew she'd touched a vulnerable nerve from the way his gaze scorched hers. He was still trying to move a little too fast. "So, maybe you weren't in the mood before."

"I was in the mood before."

"So maybe you chose the wrong men."

"I have been careful—and caring—always about the man."

"So maybe it was a long time."

"Maybe it was you."

When she awakened, she found that the pillow beside her was deserted and that the sheets next to her were cool. Turning over, she read the dial on the clock. It was past five in the morning.

She climbed out of bed and grabbed a robe. Scott couldn't be up and around. She thought dryly that a man with his sexual stamina should not only be sleeping, but comatose.

When they had come in from the woods, she had been trying, hard, to pursue a conversation with him. Scott had diverted her into the shower, and she had discovered very quickly that letting the man anywhere near water was as dangerous as allowing a toddler near cookie dough. His imagination was limitless with water, soap and slippery skin. They had laughed and loved until the water ran cold.

She had been exhausted by the time they'd curled between her ice-pink sheets. Not him. A sleepy cuddle had turned into a slow dream of a woman's fantasy. There wasn't a creak, crevice or hollow of her body that he hadn't explored—and loved—thoroughly and with reverence. He'd made her laugh in the shower, and in the darkness of her bedroom, he'd made her cry.

She had fallen asleep with her arms wrapped securely, protectively and lovingly around him. Her virile lover seemed dead beat. He had also given her no possible chance to pursue that conversation started in the woods—no possible chance to tell him that she loved him, for example.

He knew her quite well.

He'd just forgotten that one coin always had two sides. She knew him quite well, too. Scott did not hide his emotions easily. And he could never hide them in bed. He may have proved to her that she had a lusty, lascivious, shamelessly earthy streak . . . But Jacqui had also proved something to herself.

Most men drove blindly toward satisfaction—hooked a woman behind while they steered the horse and basically hoped she'd stick on for the ride. Scott made love with his eyes open. A woman was never going to escape those eyes, not in his bed. He had no appreciation for shyness, embarrassment, hesitation. A woman in his bed risked it all...but then, so did Scott. If he didn't want to talk about love, he had certainly shown her his version of it. And it had opened her heart as to the kind of sensitive, vulnerable and infinitely deep man that Scott was.

Finding him now was no problem, because the only light on in the entire house glowed from her studio. It stood to reason that he was in there. As she hesitated in the doorway, she felt her heart open just a little bit more. She knew he'd fallen asleep content, exhausted and sated. And now he wasn't content, but disturbed and upset.

He was standing at an angle where he couldn't see her. His thumbs were hooked in his belt loops, and he was staring at her sculptures. His jeans were zipped but not buttoned. The smooth, toned muscles covering his shoulders and upper arms were flexed and rigid, and his eyebrows were plunged in a frown.

"Hey," she murmured from the doorway. "I already told you I was a rotten artist. Staring at them won't make any of them look any better."

His head whipped around, and his eyes found hers. For a brief moment, she had him again—the vulnerable, virile lover who had come apart for her last night just as surely as she had come apart for him. His eyes found her, treasured her, and for a moment the anxiety in his expression eased.

But not for long. As if to fool her, he produced a grin and motioned her closer with a two finger come-on. "Far as I'm concerned, all this stuff of yours belongs in the Metropolitan Museum of Art."

"What do you know about the Metropolitan Museum of Art?"

"Zilch." When she chuckled, he tugged her next to him. His bare chest was warm, but his muscles were too tight, too taut, and the lazy kiss he dropped on her cheek was distracted. "You should be sleeping," he scolded.

"I was sleeping, until I realized you were gone. What's wrong?"

"Nothing." His fingers sifted gently through her hair, then stopped. "Everything. Dammit, the bastard is *here*, Jacqui. Right here in your studio."

"Who's here?" she asked bewilderedly.

"Your pyro." He dropped his hand from her hair and shifted three steps away from her. "I may shoot you for not telling me until last night that your prowler had been in this room. Don't you see what that means?" His fist slapped against his open palm in a clap of frustration as he continued.

"It means that I've been heading down a hundred wrong alleys. Your torch isn't some guy you see every week in a grocery store. He isn't Roberts or West or any other arsonist on the books who picks out a victim by a type. You're not a type to this guy, Petunia, you're *you*. Why would he bother with this room unless he knew it meant something to you? And he knows you damn well, if he knew that bridging this locked door would get to you."

She took a long breath. Scott was as revved up as a funneling tornado.

"He's here." Agitated, Scott waved a hand toward her shelves. "Don't you remember what you told me last night? That you sculpted some of your patients, but not all. You sculpt people you know and care about—but not all. The other subjects you choose are the people who give you grief or cause you trouble or are tough to deal with. People who bother you."

"In a way, yes—"

"So he's here. He's one of these clay busts. Don't you see how logical it is? You spent time molding him in clay because there was something wrong, something you couldn't put your finger on, something that troubled you about him. I'm telling you, he's up there." He pivoted to face her. "You ready for a marathon? Because I want you to tell me about each person you sculpted. Yes, obviously concentrating on the men but not ruling out the women. I want to hear every detail, every why, when and where you can think of—"

"Could you just hold up a minute there, Geronimo?" He was going so fast that she couldn't think. The possibility Scott was suggesting nagged her like but the buzz of a mosquito, unignorable and aggravatingly real. "But I may have misled you," she said cautiously. "Yes, I worked on people who worried me, but that was for all kinds of reasons. I sculpted my brother the year he had a divorce, for instance. You don't want to hear about my brother—"

"Yes, I do."

"Timm, the senior member of our practice, is up there. He's like a second father to me. I did Jonathan the first year I worked with him, and a half dozen others of these are just friends. You don't want to hear—"

"Yes, I do."

"Llewellyn . . ." But for a moment there was no one to argue with. Scott disappeared from the room, returning shortly with a steaming mug of coffee that he pressed into her hand.

The coffee was as dark as mud and loaded with caffeine. Perched on the stool with her robe wrapped around her knees, she sipped at the wake-up sludge and willed it to stir some enthusiasm in her blood.

That shouldn't have been hard. The effect that the fire setter had on her life was constant and measurable. She desperately wanted him found and caught. She wanted security restored to her life and her mind freed of that constant worry. With irrational feminine perverseness, though, she just didn't want to worry about him now. She wanted to still be curled up next to Scott.

You want your lover back, not this merciless inquisitioner, she thought dryly, and yet again tried to rally for his sake. She would have been unrealistic to expect Scott to wake up loving and lazy. His job, by necessity, dominated his life with Devil's Night only weeks away. She understood dedication. She respected it. And for an hour she tried to ignore the gnawing worry that Scott was driven less by his job than by demons at another level entirely.

Never still, he picked up each clay figure, fingered it, turned it, examined it. "About the judge—"

"Judge Henshall has a fast inclination to throw away the key on kids in trouble. I sculpted him to figure out how to get through to the old turkey, and that's *all*. Trust me. The only thing Henshall lights up is his pipe."

Any other time he would have smiled. Instead he pounced on the bust of McGraff. "That old man's always bothered me, Petunia, and he could easily know about your studio."

"I've told you. No one knows about the studio. True, I don't guard it like it's Fort Knox. But I do keep it locked."

"A baby could have picked any lock you had until we got you the security system, and McGraff has access. He may not be around the house every single day, but he's here most days for at least a few hours."

"Well, we could certainly convict him on that basis alone, which you have tried to do before," Jacqui said with exasperation. "Of course, you questioned him yourself and so did the police, who also checked his fingerprints and didn't find any kind of record."

"He's a clear-cut stray dog, Petunia. You don't know him."

"I know him well enough to know he's an eccentric. That's not a crime. And he's badly introverted, but that's not a crime, either. He's just an old man crippled up with arthritis."

"Okay, okay. We'll move on."

But the inquisition had stopped being "okay" for Jacqui. To hell with her arsonist. He wasn't worth a man's sleep, sanity or common sense. Scott looked increasingly drawn and increasingly driven.

Three cups of coffee later, her concern for Scott had intensified. Even when they finished going through her shelves, he wasn't satisfied. He returned yet a second time to the bust of Jonathan. "You neglected to mention something about him."

"What do you mean?"

"He's in love with you." Scott glanced at her. "*That's* what you carved in his face. A man who was in love with you, and a man, Petunia, who made you damned uneasy. How hard did he put the push to you?"

It wasn't the question. It was the way he asked it, cold and without emotion. "Fairly hard," she said evenly.

"Is he still pushing?"

"Who's asking? The fire investigator or the lover?"

He missed the vulnerable nuance in her voice. Taking down the sculpture of Jonathan, he set it on her worktable. By the time he finally ran out of questions, there were four other clay figures lined up in front of her.

The one bust was Jonathan. Another was one of the first patients she'd ever had, a boy who had clung to her conscience because she had failed to help him. The third bust was of a teenager with a history of sexual abuse, who was currently in therapy with her. The fourth bust Scott had chosen was a carving she'd made from memory of her first lover, which she hadn't told Scott, never intended to tell him, and which he couldn't possibly have known. The fifth bust was of Stan.

Staring at his choices, Jacqui felt emotionally shaken. Scott had seemed to pick up on an invisible something he saw in her sculptures. She could easily dismiss several subjects as her arsonist. That wasn't the source of her jitters. Scott had unfailingly, instinctively picked those people who had troubled her—seriously troubled her—at some time in her adult life.

He knew her well. Intimately well. If she hadn't realized it before, she realized it now. She'd let him in closer than she'd ever allowed another human being.

"I was right, wasn't I?" he murmured. "Something about every one of those guys scared you good, sometime, somewhere, somehow."

"Yes."

"Look at them."

But she looked at him, instead. "The night I had the prowler," she told him thoughtfully, "one of these busts had been moved and placed deliberately under my work light."

Scott whirled around, his dark eyes searing hers like a blaze—but not a blaze of passion. "Which one, and dammit to hell, why didn't you tell me this before?"

"Because at the time, I jumped to the conclusion that it was the person responsible for the fires. And if I tell you the name now, you'll jump to the same conclusion." She carefully avoided looking at the carving of Stan. "He isn't and I was wrong."

"How do you know that?"

She said softly, from the heart, needing him to hear her. "Because I believe in him. And because there came a point, for me, when I simply had to believe in my own professional judgment. Whether or not you believe in my profession, Scott, I'm a damned good psychologist."

"For cripe's sake, I know that!" he exclaimed irritably.

She hadn't known—that he valued her career or respected what it meant to her. His automatic response told her something she'd desperately needed to know, but he didn't give her a chance to enjoy that relief for long.

"But being good at your job is not what we're talking about. Not to accuse you of being an idealist, but we both know you could find the good side in a rabid dog. Come on, Jacqui. Which one was under the light? Jonathan?, The son of a sea dog psychologist you work with?"

"Jonathan is not a son of a sea dog."

"He put the moves to you."

"I'm twenty-seven years old—not that long in the tooth—single and living in the twentieth century. Could we get a little realistic here?" she murmured wryly, If you're going to hang every man who's ever put the moves to me—"

"Quit stalling, Petunia. Was it him?" When she didn't respond, he snapped, "Whoever it was, the cops can check out where he was and what he was doing on the night you had the fires. I want the name."

She said slowly, softly, "I know you do, and I'm sorry you do, and this is absolutely the last time I will ever discuss my arsonist with you."

Scott looked as though someone had just struck him. "What in the sam hill is that supposed to mean?"

"It means that I'm in love with you, Llewellyn." Odd, how 170 pounds of bad-tempered man could instantly freeze at the sound of a little four-letter word. She set down her empty mug and slid off the stool. "I'm not long on courage, which I told you before. It takes one heck of a lot of audacity, arrogance and, yes, courage, to admit how I feel about you when you haven't said one word about a relationship or the future or loving me. You're partly to blame for my newfound courage, of course. I'm afraid you turned out to be a man worth taking just about any risk for."

"Jacqui—"

"Shut up, would you? One of the most lily-livered cowards of all times is about to risk making a total fool out of herself. We should really invite Guinness for such a world shattering event, but somehow I'd prefer this to be just between you and me." She took a long breath—her lungs seemed starved for oxygen—but there didn't seem to be anything she could do about the tremor in her voice.

"Here's the offer, Llewellyn. If you want a warm bed and a lover—I'm offering you one. I'll be your lover, any way you want, any how you want, free and clear, with no complications and no strings. That coupon's redeemable anytime through and including Devil's Night. Come November 1, we'll talk, but not before. In fact, that's the only term you have to honor to take advantage of this outstanding, one-time offer—no talk about my arsonist."

He was utterly still for a moment, but the muscle in his cheek was pulsing like a detonator, and his face was as flushed as fire. "You're not being funny."

His ominous tone unnerved her, but still, she tried to play it light. "The body isn't enough? All right, I'll throw in washing your socks. Believe me, you will never hear me make that offer again."

"Stop it."

She said fiercely, "I don't care about him. I care about you. Every time you start talking about my arsonist, you turn into a stranger, cold like a machine, ruthless like someone I don't know. I understand that you want to protect me, but this has gone past that. Nothing has happened since the security system was put in. There are police patrolling the place at all hours if someone tried to do anything. You have to get it through your head—I'm as safe as anyone can be short of renting a vault in Fort Knox."

"You're not safe. You don't understand what a bastard like this can do!"

"I can see what he's doing to you." Always, she was careful with people's sensitivities. Now, she heard herself bungle and thrash toward deep water, too upset to stop herself. "You're eating yourself up, trying to make this a replay of what happened to your sister. Don't you see the similarities? Someone you care about is in danger. You had to watch what happened to Phoebe, without being able to do anything about it. You wanted to be a hero. You talked yourself into believing that if you were brave enough, you could have saved her from being paralyzed. That was never true, and you have to deal with that. Please. Put that guilt on your conscience to bed, because I don't want a hero, Scott. I just want a lover. I need you as a lover. I'll give you everything I have as a lover in return, only—"

He strode toward her faster than she could stop him and hauled her so close she had the crazy sensation of being surrounded by a thunderstorm. Damn, he was mad. When his mouth slammed on hers, her blood raced. Every surface on his body was hard or hot or both.

He didn't like being analyzed. She already knew that. His lower body ground against hers in a most primitive announcement of male dominance. His palms held her head so his mouth could plunder, caveman-style. His kiss held enough bruising pressure to make her neck ache. The electricity between them could have toppled trees in a lightning storm.

Her good sense suggested that she knock him clear across the room for such cavalier behavior. Her instincts, though, had always been the stronger force around Scott. She didn't brace; she yielded. She didn't tighten up; she accepted the searing weight of his mouth, absorbed it and demanded more.

In the end, a kiss that began as a man's unforgivable demand for submission became something else. He was certainly angry, but not with her. He kissed with desperation and frustration and anxiety born of caring. When her arms swept around his neck, he kissed with compelling passion.

When his mouth tore free, they were both gulping for air. Her vision was misty, but she could still see that his eyes were hauntingly dark. Whatever had happened for him in that kiss had only intensified his frustration, not relieved it.

His thumb brushed the side of her jaw. His touch was tender, his voice raw. "Did you wake up this morning and say, 'This is the day I'm going to drive Llewellyn crazy'? You don't give it away free and clear, Petunia, and you don't make offers like that. Not to me. Not to any man. Not you."

"I meant it." Her voice cracked.

"Yeah, I know what you meant." His shoulders bunched all over again. "I know I come on like a ton of bricks where your pyro's concerned. I'll work on that, but you can't tie my hands as far as helping you. That's nuts."

"Possibly."

"You can't seriously expect me to pretend he doesn't exist."

"I do."

"That's even more nuts."

"Nuts, crackers and bananas, in your vernacular, but have no illusions, Scott. I meant what I said. We will not be talking about my arsonist. The subject's closed."

His head reared up and his eyes blazed. And then he moved. It didn't take him five minutes to gather up his things. When he slammed the kitchen door, she could have sworn the whole house rattled.

Silence flooded the house, slowly, like a consuming wave of loneliness. Odd things filtered through her consciousness. A crack in the ceiling, the black shine of her skylight, the austerity of her workroom. Mostly she was aware of an ache spreading through her muscles like fear and that she suddenly became cold. Her robe covered her bare flesh, but it was minimal protection against this kind of internal chill.

Moments before, it had had seemed terribly important to do whatever it took to dent his thick skull. He took his sense of responsibility too far. If something happened to her, she was terribly afraid he would blame himself, as if he was still—damn him—blaming himself for what had happened to his sister. Scott didn't value his own hide enough. How could she tell him that she valued the man just as he was—flawed, scared, human, real—and to hell with his courage? He was hurting. Was she supposed to stand there and do nothing?

Well, you sure did something, ducky. He slammed that door hard enough to bend the hinges.

She sank down onto the stool, feeling lost. For a woman who never dabbled in emotional courage, she'd just laid an awful lot on the line. All that risk, and for what?

She slid both hands through her hair, clawing it back from her face. For him, of course. In being a man who never backed down from trouble, in being a man she could trust, in being a man who gave of himself with honesty and passion and caring... he had become, unfortunately, a man worth climbing cliffs for.

Through all he had to say, she noted painfully that he had carefully avoided any mention of their future. In principle, she had expected that. A man like Scott had to prove himself before he had the right to love. He had a lot of guilt tied up between his courage and his conscience.

She understood that, but she had no idea how to make a man believe that he didn't have to be a hero to be loved.

Chapter 10

The group had been squeezed into the conference room like sardines. The hodgepodge of police, fire-fighters and city officials now filing out of the door were not the entire bulk of Scott's task force, but they were its core. The media had coined the word *army*, and in every sense that mattered, this Monday morning meeting had been a rehearsal for war.

Alone, Scott hunched over the model of Detroit that sat on the conference table. The hundreds of cardboard blocks and buildings resembled a child's paper-doll game. Seven command posts had been marked off with yellow tape. Curfew lines were marked with red. Historically hard-hit arson targets were squared off with fluorescent chalk. Fire fighting, medical and police vehicles were color coded and identified by location.

The mayor had challenged the task force with reducing fires and fire alarms by thirty-five percent on Devil's Night. Scott's crew had privately set the far more optimistic goal of a fifty-percent reduction. If it all came together as it had in their rehearsals, they just might achieve that goal.

Certainly his team believed in it. Outside the conference room, Scott could hear bedlam. A half dozen phones rang. Doors slammed. Voices snapped, barked and swore to be heard. Footsteps clicked past at a racing pace. Everyone knew there was less than two weeks to go, and the countdown atmosphere was electric. He could taste the excitement and smell the tension.

And all noise abruptly ceased when the conference door closed. A Styrofoam cup of coffee appeared in front of him—nothing drinkable; no coffee Luz made ever was. He warned himself not to touch it. His stomach was already sloshing acid, and there was a sledgehammer whacking away inside his right temple. Caffeine would make both problems worse.

He picked up the cup anyway. "You have a bone to pick about the meeting?"

"Not about the meeting, no." With easy familiarity Luz dropped into the nearest battered chair and crossed her long black legs at the ankles. Like him, she picked up a toy fire truck and relocated it on the three-dimensional map. The model would be taken to the dispatch area on Devil's Night. She couldn't get enough rehearsals.

Neither could he. Gulping the coffee, he automatically corrected the first move she made, then seriously assessed her second. Every move posed a problem. The routing and tracking of equipment was an integral key to success on Devil's Night. Dispatching a fire engine from its home base was no sweat. Once trucks and ladder companies were dispersed throughout the city, though, every new fire created enormous complications— Where was the closest backup and how to route it to the trouble

spots, always worrying you were spreading your resources too thin and knowing you had to keep your big
guns in the areas of highest liability.

Scott and Luz both continued to move pieces, even
after she started talking. "I should have told you way
back in the beginning you've done more than all right by
me through this, Llewellyn. I owe you some thanks."

Expecting the conversation, he never glanced up. Every
fire alarm went through dispatch, and the people manning those phone lines had control over on-the-spot logistics like no one else. He'd made a few waves when he'd
chosen Luz from the pool of dispatchers for his task
force. "You owe me zip."

"You went out on a limb for me," she insisted.

"Some limb. I chose the right person for the right job.
All problems should be so easy."

"You know I'm the best and I know I'm the best, but
a few people over the years have taken exception to my—
some say—abrasive personality."

"You, sweet thing?"

"I should have known you'd make it impossible to
thank you, Llewellyn. Good thing that isn't what I came
in here for." Luz unquestionably had a face that could
make a mirror wince, but she also had eyes like chocolate syrup: liquid, dark and deep. "It's going as good as
it can. Cops brought in two bad-news firebugs last night,
and they got a good lead on Roberts. Alarms have sim-
mered down this week, and you got the whole team
humming like a well-oiled machine."

"Yeah, so?"

"So when nobody's around, you get this look on your
face like you're ready to blow sky-high."

"You want big smiles, check with me on November 1. I'm supposed to be mean and tight all through this month. I read it in the job description."

Luz politely expressed her personal feelings about his job description with a four-letter word, then slouched in the chair with all the grace of a Mack truck. Moving her would probably take one.

He sighed impatiently. "Maybe I have a reason to be a little nervous. A million things have to happen and come together at the last minute. And we have a known influx of arsonists gathering in Detroit with obvious high hopes of having a summit on Devil's Night—"

"You thrive on stress, always have. Remember me? I used to be the voice on the other end of the line when you'd call in a four-alarm fire. You whistled through that stuff, Llewellyn."

"This is nothing to whistle about, and yeah, it's getting to me." Abandoning the game, he rolled his tense shoulders as he glanced out the window. The sun glinted down on his city. He heard a siren in the distance. "I hate losing, always have. And I want to believe that if we do everything right, it'll end this year. No more Devil's Night, the war over and the idea dead. Only that's not what's going to happen."

"No?"

He was barely conscious of Luz sitting there. He wanted to be talking to Jacqui. She understood most things in a way no one else ever did. Some things, of course, she understood not at all. "I'd protect her with my life," he said absently, meaning—he was sure—his city. "Only I don't see how. The fight doesn't scare me. I love a fight, but when an alarm comes in, you know your enemy—fire. You fight it with known weapons and known skills and guts, and you fight it to win. Only how the hell do you fight a war when there's no face on your enemy? I don't know who's out there setting fires, and I don't know why.''

Luz buffed a nail on her shirtsleeve. ''That's kind of deeper waters then I planned to wade into, Llewellyn. I can't help you with that kind of problem, but I can help you with her.''

''Her?''

''Yeah, *her*.'' Luz collected her cup and his between two pressed fingers and gradually eased to her feet. ''Don't give me that look. You been around here long enough to know gossip spreads through the ranks faster than sludge. You're making six calls a day to the Silver Lake cops, hounding their fire chief. You put an off-duty cop on your personal payroll, and you have the switchboard operator ordered to find you anywhere if Jacqui calls. So the whole place knows that her name is Jacqui and she's got herself some kind of problem with an arsonist and you're involved.''

She motioned at him when he tried to interrupt, making both half-filled cups slosh. ''It's not my business, okay? I'd love to say something about a stone-headed boss falling head over heels, but I didn't bring up the subject to tease. I brought up her name so you'd know I know it, and so you'd know every one of my dispatchers knows it. Her name comes up through dispatch—kosher or not—she'll get the National Guard equivalent in fire engines and ladder companies.''

Three times Scott tried to frame a reply, but by the time she reached the door all he could manage was, ''Thanks.''

The emotion in his voice almost made her turn around. She couldn't remember an occasion when she didn't have a quip on tap for Llewellyn. Not this time. "Forget it," she said gruffly, and left.

Scott swiped a hand over his face, wondered how the hell anyone could fail to value Luz as much as he did, and gazed down at the traffic jam building up ten stories below. His total focus and concentration was on his city twenty-four hours a day now. It had to be.

Of all the primates, however, nature had unfairly created man with enormous brain potential—the ability to think of two things at once, for example. Scott was fully capable of devoting his entire concentration to Devil's Night and wanting to wring Jacqui's neck at the same time.

It had been two weeks since he'd walked out of her studio. Why should he have stayed? You can't talk to a woman with the self-protective instincts of a daffodil, and Scott had never valued talk all that highly, anyway. A man acted—he didn't talk—and protecting Jacqui was not dependent on her cooperation. He'd been on the cops. He'd been with her boss. He'd hired an off-duty lieutenant to watchdog her house during the daylight hours.

She'd nicked some raw nerves, though. He didn't figure a little space was going to hurt either one of them. Only she called him. Nightly.

The calls had become his lifeblood. They were her way of telling him she was all right and that nothing had happened. Only they had also become his nemesis. She always began with his job, coaxing him to talk about the stresses and pressures, wooing the details out of him. No one could make a man talk like that champagne blonde, and then her voice got this tremor, and she started. She talked about back rubs. She talked about his preference for lemon satin or black silk in a negligee. Somewhere she'd unearthed a newly translated Indian sex manual. She talked about her favorite positions. And if he even obliquely referred to her fire setter, she rang off.

He ended every phone call hotter than a sixteen-year-old boy at a drive-in...and mad enough to shake her. He was almost positive he couldn't be in love with a woman who drove him this nuts. Further, the calls were all false advertising. The harder Jacqui worked at wild and wanton—and that woman had one hell of an imagination—the more he was aware she knew spit about sex. The calls should have made him smile.

Instead, they upset him, which was obviously her intent. Some women were naturally aggressive. Jacqui wasn't one of them. She was laying herself on the line for him—an intimate line, a line they both knew damn well was tough for her—and he didn't like it. Her message was as subtle as a blowtorch. She was willing to take risks for the man, but not for the hero. She *valued* the man, not the hero. *Forget the fire setter, he could hear her say. Scott, you have nothing to prove when you're with me.*

Only Jacqui was wrong. He did have something to prove, and the test had become more inexorably linked to her every day, every hour, every minute. Guilt was an old friend of his. He'd always believed that his cowardice was partly to blame for the extent of his sister's injuries. For the same reason, he'd sworn off a serious love relationship for years. A man had to be able to sleep nights before he could ask a woman into his life.

It's come that far, has it, Llewellyn? His gaze focused blindly on the spiraling skyscrapers through the sun-dusted window. Yeah, it had come that far. The sound of her voice alone heated his blood, and she had this certain smile that made his heart spring. She was warmth, empathy, passion. She aggravated him. She made him laugh. She didn't understand about their class differences, and she was blind sure he was a good man, making him want to be. She was always going to care far too much about other people and far too little about herself. Talk about your hopeless idealists....

He couldn't live with himself if something happened to her.

And there was the test. The cops didn't really believe her, no locks were foolproof, and no one—including Jacqui—understood the capabilities of a pyro the way he did. In his head, in his heart, he knew he stood between her and danger. And in his head, in his heart, he had to know he wouldn't fail her.

The bastard was still loose because of something he'd missed. She was still in danger because of something he was failing to see or do—and he'd lived with guilt before, but not like this. *Not her, Llewellyn. You can't fail her....*

"Scott?" Mary, the receptionist, stood in the doorway. "Here you are. When you didn't answer the phone in your office, I didn't know where to find you. There's a fire on Tenth Street, an empty warehouse. Deputy Chief called—it's a two-alarm, well under control, but they suspect arson and thought you'd like a look. The area was hit pretty hard last year on Devil's Night—"

"I'm gone."

By the time he drove back to the office, it was nearly four-thirty. His jacket was torn, his face smudged, and he knew he smelled like soot, mud and smoke. A little lady in a pink wool suit looked appalled when he climbed into the elevator with her.

She exited on three. He punched ten, watched the doors roll closed and leaned back for a rest that lasted seven floors. Exhaustion nagged at every muscle and nerve, but for the first time in weeks he felt like whistling. No fire was a picnic, but with Devil's Night looming so close, he'd felt reassured as he'd watched the veteran crew's efficiency and skill. Even better, the arsonist had been snatched from the watching crowd. Pyros were often stupid. They'd stand around and watch their creation, and then they were always surprised at getting caught. More to the point, that was one more taken out of action before October 30.

As the elevator doors whined open, he admitted to himself that the best of all was getting his hands dirty. The grit and soot felt good. Action felt good. Any action would have felt good after all these months of infernal worrying and waiting and planning. The price to pay, of course, was no dinner and a deskful of priorities that wouldn't wait.... He barely turned the corner before he saw Mary frantically waving at him from the reception area. "I saw your car drive up from the window. I've been keeping her on hold on line three."

He lopped off his whistle on an intake of breath. Mary's impersonal "her" was its own identification. His face paled and he bounded the hall at a fast stride. Jacqui's calls had always been at night, not during daylight office time. He kicked his office door closed at the same time that he reached for the phone.

Slow down, he told himself. She had to be all right; a dozen people would have contacted him if anything had happened. Still, as fast as he hefted the receiver to his ear, he barked, "You're all right? Not hurt?"

"I'm fit as a fiddle, thank you." Her voice was low and amused and made him want to strangle her.

Or love her. Hard, promptly and privately. No matter how much she drove him crazy, he missed her. Loosening his death grip on the phone, he started tugging off his jacket. "Okay, you didn't call to talk about Mr. Taboo, so what's new on the erotic tease and torture scene?"

"I know I've been trying hard to convince you otherwise, but occasionally I have my mind on things other than sex. Even where you're concerned." He caught first the nuance of humor in her voice, then the seriousness. "If you'll remember, I promised I'd try to get a few of my kids together to talk to you. I sort of did and didn't."

"How's that?"

"Schedules were too impossible to make the idea work in person, so I made a tape—with their permission—involving almost a dozen kids. If you could spare an hour, I'd like you to come over and hear it—here, at the office, with both Timm and me." She rushed on. "I really believe it would be worth your time, Scott. I know you're busy, and I know Devil's Night is around the corner, but I really believe these kids could give you some ideas. They're not just part of the cause, but part of the answer—"

"Honey, you don't have to hard sell me. I'm more than willing to listen."

"Tomorrow I have three o'clock free."

"Three's fine," he agreed.

There was a pause. "Not long ago you'd have brushed off a psychologist's input. Don't tell me we've finally dented that prejudice."

"Occasionally water gets through to a stone. Occasionally a man can even admit he's capable of being dead wrong and stupid, but not me. I've got too much pride." Her throaty chuckle singed his heart. He leaned back against the desk and closed his eyes, the phone still cradled to his ear. "You're breaking your own rules, Petunia."

"What rules?"

"You're initiating a conversation about fire."

"Not true. I've started a dozen conversations with you about fire and Devil's Night. My personal arsonist was the only subject we closed up."

"You closed it. I didn't. Jacqui—"

As though she sensed where he was headed, she barreled into a change of topic. "I can imagine how tired you are. I know what kind of long hours you put in, and I was thinking..." Her tone was light, soft, breezy blithe. A man could miss the tremor if he wasn't listening. "The next time you come in the door, I have in mind stripping you down, laying a sheet on the carpet, opening a bottle of jasmine oil and massaging every tight muscle I find—"

She went on, talking really brazenly, really wantonly. She did it well. Jacqui did most things well. Separating a man from his conscience wasn't even tricky for her, which was why he'd been careful to keep a geographical distance between them. Until her fire setter was caught, until he knew she was safe, he didn't belong in her bed.

Not the way he wanted to be in her bed, and at the moment all he wanted was a cold shower. "I'm going to spank you. I've never threatened a woman with physical harm before, so know that you're the first. I can't do it, Petunia."

"Can't hit me? Scott, I know that—"

"I can't sleep with you and not claim the rights that go with that. Make love with you and not protect you. Separate the lover from the woman who's in danger."

There was a moment's silence. "I'm not getting through, am I?" Her voice had lost the sassy suggestiveness. The buttery, vulnerable tone clawed at him far more than the sexy promises.

"If you were here, I'd have the door locked, and the papers on my desk would all be swooshed to the floor so we'd have a flat surface. Does that answer whether you're getting through or not?"

"No." Her sigh was as fragile as spring, as whispery. "It isn't sex I'm putting on the line, Scott. I thought you knew that. It's me. Because you're worth it, but I need you to believe that as much as I do."

She hung up before he could respond. He had no idea what he would have answered if she'd given him the chance.

He sat there in absolute silence, hearing people leave as five o'clock arrived. The last phone rang. Desks slammed shut, conversation buzzed, the thud and click of weary footsteps trod past his office door. The distant whir of the elevator descending was the last noise, and then the offices were empty of all sound. He still hadn't moved.

She believed in him. As no one had ever believed in him, as he didn't even believe in him.

Anxiety shot through Scott, colored by dread, weighted by fear. Jacqui was quick to make her pyro her last priority. He couldn't. She'd had no incidents for more than two weeks now, which had obviously reassured her. It didn't him. In Scott's experience, a creep who loved fire didn't quit. He started with matches and graduated to forest fires—until and unless someone took him out.

He could remember a car burning with his sister under it. He'd felt the same anxiety, dread, fear. Those emotions had overpowered him then, sucked him down, frozen him. He felt frozen now. In a rage of helplessness.

* * *

"He's five minutes late." The stack of journals flew under Jacqui's fingertips.

"And as you warned me, things happen on his job unexpectedly. If he's late, he's late, and if he's unable to make it, then you and I will have a nice, relaxing hour with our feet up."

"I'm worried about him, Timm." Jacqui slammed a book in place. "He puts himself in the middle of things. He's the kind where if there's a fight, he's in it. If there's a fire, he's holding the hose. If there was a war, he'd be on the front lines. He doesn't think—not about risk or danger—and with Devil's Night coming..." She reached for the mess of journals. "He's got a job where he should be on the sidelines. He won't be. He'll be in the thick of wherever the worse problem is, and I keep worrying." She glanced up. "It's okay to tell me to shut up, you know. I know you've heard all this before."

"I have no desire to tell you to shut up. Whenever you're wound up, you inevitably straighten all my bookshelves." Timm motioned toward his oak shelves. Every tome was in place, every book nicely lined up, the journals straightened—and Jacqui's hands were inches away from an attack on his magazines.

"If you weren't so messy..." she began, but she forgot to scold when he laughed, and then she laughed, too. She also finished straightening his magazines and then poured them both tea.

Years before, she'd had reservations about joining the practice with Timm. He was two decades older than she was, a soft man with a balding pate and an aesthetic choice in clothes. His office was as dignified as he was, dominated by pipe smoke, leather and old oak. In her office, she always threw open the drapes, let the sun in.

He preferred the curtains drawn and the old-fashioned atmosphere of couch and defused lamplight for his patients. Jacqui had been afraid he was just as rigid and old-fashioned in his approach to psychology.

She'd been hands-down wrong. Jonathan had the brilliance of insight, and Jacqui knew she had a certain skill and intuition with people—but Timm had the patience. Nothing shocked him, nothing shook him, nothing scared him. No matter what traumas a person had suffered, inherent to the psyche and body was a capacity to heal. Timm methodically, patiently searched for that capacity in every person he dealt with.

He was not only a good therapist, but a good person. Still, she wasn't absolutely sure what Scott would think of him. From the soft chin folds to the well-manicured hands, Timm wasn't exactly Scott's kind of man. Pacing to the window, she pushed at a drape. "Finally, that's his car driving in."

"You have the tape?"

"Of course." Automatically she started to straighten, tug, smooth. Her scarlet dress was a flannel knit with a cowl collar and long sleeves; a strip of soft leather cinched her waist. The outfit left her little to fuss with, and she hadn't run her stockings since checking five minutes ago.

Her choice of red was a mistake, though, which she discovered the moment Scott strode through the doorway. His eyes found her faster than a streak of lightning, then more slowly traveled every nip and curve. The knit hadn't seemed tight that morning. Now it did.

His slow smile was almost as unnerving as his cracked-tenor "Hi" and the breezy way he traveled the distance between them. There was no anticipating the devil. He shamelessly dropped a kiss on her mouth right in front of

Timm, then just as boldly shot out his hand to the senior member of the practice.

"Jacqui's talked about you often enough for me to be sure of the Timm, but I'm not sure I ever caught your last name...."

"McGarland." Timm stood up from his desk chair and transferred the pipe to his left hand so he could offer his right—and a smile. "We're pleased you could make it, Mr. Llewellyn."

The handshake was quick. Neither man by expression nor movement indicated this was anything other than their first meeting, yet Jacqui happened to know both men. Neither lied worth beans. "You didn't tell me you'd met before," she said casually to Timm, not Scott. To Scott she talked with her eyes. *I'll get you for this.*

"You didn't ask," Timm said mildly.

"Were you going to mention that you knew each other?"

"Certainly. If you asked."

Scott's hand drifted down her spine, leaving a wake of hot-pepper sensations. "Where's that tape of yours, Petunia? I'm short on time and tying you both up, besides."

She wanted to press it—when and why and how had he checked on her through Timm?—but he was right. No one had time to waste, and she badly wanted him to hear the tape she'd put together.

Timm eased back in his desk chair, and she took the couch cushion next to Scott, where both of them could easily punch the On/Off button on the recorder. Once the tape started, all three fell silent. The voices were mixed, boys and girls, some angry, some flat, some high-pitched, some low. Prep school accents followed the gutter grammar of the generic poor. The voices only had two things in common: they were all young, and the subject was fire....

"He hit me. He kept hitting me and hitting me, and I felt so helpless. I told myself I'd do something to get him back..."

"My mom's boyfriend played ball with me when she was around, but when she was gone, man, it was duck fast or take the bruises. I set my first fire in his car..."

"So my dad left and my mom left. There was just Gram, and she didn't want me..."

"I faked it through school, but I couldn't read. The teachers all knew it, but they didn't care. I got out anyway, only everybody else was getting a job and I wasn't. Everybody else had some kind of power, and I saw no way—no way, man—in my whole life would I have anything. So I stole some propane and I..."

"When she left us, he started drinking. He did more than take a swipe at me when I was a kid—I used to hate him for that—but nothing was like this. He'd come home from work and look right through me like I wasn't even there. The neighbors had this fancy thing outside, like a gazebo. That was the first thing I set on fire..."

Scott stopped the tape, his eyes as sharp as black blades. "That's him, isn't it? The one with the swastika. The one in your studio. The one you think you trust."

If he'd looked any less worn, any less pressured—or if she could have just managed to love him less—she would have scolded him a lot louder than she did. "I did not bring you here to worry about me, but to worry about them. Just listen, would you?"

He did, not expecting to be moved by the children's voices, but moved by nearly all of them. "They've really been kicked around," he said when Jacqui brought him a mug of coffee.

"A lot of kids are kicked around. They don't all turn to setting fires. The common reason these kids turned to arson is in their voices—couldn't you hear it? The hopelessness? They've stopped believing that they have the power to make their lives better. That's why they're lashing out, Scott, and dealing with the real problem is the only way you're going to stop them."

She'd forgotten Timm was in the room. She'd forgotten everything but her kids—and Scott. He'd listened, she knew. The kids had gotten through to him, because the caring was in his eyes, and she knew every nuance of expression in his eyes, because he had yet to stop looking at her. His arm was stretched out on the back of the couch. His fingers drifted down to brush her shoulder and lingered. "I hear you, but it would be a little tricky to fight fires with a squad of psychologists, Petunia."

"Are you trying to be funny?"

"No, but I honestly don't know what you want me to do, and it's pretty obvious from that glow in your eyes that you have something on your mind."

She nodded. "How many kids do you catch on Devil's Night? How are they handled? What happens to them?"

"The numbers vary. If I remember right, '86 was one of the worst years as far as kids—around five hundred arrested for violating curfew. As far as how they're handled, I guess they're swept off to juvenile hall. The penalty's stiff because it has to be. Ninety days in jail, a five-hundred-dollar fine." He shook his head. "I haven't exactly been involved in the kids' side of things in years past. There are big boys out there setting big fires, and when your city's burning, you have to set a few priorities."

Jacqui dismissed anyone over twenty-one with a flip of her hand. Her priorities were in an entirely different corner. "Don't you see what you have? Five hundred kids. All in one place, all in one night. You could reach all of those kids at one time, identify them, have counselors follow them up—"

They argued, wrangled, discussed. He claimed only an idealist would come up with her plan. She claimed she was the realist. "How you handle those kids—how, with whom and in what way—could affect whether they set the next fire. Whether there even is another Devil's Night."

She made sense. So did he. Ideas formed with long-term potential, yet there was nothing that could be resolved on a Tuesday afternoon in Timm McGarland's office. Both knew it, yet still they talked.

His eyes lingered, savored, hungered on her face. He made no secret of wanting her or missing her. He created excuses for a knee to brush a knee, a hand to find her shoulder. Yet there was as much determination in his gaze as in her own. They talked of nothing but kids and fires and Devil's Night, yet there was another kind of communication happening. *No matter what you say or do, I will find a way to protect you, Sweet Pea.*

Come home with me. I want you to come home with me. But not if you see me as a responsibility, a cause. You're not going to prove your courage through me.

Petunia, that's horseradish.

If it was horseradish, you'd have been in my bed these past two weeks. Llewellyn, can't you understand that I'm scared? Not of some stupid arsonist. Of you and me. I have to know that I mean more to you than a woman you feel guilt-driven to protect. Do I?

Jacqui—

"What's going on here? I could hear voices all the way down the hall. Are we having a debate or a party, and can anyone join?" Jacqui glanced up to find Jonathan ambling into the room, his cool blue eyes shifting immediately to Scott. "This is your Llewellyn, love?"

Timm rose at the same time that Scott squeezed her shoulder, hard, and then surged to his feet. The next few minutes were mystifyingly disorienting to Jacqui.

Jonathan had already heard her tape, and in the casual way the three ran their practice, would automatically have joined the group if he hadn't had a scheduled patient. His patient was obviously gone, yet her assumption that Jonathan would make an insightful fourth to their group suffered a confusing letdown.

Something was wrong. Scott coiled up, and his greeting to Jonathan was clipped. A conversational ball batted back and forth, but it was all bad tennis; nothing connected. Scott shared a look with Timm. Timm's eyes narrowed on Jonathan. Jonathan never took his eyes off Scott. And Jacqui stood in the middle of them, feeling as though someone had thrown her into an abrupt fog.

Timm eventually said, "Sandy just signaled. You must have a five o'clock appointment, Jacqui? And I think it's time we wound this up. Jonathan, we'll catch you up with all the details tomorrow...." The older man, ever soothing, relentlessly steered the group toward the door.

Jonathan was the first one out, then Jacqui. When she turned to share a last word with Scott, though, he seemed to be on the other side of Timm's half-closed door. And the senior member of her practice was standing between that half-closed door and Scott.

Her heart stopped for a full beat and then restarted double time, probably because she felt doubly betrayed, and that feeling intensified when Timm closed the door so Scott wouldn't realize she was there. "He's staying to talk with you?" she asked quietly.

"Yes."

"And you've talked with him before. More than once."

"Yes."

"You could have told me—"

Timm said patiently, "If you'd thought about it, I shouldn't have needed to tell you. You know your man, Jacqui. You might have clipped his wings by refusing to talk to him direct, but he was never going to give up flying. I was very naturally one of the people he would question. He suspects your arsonist is someone professionally involved with you—"

"He suspects everyone. That's why I stopped talking with him. I don't care about the damn arsonist. I care about him!" She rapidly lowered her voice. "And I still think that ethically you should have told me he was talking with you."

"Ethics have to do with our professional relationship. Scott approached me on a personal level, and that's what our conversations have been—personal. I'm as concerned as he is—"

"Shove it, Timm. I am perfectly fine and perfectly safe, and that isn't even the issue. At least not the issue that matters." She took a long breath. "Nothing is going to happen to me. Make him see it. And make him see that it wouldn't be his fault if it did. My situation is nothing like his sister's."

His eyes, so serious, suddenly caught a sparkle of humor. "Honey, I am a hundred percent sure he doesn't see you as a sister."

Her heart was in her voice. "And I am a hundred percent sure that I have failed to be his catcher in the rye."

"I don't understand."

"You don't have to. I do," she said sadly, and walked down the hall toward her office.

Chapter 11

He hadn't counted on the outside entrance to her attic being hooked to the security system, and he sure as heck hadn't figured on the day being so cold. It was hard to splice electrical wires with clumsy, numbed fingers. The spare light didn't help, and he was jittery with nerves.

Too jittery. Jacqui worked all day, every day. There shouldn't have been anyone around, yet the surprise of interruptions was constant. If it wasn't the meter man, it was the mail lady, then someone doing this or selling that. And then there was the off-duty cop. The Welshman must have hired the weight lifter in the pale gray car who kept cruising by, munching on doughnuts and sipping coffee. Outwitting the cop had become kind of fun, a game of who was watching who, but he wasn't having any fun today. The gray car always disappeared for a few minutes after one to pick up a take-out lunch, but the errand never took long. Time was critical.

Both the hot and ground wires already ran across the joists of the unfinished attic. All he had to do was splice them to the single-burner hot plate. When he reached back for the plate, though, the razor pain in his skull nearly blinded him. He had to stop, suck in his breath.

For a few brief moments, nothing made sense. He shouldn't be here. He couldn't be here. Hadn't he promised himself he could wait? And Devil's Night was Saturday, just six days away now. He'd screw everything up if he was caught now. He couldn't risk setting another fire this close to Saturday.

The head-splitting pain started to ease. He'd begun to think of his headaches as red. Red had stopped being the color of fire and was becoming the color of emotions like anger and passion. He'd wakened that morning to this snake of red rage climbing through his blood. Nothing loosened its hold until his father's voice—so virile...so strong!—had started talking inside his mind.

His father reminded him of how powerful he had become. No one could catch him now, and he had neglected to start a fire just for Jacqui. The other times he'd done three, four, five mimic fires in a night. He had to set one just for her, just between him and her, intimatelike. He liked that image. Intimate. And his father had pressed it.

She was everything. The woman he'd never had. The caring that had never been offered him, and just thinking about setting a fire for her had him hot...an idea that amused him no end.

Squatting, he finished attaching the switch wires to the hot plate, then dropped some matchsticks onto the metal surface. He inserted a rag soaked with diesel fuel. Gas or propane could explode on ignition. Diesel fuel took a nice long time to catch.

The miracle—the brilliance—of this particular scenario was that he would be miles away when the fire started. Nothing would happen to the hot plate until Jacqui used the wall switch for her bedroom overhead light. When she turned on the light, the switch would activate the hot plate. Slowly, it would start to heat and glow. In due time, the matches and then the oily rag would catch. Smoke would start to fill the attic. Nothing like diesel to create a lot of smoke.

Nothing, of course, would ultimately happen. Fiberglas insulation was packed between her attic joists. The stuff would smolder well, but not take. Sooner or later the smoke would filter downstairs through cracks and crevices and floorboards, until it finally wisped around one of her smoke alarms. She'd get out okay.

He wanted her to get out okay. Tonight.

Once he had reconnected the wires affecting her security system, he stowed his tools and scanned the dark, peaked attic for anything he might have missed. Hurry, hissed the snake in his blood. He knew he had to get out of there before the cop reappeared, yet that wasn't his cause for haste. The cramping pain was scissoring through his skull. He had increasing visions of his brain split clean in two, and if he didn't hurry he'd be sucked into that bleak, black vacuum.

Starting little fires used to be all it took to regain control. No longer. The snake inside him had become insatiable, rapacious. Power was delicious. Six more days, he told himself. Six more days and he'd show them all endless power, total power. They'd all be sorry.

Poor Jacqui. She'd be sorry, too.

Not too sorry after Saturday night, of course. Because after Saturday night, she'd be dead.

* * *

Jacqui set the dial to Delicate and measured a capful of pink soap. She'd just dropped two sweaters into the machine when she glanced at the sweater dress she'd worn to work. It wasn't dirty, but it could use a freshening up, too. Tugging it over her head, she added the dress to the wash.

By the time she finished a few little cleanups, she was shivering—the basement was too cold to putter around in in nothing but a slip. She tugged the light cord and headed for the stairs.

Her mood hovered somewhere between a well pit and a cave. Stan hadn't shown for an appointment today. Jonathan had been in one of his moods, and Scott . . . it was best not to think of Scott.

All those phone calls. All the throat-drying, cheek-burning, stomach-knotting nerves it had taken for her to make those phone calls, and what had she accomplished? *Egg on your face, kiddo.*

Still shivering, she headed for the bathroom. Her eyes glared in the mirror's reflection as she brushed her teeth. He cared. That came through in the timbre of his voice, the way he looked at her, the way he was around her . . . and the blasted way he went behind her back.

She didn't mind the egg on her face. She minded, badly, being part of something that hurt him. The silly phone calls had never been an answer, but she just didn't know what was. *It seems to me, Duckie, that the right woman for him would find a way to be part of his healing, not part of his stress.*

Her fingers trembled, hanging up the toothbrush, and abruptly she realized that goose bumps were shivering all over her flesh. She was either unquestionably cold or unquestionably fast running out of courage.

Being cold was by far the easier problem to solve. In search of her robe, she strode for the bedroom and switched on the overhead light.

At one in the morning, Scott's phone jangled. Without opening his eyes, he groped for the receiver and tucked it between the pillow and his ear. "Llewellyn."

"Sir? I hope I'm not disturbing you in the middle of the night for nothing, but I have a note that you're to be contacted... There was a fire reported fifteen minutes ago on Oak Ridge in Silver Lake Township, the home of a Ms. Jacqui—"

"I know whose house it is. What's the report?" He reached for the light.

"One-alarm. Dispatched through the Silver Lake station. An attic fire, cause unknown, possibly electrical, and since it was just reported in, that's all I have. If you want me to call you back after there's been some follow-up—"

"No need. I'll be there. And thanks. You did just right." His feet hit the floor before the receiver clattered in place.

Ten days ago, the temperatures had been Indian-summer mild. Tonight, snow sploshed onto his windshield during the drive. Nothing that stayed frozen—snow rarely stayed frozen in October—but the dribble and splash was enough to make visibility difficult. His car might not have been able to bridge sixty, but his heart was going 110.

A cluster of shops marked the turn into her suburb, but that was the end of the look of city. Neon signs disappeared and the darkness closed in. Huge old trees blocked the streetlights, and the blacktop was slick with wet, fallen leaves. Jacqui's house was at the end of a long, twisting road around the lake, and halfway there he could smell the smoke. The smell knotted a rope in his stomach that didn't let go.

Neighbors Jacqui probably didn't know she had were clustered in the street. As he climbed from his car, he automatically searched the crowd, hoping that someone would click as more suspicious than the average disaster-loving bystander. No one did, so he mentally catalogued the rest of the scene.

The light was still whirling on the yellow pumper engine. No one was manning the deluge gun, but the downstairs stang hose had been used and was still unraveled. Two ladders stretched to her attic vents, and as dark as it was, he could see the scorch and char of her eaves and roof.

Nothing was noisier than a fire and a fire fighting scene. Nothing was more eerily quiet than those few minutes after a fire was totally out. Scott knew that, except for a man radioing in from the open cab, the squad was inside, checking the nooks and corners. At a glance he could determine the progress of the fire, from how bad it had been to how it had been handled, but that didn't give him answers to his questions about Jacqui.

Pelting toward the back steps, he met the chief striding through from the other side. "Was she hurt? Where is she?"

"Jacqui? I don't know where she is—outside here somewhere—but she's fine." The chief, recognizing him, said wearily, "I owe you an apology, Llewellyn. I thought it was kids' pranks before. We all did. I also kept thinking that if she had a real problem, the cops would take the obvious ball . . ."

The older man shared the details of the fire. Scott listened, but he still scanned the white faces of the people huddled in the driveway, searching for her.

"I don't need to see an attic any hotter than that. For a few minutes I thought we had a threat of flashover." The older man lifted his helmet to wipe his sweat-stained brow. "Whoever insulated the place had the sense to use Fiberglas, but he was stingy, skimped on materials—"

"Cause?" Both moved several feet from her back porch as the team flushed past and out. The boys were full of themselves, talking fast, moving fast. Ladders had to be put back on, the stang hose wound up, extinguishers clicked in place and the hose-bed tarp battened on. When the light stopped whirling on the engine, it was all over but the shouting—and he still hadn't spotted Jacqui.

"No question of the cause—a rigged-up hot plate. He left a calling card behind, though, not that it'll be of much help...."

"What?" For an instant the chief had his full attention.

"Boys found a small brown medicine bottle in the driveway, the same like you get from any pharmacist. It's not hers—we asked, and she can't place it with anyone she knows. Looked like pain pills to me, but what do I know? One of the boys got it in the cab in a bag; we'll have it to the lab in the morning—"

Scott instantly corrected him. "Tonight."

The chief hesitated, accurately read the expression on Scott's face and sighed. "All right, the lab boys won't like it, but tonight. Don't count on big answers, though. The label had been taken off the bottle. I don't see any way to trace the who, what or when."

"It's still something. The first mistake he's made, the first clue we've had. And I want to be called as soon as the lab—"

His voice cut off abruptly. In the road, one cop was climbing into his patrol car, and his partner was shooing the last of the neighbors home. When the small crowd finally dispersed, he could see the lone figure sink to the curb.

She had a winter coat pulled on over her long blue robe, and huddled there, she simply put her head in her arms. Yard lights illuminated her tangled shine of champagne hair, but he couldn't see her face—and didn't need to. Her hunched shoulders framed a picture of despair and defeat and overwhelming exhaustion.

The chief spotted her at the same time Scott did. "I guess I just figured her neighbors—"

"She barely knows them, and anyway, they might have tried. You don't know her. She's not real quick on accepting help." Scott was already slicing the distance between them.

"I'll get back to you about the lab."

"Tonight," Scott reminded him, and then temporarily blanked the subject from his mind. Jacqui was his priority now, his only priority, and he jogged toward her with that rope lashing tighter in his stomach. The label on that rope was guilt, and guilt whipped through every nerve in his body when her head shot up.

"Scott? How long have you been here? How did you know...?"

She hadn't wanted him to know—it was in her voice—and that tore through him, but not as much as the look of her. Her face had a porcelain pallor, the eternal optimist's sparkle was gone, and her eyes were a smudged, bruised green. His heart lashed out that she looked this way because of him. Because he'd failed to protect her. Whether she'd tied his hands, whether criminals slipped through law enforcement efforts all the time wasn't the point. Scott was the closest to the facts, to the total picture and understanding of her pyro, and to her.

"Did you see the house?" She slowly uncoiled into a standing position. He could have helped her. He wanted to help her. He didn't.

"Just the outside. I haven't been in yet." He saw from her expression that she assumed he'd hold out his arms to her, but guilt had frozen every muscle in his body. When he didn't move, her eyes flew to his—unsure, uncertain, rebuffed. Slowly, very slowly, her arms wrapped tightly around her chest.

He started talking, fast and tough. "Dammit, you're in slippers. My car's right over there—the keys are in it. Get in and start the heat."

"I can't, Scott. It's all over. I have to go back in the house."

"There's no way on this earth you're going back in that house tonight. You're coming with me. Now."

Maybe it was his cold voice that made her swallow, hard. "I can't go anywhere without clothes—"

"I'll get your clothes."

"It's more than clothes. It's a purse and briefcase and shoes—"

Women. In her house, he did a cursory assessment of the fire and smoke damages and then found a grocery bag. He started with a pair of shoes, pulled some stuff off hangers, raided her underwear drawer and then moved toward the bathroom. The cosmetics confounded him, so he simply swept in the whole batch. He switched off the lights, collected her purse and briefcase and headed back out to her.

The fire truck had pulled out by then, but Ms. Dis-obedience was still standing on the frozen lawn in her slippers, nowhere near his car.

"Did you lock the door?" she asked him.

"There'll be a man there for hours in case of a flare-up. He'll lock up—not that it matters. Our boy loves locked doors. The chief said the security system was intact, and he still had his fun with matches. Would you get in the car?"

"I—"

"I'd like you to argue with me. I mean it, I'd love it. Just try giving me the smallest hassle you can think of, and see what happens."

She climbed into the car. Actually what she did was climb into the car and collapse against the passenger door. Scott strapped her in with the safety belt just like that, glowering as he did so. Moments before, she had known herself to be snowed under by a mood of drained, exhausted despair. If Scott's cold bite had a cruel edge, his unexpected attitude at least took her mind off her-self.

The despair of this fire was far different than the oth-ers. No matter what had happened before, the helpless feeling of victim hadn't sunk in until tonight. Although she'd never tell him, that was partly Scott's fault. He had often accused her of being a Pollyanna, but he had also been positive that the culprit was someone she knew. She had, simply, absorbed that judgment as the most ele-mental kind of reassurance. It was just not possible for her to feel helpless—or in any serious danger—if it was someone she knew. Every woman feared the "mad rap-ist," but how could a woman be afraid of people she spent hours with every day, cared for and cared about, smiled at and—dammit—probably hugged?

That was the first thing she'd thought when she awakened to the alarms and the smoke swirling and blanketing her ceilings. She'd probably hugged someone who hated her.

Dammit, what had she ever done to be stabbed in the back like this?

She wanted to hang on to that thought. What, after all, was wrong with a good solid dose of self-pity? It wasn't as if she indulged daily, but as Scott lapped up the miles to the east side of town, she was increasingly conscious that he was the seriously wounded one.

He'd come on really macho, really tough. He hadn't touched her. He hadn't offered one soft word, one hug, one caring look. He also had yet to meet her eyes, but the look in his was the look of a man taking a slow stroll through hell.

At first he didn't talk—at least to her. He was too busy talking to his car phone. She heard him line up an investigative team to be at her place at daybreak. He talked to a lab. He checked through dispatch for the protocol report of her fire. And he raised holy hell with some off-duty cop. If she didn't understand the gist of the last conversation, she knew the lieutenant on the other end was extremely lucky to be a solid physical distance from Scott at the moment. And when Scott finished with him, he rounded back on her.

"I'm telling you now, I'm going to hit the cops in the morning to haul in three for questioning. Your caretaker, McGraff. Stan Witkowski... and don't climb on Timm for giving me the name—*you* should have. And that blue-eyed Harvard type you work with."

"No, no and maybe," she murmured.

"I was telling you, Jacqui, not asking you."

"Scott, if the police call in Stan, he'll end up back in juvenile hall. It's the worst place for him, the wrong place for him, and he isn't the one."

"I don't care."

"And you'd scare McGraff half to death. He's already been questioned—you know that. What did anyone turn up except that he's a beaten, arthritic old man? Don't do it to him—"

"I don't care."

"Jonathan—fine. He'll love it. In fact, he'd considered it high camp to be questioned by the police, so go ahead."

"I will."

"But he's not an arsonist. Given certain circumstances, pressured to the wall, I am not absolutely positive of what Jonathan is capable of. But he would never choose fire, Scott. He has different weapons in his arsenal that would make far more sense."

"That's nice. Everything you've said about all three is nice. I'm still having all three hauled in."

"Llewellyn—"

"I listened to you before. We did it your way before. Now we're doing it mine."

Put Scott in one cage and a starving leopard in the other, and she decided she'd rather handle the leopard. And it was odd, but the tighter and more furious he sounded, the more a soft, soft calm settled inside of her. The fire mattered, her home mattered, danger and fear and despair—all of it all mattered. It all had to be dealt with, none of it had disappeared, but the man she loved, who was doing a good job of tearing himself in two, mattered more.

Minutes later, she took the steps to his building. She saw tans and burgundies as she walked into his apartment, then the blur-bright blink of a lamp he switched on. "I'm getting you a whiskey, then putting you to bed."

"I really don't want—"

"I don't care what you want—you're getting it."

In the dark he'd looked intimidatingly fierce, a fighter begging for a fight, wired for it, prowling for it. Lamplight didn't change that picture, but illuminated other details. His complexion was chalk, his mouth taut and his eyes so tortured and dark that she couldn't bear it. Still, the shot glass he forced into her hand looked as palatable as ammonia and smelled worse. She loved wine. Given three or four hours, she could easily finish a glass of wine.

She took a sip because he was glaring at her, then made a gargoyle face on the thousand-to-one chance she could woo a smile from him. He didn't smile. "Finish it," he said tersely.

"I thought you didn't advocate alcohol for shock."

"You're not in shock—you're shook. There's a difference. If I could talk you into it, I'd get you good and drunk."

"Sounds fine by me, but please. Not on this."

"Finish it."

She upended the shot glass. Her eyes blinked wide when the scald hit her throat. Four gulps. Every one of them stung. The stuff was rancid, making her lungs fire and her eyes tear.

He showed no sympathy. "I want you to have another."

"I'd rather pound tacks in my thumbs."

He sighed, loudly. "Well, being the heavy drinker you are, maybe one'll do it. Come on. We'll get you to bed."

The place had no knickknacks. No pictures. The couch and TV had cost him good money, and he kept his kitchen neat, but his bookcase was the real shocker. The issues of *Firehouse* and *Fire Engineering* she could have expected, but he had several shelves of fiction. She glimpsed Angelou and Gabriel García Marquez, Sayers and William Styron . . . and Salinger. He would have Salinger.

"Jacqui—"

Obediently she whipped her eyes away from the bookshelf and allowed herself to be led down a minihall. The bathroom was off the left, the single bedroom off the right, and Scott had obviously been woken from a sound sleep for her fire alarm. The silver-gray sheets on his four-poster were all rumpled, his phone lay cockeyed on a pillow, the rough wool blanket was thrown back.

He dropped the grocery bag of her stuff on an old federal-style dresser and started closing closets and drawers, grabbing shirts, sweeping the phone back onto his bedside table. At least he'd stopped yelling at her, but his voice was still jerky and tight. It was a stranger's voice, and he might as well have been talking to a stranger. "The phone may ring in the night. Don't sweat it. I'll get it from the living room. There's food in the fridge, and don't get silly about asking me for things like toothpaste and hairbrushes. . . ."

She pulled off her wool coat and folded it on a chair, never taking her eyes off him. She reminded herself of several things. He was exhausted, so was she. She had also just been through the heart-pounding terror of a fire. Her stomach was still uneasy. Her hair smelled like smoke, and she probably had soot on her face. In other words, neither of them were "in the mood," and she had to look as attractive as a bag lady.

Those seemed useful things to remind herself about. It also seemed a brilliant time to recall that there were certain things she didn't risk. Ever. She didn't walk into dark, hollow caves, for example. She didn't light fuses she had no chance to control; she didn't tease tigers; and being a woman of pride, she didn't beg for rejection. Particularly the kind of rejection that would cut straight into her soul.

"There's breakfast stuff in the refrigerator. You don't have to worry about it. I'll be up before you will."

"Okay," she murmured. Then she slowly, thoughtfully reached for the sash of her robe.

"There's food in the fridge."

"I believe you've told me that three times now, Scott."

"Did I?" He straightened from where he had been pulling up the sheets, saw her standing in the pink-scalloped slip, and instantly averted his eyes. "You're ready for bed."

"About as ready for bed as you are," she agreed.

"So just shout if you need anything else. I'll get out of your way."

"The hell you will," she said softly.

He froze, but she didn't really understand why until she severed the space between them and slid her arms around his waist. He *was* ice cold. Even through his oxford shirt and jeans, she could feel the chill of shock in his body. "Put your arms around me," she ordered.

"I don't want—"

"Yes, you do."

"I can't—"

"Yes, you can."

He clenched her arms as if to jerk her away from him, but that wasn't what happened. The shudder that took him was as wild as fire, as lost as pain. He loosened his hands and swept his arms around her, crushing her breasts against the roar of his heartbeat. "Dammit, what if something had happened to you?" His mouth pressed against hers, not once, but again and again. "You think I could have lived if something had happened to you? I failed to protect you, Jacqui."

"Yes, you did," she said fiercely.

His head whipped up, his eyes a mirror of black onyx. She saw herself in that mirror; she also saw guilt. Something snapped inside her. She'd had enough. Months from now she would remember this moment as not at all the crisis she expected. Finding the courage to be angry with him wasn't the issue. It was having the love.

She had the strength and fury of that love, and it poured out of her. "Llewellyn, you are always going to fail if you keep expecting to protect the people you love from the impossible things." She jerked open one button on his shirt, then another. "You can't protect me. Not from earthquakes and tornadoes. Not from evil. Not from one of a thousand things that happen to people by chance." She ripped the shirt out from his jeans. "Men! You were all raised wrong. You grow up hung up on being heroes, all revved up on physical bravery and macho tests. And *you*. You're worse than all of them! You took what happened to your sister and let yourself get all screwed up!" His stupid shirt had tight buttons at the cuff. They were that much harder to deal with because her stupid eyes were spattering tears. "Well, let me tell you something, buster. I don't want a hero. I want a coward. I want somebody I can talk to, someone I can say, 'Look, I was scared out of my mind tonight.' And I want him to be able to say, 'Look, I was scared out of my mind tonight.' I want to be able to say that I'm not sure I can get through this alone. And I want him to have the cowardice to admit that just maybe he can't handle this alone, either.''

"Jacqui—"

When she finally had the shirt, she hurled it. "You can take your whole hero's scene—"

"I was scared out of my mind tonight—"

"And shove it!"

"And there is no chance—none—that I can make it through this night without you."

She was standing with her fists on her hips when his words filtered through. It wasn't the words that told her that she'd finally gotten through, but the look of him. With the lamplight behind him, his face and bare chest were shadowed, but she could see the pulse in his throat. It was beating like a sick clock. He was standing as still as a statue, and his eyes...the look in his eyes had the shine, the power, the honesty of emotion.

"I love you, Jacqui," he said quietly. "And yes, I'm scared. Scared for you, scared with you, and maybe even scared of how overwhelmingly strong that love is. I was never all that sure I could possibly be the right man for you—"

She never gave him the chance to finish. She surged toward him, arms up so her hands could slide into his hair and hold his head still. She pelted his face with kiss after kiss, soft kisses, lost kisses, silk and silvery kisses. She caught a swift smile creasing his cheek—she kissed that, too—but she was dominantly aware how quickly his smile faded.

His hands were moving, sweeping her flesh, skimming over satin. He held her as if she were a treasure lost, now found. He touched her as if every inch of flesh was precious and fragile. And his hands—Scott's always strong, always sure hands—were shaking.

The instinct and need to protect was so strong in him. She had criticized him for it, yet now she felt the matching urge, instinct and need from a feminine point of view. However strong, he was a vulnerable man. She wanted to guard him. Keep him safe. Protect him.

She wanted those things fiercely enough to catch his hands and lock them still. Green eyes met black. "Let me," she whispered. He didn't answer, but when she laid her lips on his throat, his pulse leaped for that contact.

Her slip was satin, but satin could also be a frame of mind. She made her body into satin, cool and slippery and soft. She rubbed against him, slinkily like a cat, brazenly—like a woman in love. His breath rasped against her cheek, and heat coiled in his body.

She released his hands long enough to give him a little push. There was nothing like the power of a woman; he fell back, landing with a definite thump on the dark gray blanket. She saw that spark of his dance in his eyes; he was enjoying her power. So was she.

She climbed on and indulged in feeling good and making him feel good. In wanting to show him what he brought to her as a woman, in wanting to show him those matching, deliciously strong feelings as a man.

She took her time. She pressed kisses on the roar of his heartbeat, the slick-soft skin of a scar near his right breast. She skimmed her palms down his ribs, down his sides, down his hips. She kissed his rough whiskers. She kissed his navel. And she kissed his mouth, slowly and reverently and often, while she most irreverently stretched against him, teasing a satin-clad breast against his chest, rubbing a leg between his jeaned thighs.

His jeans, of necessity and inevitably, drew her attention. He had worn no belt; he'd dressed too fast. Opening the snap seemed to make as loud a sound as a firecracker. Her eyes flew to his. Scott's eyes, as it happened, were closed. Fiercely, tightly closed. The swell beneath his zipper was unmistakable, so she was careful. Tortuously careful, releasing slow zipper tooth by slow zipper tooth.

"Jacqui?"

"Hmm?"

"You like it."

"What?"

"Courting danger."

"Of a kind," she agreed.

"I can't believe you ever doubted it. That you were beautiful, inside and out. That you could make a man love you, inside and out. That you could make a man shake good and hard, inside and out. You don't have any more doubts, do you?"

"No."

"Good."

That fast, he usurped her role as king of the mountain. His kiss brought her down, and when he'd finished ravaging her mouth, she was the one lying flat and breathless. He handled his zipper far more efficiently than she did. In fact, he handled his jeans far more efficiently than she could.

When he came back down beside her, the only thing between them was her slip. He slipped down the shoulder straps and applied his tongue everywhere he found skin. Her breasts suffered, exquisitely, under an assault of ardent licks, damp lashes.

Long before he straddled her legs, she felt mist blurring her eyes and the heady, soaring sensation of flying off a cliff. That sensation only intensified when she felt his weight and fullness and hardness stretch her soft core.

Tenderness turned to hunger, want to need, and a night that had been chill with fear turned hot, passionately hot, with what each wanted to bring to the other. His slow, tortuously deliberate thrusts changed to a fierce, hurtling tempo. They flew off the abyss, clinging to each other.

As she already knew, he would be there to catch her. This time, though, she was his catcher, too.

"You're just a little dangerous when you're mad, Petunia."

"You think so?"

"I know so. I also think that slip would be banned in Boston."

She smiled in the darkness, her cheek against his chest. "You liked the slip?"

"I liked it. I liked the body in it more."

"Don't be so stingy, Llewellyn. You more than liked the body."

"Loved." His lips exhibited the emotion on her temple.

"I do like that word."

"Yes." His whisper was low and amused. "You made very clear what you like, you heartless woman. You like a coward—wasn't that what you said? You like your men good and helpless—"

"No." She raised her head, her soft, sleepy eyes suddenly serious. "Don't misunderstand. Even when we're laughing, even when we're teasing, don't misunderstand. I want you as strong as you can be, love, but I also want you to know that you don't have to be that way around me."

"Are you trying to tell me you love me, Petunia?"

She heaved a sigh, full of exasperation, but she raised her head exultant and high. "There's never been any point in telling you anything." She weaved a leg between both of his and cradled his head in her arms. "I'll just have to show you."

"You sure you're not too tired?"

"I'm sure."

"You sure I'm not too tired?"

"Llewellyn, I'm beginning to discover that you are never tired where this subject is concerned. Now if you would please stop talking, I believe we have everything settled...."

"Not quite," he murmured. He didn't know how she'd lightened the load on his conscience, how she'd managed to make his old dragons seem ... not silly, but definitely out of perspective. Selfishly out of perspective, because his head, for too long, had been distracted from what mattered.

She mattered. As he swept her beneath him, he sought to prove that to her with passion and warmth, honesty and intimacy. He'd tested himself for years. Tonight he set a different kind of test for himself: how high, how hard and how hot he could make her before she demanded to be taken. She didn't need a man hung up on old ghosts. She needed a man she could share any and everything with. The cherishing he meant to ravage on her body was the silver side of the same coin. God help her, she was a woman with whom a man could share any and everything.

Devil's Night was still to come. Her pyro was yet to be caught. A man could learn to share fear, though, with a woman who matched him in emotion, strength and—almost—love. It was extremely hard for him to believe she could possibly love him as much as he did her.

Chapter 12

Scott's break for dinner consisted of filching a Big Mac out of a bag that someone was passing around. Juggling the burger and an open cup of coffee, he pushed open the door to dispatch.

The dispatch center was an oasis of calm in comparison to the madhouse atmosphere of the Detroit Fire Department Central Office. The dispatchers' ability to hear and concentrate could mean the difference between life and death. So there was quiet of a kind, but the high-stress, high-strung mood was as volatile as electricity. Decisions made in this room had the power to affect an entire city. Some had to be made faster than the flip of a dime. Many were irrevocable, and everyone knew it.

Alternately taking a bite of hamburger and a sip of coffee, Scott never broke stride as he passed the half dozen people wired up to the switchboard control panels. Only Luz glanced up to shoot him a wink. "We can handle this with our hands tied behind our backs," she said. "Go take ten and put your feet up."

He might have, if he hadn't been going nuts. Gulping coffee, he hunkered down over the relief model of Detroit. Rehearsals were done. Every change on the board now represented real action.

The real action during the past two days hadn't added up to fifty fires. Cupcake common for average times, and a result, Scott knew, of the forty-eight-hour-deluge of rain he'd prayed for. Today, though, was Devil's Night proper. The gods had tired of giving out free breaks with the weather. The morning had dawned dangeroulsy bright and clear.

The first call had been a whopper: a four-alarm for a warehouse on East Grand Boulevard that even this late had a truck and ladder company engaged. He bit another chunk of hamburger, gulped it. A factory on French Road had been hit around noon. Arson. A gang of derelict kids started throwing pipe bombs in deserted houses in Highland Park around three. A group of vandals had descended on Gratiot to prowl and loot just before dinner. There were literally dozens of other splashes of red all over the map, all of which had taken out equipment and manpower, but nothing that even came close to stressing his team.

No Devil's Night had gone this smoothly in a decade. Scott told himself that he shouldn't be surprised. An efficiently managed curfew had a powerful effect. Media education had swung its weight. The two-day rain had been a personal gift from God, and God also knew there were some eleven thousand police, fire fighters, medics, city employees and volunteers involved in winning this war.

He shoved a hand through his hair. The worst had been in '85. So many fires erupted all at once that some went unanswered. There simply hadn't been enough units, enough personnel. Tonight, he could see that there were abundant units waiting and sitting idle at every command post but one—the one Luz reached over his shoulder to pick up. Instead of relocating the pieces on the board, though, she removed them altogether.

"What?" He didn't need to frame the whole question.

"We're loaning out two ladder companies. Grosse Pointe and East Detroit. They both called in for help within ten minutes of each other." Without asking, Luz offered him two antacid tablets. She rolled her eyes as he gulped them with coffee. "Quite a change of pace for the suburbs to take the licking on Devil's Night instead of us. Burned their butts to ask for help."

He wanted to snap, "Don't short us," but he could easily see that Detroit's southeastern quadrant was still well equipped to handle double the standard number of calls.

Still, he was tempted to slap a fist in his palm. Dammit, where were they? The state cops had warned of an influx of arsonists. Kids looking for trouble didn't automatically change their minds and decide to stay home to play Monopoly. The city had been hot for weeks. The cops were out searching for known, active devils, who were evidently sitting with their feet up, watching TV. And him—Jacqui's pyro—where was he?

"Damn, would you relax?" Luz's palm descended on the tight muscles in his nape like a cuff. "It's going a hundred times better than we all dreamed. Ease up."

But he couldn't ease up. It was going well.

Too well.

* * *

Jacqui lifted the bite of lasagna, using her finger to cut the stringy swirl of cheese stretching up from the plate. "This is how I want to go. Stuffed on lasagna."

"And mounds of garlic bread, preferably oozing hot butter," Phoebe enthused. "Can you smell the calories in this room or what? I'll tell you right now—I know exactly where this meal is going to end up on me, and I'm going to fiercely resent having a svelte sister-in-law who can eat anything she wants."

"I keep telling you. He hasn't asked me. And furthermore, 'svelte' is just another word for skinny."

"Not to my brother, it isn't," Phoebe teased.

"Your brother likes his steaks ruined, which says a lot about his opinion—and taste—in general." The news flashed from the mute television in the corner. The drawn curtains and soft lamplight shut out the cold, crystal-clear night. Her dinner was held on a plate on her lap.

"Trivia or Scruples after dinner?"

"Whichever." It was an extraordinary night to feel perfectly relaxed, yet Jacqui kept telling herself that she was.

Scott sat on a hot seat tonight—alone. Every newscast had been exhilarating. The reports were that the pattern of Devil's Night had been broken. The cycle had never had a chance to build. This was the year they were winning the war. His war, she thought fleetingly, and indulged in a shameless surge of pride in him.

She had, unfortunately, a daunting personal crisis of her own to worry about. Fear had never been far from her mind since the last fire. She had foolishly underestimated the menace of her pyro before. That would never happen again.

Scott's frustration matched her own. So did his anxiety and fear. She'd been camping out of suitcases at his apartment for a week. He didn't want her alone, and her house was going to take weeks of repair and redecorating before it was livable again. Living together, Jacqui mused, hadn't helped catch a pyro. It hadn't made fear disappear. But it had taught her, most irrevocably, that you could live through hell if someone loved you.

They had lived through more heaven than hell last week, but she had easily admitted that this was one night she felt uneasy about being alone. The solution had been easy. Scott's parents had all but demanded that she stay overnight with them on Devil's Night. As it happened, the Llewellyns had been called out of town for a sick relative, so Phoebe had even needed someone to stay with her. Her pyro couldn't possibly know she was here. No one did.

Chuckling at something Phoebe said, Jacqui lifted her empty plate to a nearby table. The two women had been having a wonderful time. Good company, good food, lazy conversation and an utterly delicious feeling of safety dominated Jacqui's entire mood.

The phone rang and she jumped like a sprung rabbit.

Phoebe shook her head as she lifted the receiver. "Yes, she's here, bro. And almost as skittery as you are. She was just telling me how good you were in bed—sure amazed me." Phoebe winked at Jacqui. "Now, why would you want to talk to her when you have me...? All right, all right...." Phoebe dangled the receiver, looking smugly amused. "It's no good. For some unknown reason, he wants to hear the sound of your voice."

"I'd like to do a lot more than hear the sound of your voice," was the first thing he said to her. "You going to make it through this night, Sweet Pea?"

"The biggest problem I have is doling out French nougats at a rate to please your sister. You're the one on the front line tonight, not me. I know the action anted up after dusk. How bad?"

"Child's play. I'll worry about Devil's Night. You just concentrate on managing to stay safe for me."

"That won't be hard. Not a soul knows I'm here," she reminded him.

"So I keep telling myself, too. But that's not what I called to hear you say...."

She filled that breath of silence with a whisper. "I love you."

"And I love you, Petunia. Believe it."

When Jacqui hung up, Phoebe had a lot to say about full moons and moonstruck Welshmen. Jacqui opened the Scruples box to distract her—and maybe herself, too. Scott's voice had soothed and calmed her as nothing else could have, yet she still jerked up for the peal of a doorbell an hour later.

Phoebe's compassionate eyes latched on to hers, and she motioned Jacqui back to sitting with an imperial finger. "It'll quit around ten, I told you. This is, after all, Devil's Night, and every preteen kid in the neighborhood is going to ring doorbells until their parents drag them back home. The thing to do is ignore it. The lights are off, aren't they?"

"Yes."

"And the drapes are all closed, the doors locked." Phoebe returned to her Scruples card. "Well? Your boss wants an affair, and your job is keeping you and your three children from starvation. What's it to be—give in to the sucker or stand your ground? And keep in mind that I can't wait to tell Scott your answer."

Heat up weren't the words for it. By eleven o'clock another forty red flags were strewed across the relief map. Spread over a space of time, the action could have been handled easily. Instead, it was happening all at once. Sirens screamed through the city. Dispatch was a hive of tense, intense activity but not panic. No one had time to panic. Every command post had units out. Total control was now critical.

Scott was wearing earphones with a mike in front of him when a department detective walked in, a long-nosed, sharp-eyed, thirty-year-old man named Brown. "Can it wait?"

"I got a line on Joe McGraff. I think you'll want to hear it."

The gaze Scott shot him was electric. "Wait." He couldn't cut short the batallion chief reporting in from a River Rouge fire, but the moment that was done, he passed the ear set to Gunderson with a sharp set of instructions. Beyond the main dispatch center was a glass-partitioned area, where he herded Brown. "Now, and fast," Scott told him.

"Maybe I'm making a lot out of nothing. I don't have that much yet."

"Tell me."

Brown was a worrier, not a fast talker. "It was the pills, see. Yesterday we were all shooting the bull at lunch, when Sam—you know Sam Rivers—he remembered a crippled kid who used to set fires about a million years ago. The kid wasn't bad crippled, more maimed. Father used to take a lot of life out on him. It was kept hush-hush—the family had money. No, the kid's name wasn't McGraff. It was McGaffrey, so I don't even know why Sam's old story bothered me, but it did."

Scott could see the firework of lights on the switchboard panels. "*Dammit*, get to the point."

"The point is that I went back to McGraff's file. He'd checked out clean on everything, see, only it suddenly occurred to me that there was a gap, nothing to check out before the man was twenty-one. Courthouse was closed today, but I pulled a string or two, found out that Joe McGraff got born on the day he was twenty-one, so to speak, meaning he legally changed his name. The original name was Joe McGaffrey."

"And?"

"And nothing. That's all I got," Brown admitted. "Nothing criminal about a man changing his name, and as far as I can tell, this McGraff's led a model life for thirty years. After that, there's nothing, nowhere. Except for the doctor."

"What doctor?"

"I called a doctor, an old friend of mine, gave him the name of those pills. I know you already have the report from the lab—pills were a heavy dose painkiller—but my doc also told me they weren't meant for long-term use. First, you got a problem with dependency, but you also got a problem from using a chemical depressant long-term, maybe especially if this guy already had a screw loose. I'm not saying the guy was on it long-term. I mean, how would I know? But—"

"Llewellyn." Luz half flew in the door, her black eyes frantic. "We're in trouble. Now."

"Like I said . . ." Brown started uneasily.

"Stick close. Don't go anywhere. I'll be right back."

But he wasn't right back. Luz hit him fast and furious before he turned the corner into dispatch. "Something's going on. It's fast and it's ugly. The problem isn't us, it's them—the suburbs. Southfield, Oak Park, Ferndale, and now a call from Redford Township. This afternoon it was Grosse Pointe and East Detroit. I even knew the G.P. fire was a gasoline explosive, but I didn't happen to handle the other dispatch. I wish I had, dammit, because that's the pattern—gasoline explosives. That's what they're all calling in, fires too fast and too hot for their own units to handle. They want help, only how the hell can I short us of equipment now, when the city's as hot as a fire-cracker?"

"Shh."

"We have three command posts down to near skeleton units now. We can cover our ass or we can cover theirs. That's what it's coming down to. Dammit, the suburbs are never hit like this. I have to know what you want us to do."

"Shh."

His eyes were frozen on the relief model. In his mind, he put in an imaginary pin on Grosse Pointe, another on East Detroit and then followed the trail of the specific suburbs she'd mentioned. The picture in his head made the mental arc of an unfinished rainbow haloing Detroit. If the arc was completed, the next strike would be Dearborn Heights.

Jacqui was in Dearborn Heights.

So was his sister.

"Llewellyn, I'm telling you we can't spread ourselves this thin. It's not just loaning out the units, but the distance and time it'll take to get them back—"

His first impulse was to call her, *get* to her. That impulse had to do with love, though, not good sense. He hit the phones, fast. He started with the state police, spelling out everything about McGraff so they could nab him, and he followed up that call by contacting the Dearborn Heights and Redford Township cops with the same information. Then, the Dearborn Heights fire station had to be alerted and warned to prepare.

Each of those calls took time, because he couldn't function in a vacuum. Outside, sirens now wailed ceaselessly. Each crisis ricocheted off another crisis. As fast as he made one decision, four more waited for him. Once Luz picked up what was going on, she alerted the dispatchers. For a few minutes the room was a frenzy, and Scott told himself a dozen times that Jacqui would be okay. She couldn't help but be okay. He'd mobilized three sets of cops and a fire department to protect her—all geographically close to her, which he couldn't be. It was egotistical and just plain stupid to think that she needed him physically there, when he was in the best of all places to guarantee her protection from right where he was.

Still, by the time he buzzed her, adrenaline had totally replaced the blood flow in his veins, and his shirt was damp with sweat. The sweat was hot.

From day one, he'd known this was his city's worse danger. From day one, he'd known that the only thing they could not prepare for or control was an unhinged pyro. And from day one, he'd expected trouble—but from inside the city, not outside. It had never once occurred to him that the bastard planned to win by never touching the city itself. Divide and conquer. Divide the city's resources, and the city would be cheated of its ability to handle its own fires. Divide him from Jacqui.

And Jacqui was left alone and undefended.

She is protected, he told himself, but the sweat on his brow turned ice-cold when he didn't reach her, when he finally understood that he wasn't going to reach her. The telephone operator's voice was cheerful, but robotically firm. The phone line was temporarily malfunctional.

The bastard had cut it.

He was *there*.

Scott checked the time on his watch. It was 11:17. *Past time someone took you out.*

Phoebe fell asleep just before ten. Jacqui didn't even try to follow suit. Alone in the Llewellyn living room, she tried switching on the television, but she was too high strung to listen or watch. *Get ready for bed, Hughes,* droned the bored voice in her head. *He's fine, you're fine, and the whole night will be over soon if you'll just let it.*

Still, she couldn't sit. She tiptoed down the hall to make sure Phoebe was sleeping, wandered into the spare bedroom, wandered out. She tried resettling in front of the TV and ultimately ended up standing in front of the Llewellyn's refrigerator, reaching in for a carton of milk.

With the carton in hand, she searched for a glass, feeling massively uncomfortable at opening cupboards in a strange house. She felt worse when she spilled a small puddle of milk—you'd think she was ice-cold, her hands were so unsteady—and she was just grabbing for a dishcloth when she heard the sound.

She was so nervous that almost any sound at that moment would have made her jump sky-high. This one, contrarily, made her freeze on the blink of a heartbeat. All she heard was a whoosh. A ghostly, eerily inhuman whoosh.

When she yanked at the insulated kitchen curtain, everything in her stomach curdled. All she could see was a blaze-bright sea of yellow—a living, moving wall of flames. She spun on her heel and raced for the living room to drag at those heavy draperies. Another blazing wall. She tripped trying to reach the window in the bathroom, then scrambled to the windows in Scott's parents' bedroom and the spare. Everywhere, fire. The blaze circled the house.

"Jacqui!"

"Phoebe, I know and I'll be there—just hold on!" She may not know the house, but she knew where the wall-mounted phone was in the kitchen. When she punched the buttons, though, nothing happened.

She batted the buttons again. Again. She could smell the gasoline now, sharp and strong. Smoke was starting to sneak in in wisps along the ceiling, gush in under the door. Outside, that soft whoosh of explosion had turned into a menacing witch's cackle. The night had turned brighter than white, and inside the heat was rising to sweat temperatures. . . . She jabbed the buttons again.

"Jacqui!"

Leaving the phone hanging, she raced back to Scott's sister. Phoebe's face was as white as the bed sheets, and her eyes were a stark, scared black. "How bad?" she whispered.

"Bad."

"The phones—"

"Out, but that doesn't matter. Every neighbor for five miles around has probably already called the fire department." She prayed. "Nothing's going to happen to us." She prayed. "The only thing we can't do is panic." She prayed again. "Not that help won't be here, but if you know where there are extinguishers in the house—"

"One's in the broom closet in the kitchen, another's in the basement, and I know there's a big one upstairs."

"Not to worry, okay? I'll be right back." But she wanted that big extinguisher the way she'd once wanted to see Santa Claus at Christmas. She pelted up the unfamiliar steps to the second floor and flipped the light switch at the top. The upper story was one huge room and a closet, nothing more. She found the huge extinguisher in the closet and unbelted it from its holder. Before hurtling back for the stairs, though, she made the mistake of glancing out the window.

The house was frame, not brick. She had no idea how fast a fire could destroy a wooden house, but the view below sucked all the air from her lungs. The extinguisher in her hands was never going to be more help than a child's toy.

Red-and-gold flames lapped against the black night; spits and sparks flew everywhere. She could see no gaps in the wreath of fire. A streak of fire climbed a shutter, another raced along a windowsill. The blaze was alive and moving. Like a hungry devil, it was consuming everything in its path. How long did it take before a frame house became an inferno?

Her gaze caught, then fixed fiercely just outside. The second-story roof had a slope leading from the window. If she moved quickly enough, she could climb out the window, down the slope and jump free of that devil's circle. She might break a leg, but she'd live. She could get out. She wouldn't burn—but as fast as that thought occurred, so did another.

She couldn't get Phoebe out.

Not that way. There was no way she could lift Phoebe, much less carry her up the stairs. Even if that was possible, it wouldn't help, because Phoebe couldn't jump, couldn't leap free, and simply pushing her would drop her right into the wall of flames.

She heard an explosion below. Rushing back down the stairs, she heard another explosion, then the crinkle of splintering glass. The devil had moved inside—the back bedroom. She knew from the sudden blasts of heat and smoke, from the too close crackle of fire. Fumes sucked at her lungs, burned her eyes.

All electricity died as she turned the corner into Phoebe's room, and then she had to contend with Phoebe's too slow, too strong voice coming from the darkness.

"It's completely surrounding us?"

"Yes."

"A few extinguishers aren't going to help."

"No."

"If it weren't for me, you could get out. Upstairs, couldn't you, the roof?" When Jacqui didn't immediately answer, Phoebe said, "Do it, Jacqui. Do it. Get out, get help. What possible sense does it make for both of us to be trapped? What possible sense would it make for both of us to die?"

The word "die" snapped the hold of terror on her mind as nothing else could have. "What is this drivel?" she said fiercely. "You're not going to die, and neither am I. We're getting out of here—"

"How?"

"I don't know."

"You can't handle both of us. You can't even lift me."

"I can. I don't know how, but I can."

"But it's too late."

But those two words echoed a memory of Scott's voice in her mind. He wouldn't believe it. Scott didn't believe there was any such thing as "too late" in a fire. *As long as there's life, you fight, Sweet Pea. There's just no other way to play it. When you have no other weapons left, you fight with the courage to live.*

Jacqui moved, suddenly and fast, stealing the bed sheets and blankets from Phoebe's bed. Groping in the dark, she hauled them into the bathtub in the bathroom and jerked the faucets on full, then raced back to Phoebe.

"Where's your wheelchair?"

"Against the far wall. It snaps open, and then there's a catch to lock it. But what—"

"You have ramps at the front and back of the house, or just the back?" She found the wheelchair, but maneuvering it into an open position was easier said than done in the dark. Phoebe was coughing almost as hard as she was.

"Both."

"So that's how we're getting out, whichever way is most clear. Moses walked through water. We're walking through fire. Sound like fun?"

"Jacqui—"

"You won't get burned," she said fiercely. "I'll swaddle you completely in wet sheets and blankets. We'll pack you up with pillows under that—" Something crashed, hard and loud, in the living room. She knew from the ghost-bright shadows in the doorway that the fire was spreading inside the house. "We're getting out of here. Now!"

The instant she had the catch locked on the wheelchair, she hauled the unwieldy thing to the bed.

"Just hold it steady. I can get into it." If Phoebe's voice was a shaky rasp, determination had replaced the cry of panic. Using her metal exercise bar, Phoebe lowered herself into the chair. "I always said I could do anything—anything—but live through being trapped in another fire."

"That's not going to be your problem. Being drowned is about to be your problem, kiddo. Just hang in there." She grabbed both bed pillows to pad Phoebe's upper body and lap, then flew for the dark bathroom. The sheet she grabbed from the tub was lushly heavy and dripping cold. In seconds she was tucking it around Phoebe, everywhere—feet, shoulders, head. Over the sheet she tucked the sopping blanket, grabbed the last sheet for herself and steered the wheelchair through the hall like Parnelli Jones.

In the living room, ribbons of fire were licking up curtains, dancing on window shades, rolling down moldings. The smoke was worse than the flames, the fumes blinding and lung burning.... Something crashed, blocking the front door. She backed up and rammed the chair toward the kitchen.

She loved Scott.

The thought—the emotion—came to her at the precise moment when she lost all courage. She seared her hand on the doorknob, but that it wasn't it. It wasn't opening that back door, seeing the impenetrable wall of fire, hearing the devil's scream-crackle, feeling the inferno of heat suck at them like a vacuum.

Fast, while that emotion of love still sustained her, she grappled the wet sheet over her head as if she were playing a ghost on Halloween. Bracing herself against the wheelchair, she pushed with everything she had.

She tasted hell—a taste she would never in her life forget—but they burst through. They must have, because the next thing she remembered was the jarring slam of ground. Air, fresh air. Cold. And crawling toward the overturned wheelchair.

"Phoebe—dammit—please, please, oh God, please...."

She burrowed through the blanket, the sheet, pillows. Phoebe's face suddenly appeared under the mass of sodden bedding, her face whiter than chalk, her hair dripping. Her smile was shaky, but there. "You know what?" she whispered.

"What?"

"We're alive."

Later, she remembered laughing. Later, she remembered a lot of things. A circus of flashing lights—more fire trucks and police than she'd ever seen in one place. Total confusion. Racing firemen and high-powered hoses and whirling siren lights. A horde of neighbors, people flushing out of their homes, bringing blankets and thermoses. Phoebe, coughing so hard, and protesting just as hard that there was no reason on earth she had to go off in the ambulance, but they took her. And then a pock-faced man in a turnout coat looming over Jacqui. "Hell, where's that medic?"

She blanked out; it wasn't for long. She came to with a oxygen mask pressed over her face. The wet sheet was replaced by a dry blanket; someone coated her palms, then cut at her jeans to get at her ankles and feet. She wanted the salve; the burns were fierce, yet between shoulders and strange faces, she could still see flames shooting from the house.

The night was still on fire. Weakness flooded her body; she knew she was crying, tears of relief to be alive, tears of grief for the Llewellyn home, tears...because she just didn't have the strength to stop herself from crying. Her throat hurt, her lungs ached, and the crush of bodies was smothering. So many people were being helpful, but she craved two seconds alone, just two seconds where there was no noise and no fire and no confusion....

It was perhaps accidental that she had her wish. The two hovering policemen moved off to contain the building crowd of neighbors; both medics were carrying things to the back of their truck. In those few brief seconds, the whole world seemed to stop, blur, tip—all at once.

"Jacqui?" The eerie whisper came from behind her, a man's whisper, low and insistent, both familiar and strange. "Jacqui...." At the same instant, she saw a black car gunning toward her—Scott's car, she knew from the insignia—and not driving the road but crashing down lawns. The car bounced, he braked so hard, and then he was running, bodies in front of him scattering like leaves in a wind. "Jacqui...." And someone screamed. A man's hand covered her mouth, stinking of gasoline. All she could see was Scott running, running, his white face backdropped by fire and night. She clawed at the hand covering her mouth, desperate to breathe; yet too much had happened for her to have any reserve of strength. She felt herself being pulled, dragged down...and abruptly freed.

Scott had to have hit him with the impact of a bullet, because McGraff didn't just fall but flew...and then landed. Hard. She heard McGraff's high-pitched cry, not unlike the wail of a siren, of grief. And then she covered her face with her hands.

"They'll kick you out if they find you in here."

"They can try."

"Llewellyn, you're exhausted. You need to go home and get some sleep—"

"If you don't quit talking, I'm going to get tough. Your voice sounds like sandpaper. Now shh."

Jacqui lifted her head to see the man with such big plans about "getting tough." Scott's tousled hair hadn't seen a brush in hours, and his face was etched white with exhaustion. The bruise on his cheek had swollen and looked painful. Tough? Every time he tried to talk to her, his voice turned into a watery gravel, and he was holding on to her tight enough to crush ribs.

Her arms were wrapped just as securely around him. The hospital bed was empty. The emergency room doctor who treated her burns had announced she'd taken in a lungful of smoke, had a heck of a raw throat and shipped her upstairs for a solid night of rest. At the time she'd been too woozy from a shot to protest. When she started arguing that a hospital bed was the last place on earth she wanted to be, Scott had resolved the matter his own way.

There was only one chair in the austere hospital room. They were in it. Draped on his lap, her cheek found a natural pillow in his shoulder, her arms a natural home around his chest. Although she'd been cleaned up, she lacked a certain glamour. Both her feet and lower legs were bandaged. Her right hand had the look of a white boxer's mitt. Scott had tucked the sheet and blanket around her, but most typical of Mr. Llewellyn, his hand was on the inside. In fact, his hand had unerringly found the gaping back of the hospital gown. He wanted— needed—the touch of her warm flesh.

She wanted—needed—that skin-to-skin contact just as much. "I'm too heavy," she murmured.

"There's no way you could be too heavy, Petunia." His eyes suddenly burned, so he closed them. His lips moved to her hair, on her temples. Every kiss affirmed love almost lost, a shadowed night and echoing memories. It was going to be very hard to let her out of his sight for a long time, and tonight there wasn't the remotest possibility of that. As much as she needed sleep, Scott knew his love quite well. She wasn't going to sleep as long as she was hurting. "I think you'd better deal with it, honey."

"Deal with—"

"Guilt." He nipped her throat with infinite tenderness. "Guilt and I are old friends. Especially misplaced guilt, which is what I keep seeing in your eyes. About my parents' house.... It's not your fault the bastard took it out, nor is the loss of that house the tragedy you're building up in your head. My folks have had a dream of building their own place for a thousand years. They'll have the insurance money to do it. And more relevant, you saved their daughter's life. You think they give a hoot about their house? So put that one to bed."

"I..." She swallowed, hard. "That's part of what's been in on my mind. A lot of it, but not all."

"Yeah, I know." Her skin tasted like soap and water. And Jacqui. He lapped, nipped, teased at her throat with his lips. "You heard the stupid cop going on about the rampage McGraff ran on the city. You figure that's your fault, right? Because you were guilty of trusting him." He made a necklace of kisses along the line of her jaw.

"I did trust him."

"So you have a slight tendency to take in every stray. To believe in every lost lamb. To trust and want to help every mongrel. Like McGraff."

"Yes."

"Yeah," he echoed, and stopped kissing her long enough to cup her cheek in his palm. "When I saw his filthy hands on you, I don't deny I wanted him taken out, permanently and preferably by me. If the cop hadn't pulled me off him... But never mind that. The point is that you are not me, Sweet Pea, and from your viewpoint it isn't that simple, is it? He was one sad case. He had it ugly from the day he was born. Sure, I think he deserves to rot in hell, but it's a real strange feeling. Knowing he's already been there, that he's lived a whole life of nothing but hell."

"Llewellyn?" She turned her cheek to press a kiss in his palm. A fine way to turn a man's insides to butter.

"What?"

"I think that prejudice of yours is slipping badly on the side of the psychologists and sociologists and social workers—"

"Just psychologists. And keep it at a whisper, would you?" Beneath the voluminous bed coverings, his palm stroked down her side and hip. "What I'm trying to tell you is to stay just like you are, Jacqui. Stay who you are and be who you are. It must have hit me a hundred times in the past few hours. If he'd known you when he was young, maybe he'd never have turned into such a monster. And maybe there wouldn't be a Devil's Night."

"Llewellyn—"

"Sweetheart, take your hand off my thigh, or I just can't be responsible."

That grin of his was slow, lazy and lethal to a woman's common sense. It was one of the first things she'd noticed about him, but not the last. Hadn't he always done it? Made her feel strong where she was the most vulnerable? Believed in her more than she'd even believed in herself?

Eyes shimmering tears, she nudged his chin and angled her lips over his. Fire flared on contact. A good fire. A soul-warming, heart-swelling, conflagration-of-emotion type of fire.

"Llewellyn," she repeated, "Devil's Night is over—"

"I know. Which means that we're both free to discuss licenses, blood tests and little Llewellyns. Classy little Llewellyns with green eyes. I'm not asking you until tomorrow, you understand. This isn't the place. I have in mind both of us rested, a romantic dinner, champagne for me and milk served for you in a fluted glass. I'll order my steak ruined—that's an embarrassment for you, but I've warned you from the day I met you about who I am, Petunia. It's not my fault you didn't run when you had the chance." He hesitated. "You have no idea how romantic I plan to make our night tomorrow. But you could help me prepare an enormous amount if you'd sort of sneak in a preliminary yes so I wouldn't have to die of anxiety for the next twenty-four hours."

"Yes."

"Yes? Just like that?"

"Yes, just like that," she affirmed. "And now, back to the more critical subject. Devil's Night is over. It's now Halloween. Through this entire country, there is a well-known and universally celebrated custom known as trick or treat. You have the choice, Llewellyn, to either lock that hospital door or take me home—"

"Behave. Remember how exhausted you are."

"You provide the tricks. I'll provide the treats. Trust me, you're going to like the custom. . . ."

He catered to her, similar to the way he planned to cater to her for the next sixty or seventy years. Heaven knew where she got the energy, much less the brazen imagination. She claimed both came from him.

Love came from her. He'd known it for a long time, just as he knew that a man with any courage at all would always protect, guard and treasure such a woman for a lifetime. If he had his way, maybe even beyond.

*   *   *   *   *

COMING
NEXT MONTH

#309 THE ICE CREAM MAN—Kathleen Korbel

Could the handsome new ice cream man in Jenny Lake's neighborhood be selling more than chocolate and vanilla? She didn't want to believe the rumors that he could be a drug dealer, but there was something strange about an ice cream man who clearly disliked children. For undercover detective Nick Barnett, this assignment was unrelieved misery—except for Jenny, who was charmingly capable of making his life sweeter than it had ever been.

#310 SOMEBODY'S BABY—Marilyn Pappano

Giving up custody of her infant daughter to care for her critically ill son had been Sarah Lawson's only choice. Now, a year later, she was back to claim Katie from her father, Daniel Ryan, as per their custody arrangement. But Daniel had no intention of giving up his adorable daughter, agreement or not! Then, through their mutual love for Katie, they began to learn that the only arrangement that really worked was to become a family—forever.

#311 MAGIC IN THE AIR—Marilyn Tracy

Bound by events in the past, Jeannie Donnelly tried to avenge an ancient wrong and become the rightful leader of the Natuwa tribe. But she found her plans blocked by Michael O'Shea, surrogate son of the man she had to depose. The pain of yesterday could only be put to rest when they learned that trust and compromise—and love—were the only keys to the future.

#312 MISTRESS OF FOXGROVE—Lee Magner

The hired help didn't mix with the upper class—at least that was what stable manager Beau Lamond believed before he fell for heiress Elaine Faust. Surrounded by malicious gossip and still hurting from a shattered marriage, Elaine turned to Beau for the friendship and love she so desperately needed. But Beau was not what he seemed, and the secret he was keeping might destroy their burgeoning love.

AVAILABLE THIS MONTH:

SILHOUETTE® Desire™

ANOTHER BRIDE FOR A BRANIGAN BROTHER!

Branigan's Touch
by Leslie Davis Guccione

Available in October 1989

You've written in asking for more about the Branigan brothers, so we decided to give you Jody's story—from *his* perspective.

Look for Mr. October—*Branigan's Touch*—a *Man of the Month*, coming from Silhouette Desire.

Following #311 *Bittersweet Harvest*, #353 *Still Waters* and #376 *Something in Common*, *Branigan's Touch* still stands on its own. You'll enjoy the warmth and charm of the Branigan clan—and watch the sparks fly when another Branigan man meets his match with an O'Connor woman!

SD523-I